ACCLAIM FOR ELIZABETH INNESS-BROWN'S

Burning Marguerite

"Enchanting, intensely written. . . . [The characters'] stories unfold in a combination of grand sweep and everyday detail, which not only underscores the novel's charm and indelibility but reminds us that even everyday life, in retrospect, can lead to epic crossroads—and beautifully written novels."   —*Chicago Tribune*

"This careful interweaving of past and present, of death and of the life that preceded it, is masterfully conceived and structured, and *Burning Marguerite* is a moving, satisfying and deeply affecting love story."
                    —*The Trenton Times*

"Elizabeth Inness-Brown proves herself already a master of description."   —*Time Out New York*

"To read this book is to feel the quiet at its center, like a cathedral, empty but filled with the wound of silence. At its heart is an elegant and understated examination of the obligations and endurance of love."
                    —*The Times-Picayune*

ELIZABETH INNESS-BROWN

Burning Marguerite

Elizabeth Inness-Brown is the author of two acclaimed collections of short stories, *Satin Palms* and *Here*. Raised in the North Country of New York State, she now teaches writing at Saint Michael's College and lives with her husband and son on South Hero, an island in Lake Champlain, Vermont.

BOOKS BY ELIZABETH INNESS-BROWN

Here: Stories

Satin Palms

Burning Marguerite

Burning Marguerite

BURNING
MARGUERITE

Elizabeth Inness-Brown

Vintage Books
A Division of Random House Inc.
New York

FIRST VINTAGE BOOKS EDITION, JUNE 2003

Copyright © 2002 by Elizabeth Inness-Brown Monley

All rights reserved under International and Pan-American Copyright
Conventions. Published in the United States by Vintage Books, a division
of Random House, Inc., New York, and simultaneously in Canada by
Random House of Canada Limited, Toronto. Originally published
in hardcover in the United States by Alfred A. Knopf, a division
of Random House, Inc., New York, in 2002.

Vintage and colophon are registered trademarks of Random House, Inc.

Grateful acknowledgment is made to Warner Bros. Publications U.S. Inc.
for permission to reprint an excerpt from "Just One of Those Things"
by Cole Porter, copyright © 1935 (renewed) by Warner Bros. Inc.
All rights reserved. Reprinted by permission of Warner Bros.
Publications U.S. Inc., Miami FL 33014

The Library of Congress has cataloged the Knopf edition as follows:
Inness-Brown, Elizabeth, [date]
Burning Marguerite / Elizabeth Inness-Brown. –1st ed.
p. cm.
1.Women—New England—Fiction. 2.New Orleans (La.)—Fiction.
3. New England—Fiction. 4. Boys—Fiction. I. Title.
PS3559.N47B87 2002
813'.54—dc21   2001029860

Vintage ISBN: 0-375-72622-5

Book design by Anthea Lingeman

www.vintagebooks.com

Printed in the United States of America
10 9 8 7 6 5 4 3 2 1

To Jan and Michael, and in memory

of Emily Marshall Monley Ellis

and Marguerite McKee

I cannot praise a fugitive and cloistered virtue, unexercised and unbreathed, that never sallies out and sees her adversary, but slinks out of the race, where that immortal garland is to be run for, not without dust and heat.

—John Milton, *Tractate of Education* (1644)

Burning Marguerite

I can see spring in winter.

I can see both the gray winter limbs and the limbs red with sap. I can see the sap flowing, although it is not; can see both the leafless twigs and the leaves sprouting from their twigs—the buds greening and bursting, the leaves unfurling. I can see through the snow and frozen ground to the growing roots, the burgeoning seeds. I can see it all at once, not only spring and winter but summer and fall too, the cells hardening, the leaves fading falling decaying, the frost, the thaw, the rising sap, the buds and then the leaves again, greening and failing and falling. . . .

But all at once, I can see it all at once.

Day in night, night in day. Death in life, life in death. Fire in ice.

Like a seed, I lie here on the ground. Like a seed, I am both sleeping and awake, both living and dead. The germ is alive in me but quiet, waiting at my center. The rest of me is food to it—food, husk, shell, nothing more.

Something descends, lands on me, scratching where it touches. I open my eyes to the darkness and can both see and not see. Whatever stands there stands uneasily, quivering on its uneven perch. A tidy weightless uneasy thing. The musty smell of feathers, of fear; the clack of tongue in beak. I see bird, not a bird particularly, not a kind of bird, just bird. Bird, beak, an uneasy scrabbling on the palm of my hand.

And on my arm. Moving along the scaffolding my

arm makes. Coming closer to me now, to the center of me, to the germ of me. There now. Above me now.

Its beak is quick. It does not hurt, but I hear its tapping on my husk, near and sharp, tapping into my shell, tapping its way to my germ, the sweet kernel of my life, the delicious center. With barbed tongue it raises to the light what it finds there: moments small and large, acts, regrets, glimpses, fragments. Particles of knowledge: The flowers of the nasturtium, the daylily, the viola are edible. . . . A yellow-orange-purple-red salad. The boy tasting the petals one by one, lifting them to his mouth, that reluctant but voracious creature his mouth. Oh, he says. *Oh.* They are a little sweet, *he says.* And some bitter, like pepper. But I like them. *And he eats.*

The boy who ate flowers.

I loved him. Loved him as his mother would have, as his father should have; loved him in their stead.

And in return he gave me my life.

One

The fire had gone out not long before he woke. The air in the cabin was cold enough to chill his nose but not cold enough to show his breath. The stove, when he reached out, was still as warm as his hand.

Inside the sleeping bag, his body had generated its own heat, and the goose down kept it there, cocooning him. It was good to know he could survive a night in the cabin if he wanted to, that he could survive even the deep cold of a night in February. The only difficulty was convincing himself to leave the warmth of the bag.

He did it by imagining the smell of coffee. Down at the house, Tante would have the coffee percolating on the stove, boiling it with the chicory that gave it a burnt taste that went away only when he stirred in sugar and filled his mug to the lip with milk. The kitchen would be warm, the fire hissing and popping. Tante would have forgiven him by now, as he had already forgiven her. She would be ready for him to come back, she would not say a word, and they would go on as ever. After thirty-five years, after the whole of his life and more than a third of hers, forgiveness came easily to them, and often. The passing of time pressed them to it, made nothing else important enough to stop it. All you ever really have is time; she taught him that.

He dressed inside the bag, took his boots from its bottom where he'd kept them warm, climbed out and put them on. Opened the stove door, stirred the ashes, made sure the fire was out. Rolled up the sleeping bag and put it into ripstop plastic, and put that into more plastic, and put that into the cupboard to protect it from mice and squirrels. Laid a tarp over the cot to keep the dust and droppings off. Cast his eye about the place. Pulled his coat from the hook and put it on; pulled his hat down to his eyes, wrapped the scarf around his neck and chin, stuck his hands into his gloves, and went out the door into the cold.

It was first light, a winter dawn. If he'd wanted to take the time to climb the ridge, he could have seen the blush of sunrise warm above the horizon. But here on the western slope the light was colorless, flat. His footsteps cracked the icy air. Judging from the way his breath hovered, the temperature was well below zero.

Around him the trees seemed to hold themselves still. They looked almost dead, like the trees onstage in a high school play. His high school play. Because he was good with wood and because he had a truck and because he could drive a nail straight, he had been asked to design the set. He had made a forest of trees, bringing summer into the drab auditorium. Each of the three nights, he had refreshed the dream with new-cut saplings, their leaves kept green by the moist medium in which they stood. But as powerful as the illusion was, the trees had looked dead to him. He could tell a live tree when he saw one, and those trees had looked dead, more dead even than these looked in the dead of winter.

The first slope down from the cabin to the house was slick, thin snow over leaves. He reached his hands ahead to the trees, grabbed their brittle limbs to steady himself. Twigs broke off in his hands. To inhale froze his nostrils, to exhale thawed them. The air was raw on his cheeks and lips.

When the slope leveled, he relaxed his caution. In winter you could see deep into the woods. He watched for what he might see, for what might be there, looking for nothing in particular. Sometimes you caught deer off guard, stripping the bark from young trees, or spotted woodpeckers after you heard them, drilling old trees in search of frozen insects. He was in no hurry; he had no place to be, no job to do but keeping himself and Tante warm. He liked that about being a carpenter in winter; he liked that about winter itself. The way everything slowed down, became elemental. Nothing mattered but staying warm.

The path widened. This was the old quarry road. He came into it where it hooked left toward the lower quarry, hidden some half mile back. Downhill, the road was still open; he kept it that way with his truck, to make it easier to bring down firewood. But toward the quarry the road was recognizable only because the growth was younger and thicker than the rest of the woods. Most people would have missed it.

A hum came, first soft and distant, then louder. A single-engine plane passed overhead, just under the low clouds.

He glanced left, up the overgrown road, and saw something. Something red against something white. He almost dismissed it. But the red glowed fresh and bright, and the thought that some animal might be hurt and bleeding drew him a few steps into the woods.

He kept waiting for what he was seeing to make sense to him. But even when he recognized the red rosebuds on the white flannel, even when he knew what they were, his mind refused to comprehend what his eyes saw, concocting instead other reasons that Tante's nightgown might be out there in the woods. The wind, a wild dog, birds. Something had taken the gown from the clothesline, had dragged it here and left it. For several long minutes his mind did not accept what else was there, accepted only the nightgown amid some strangely shaped and tinted rocks. Rocks whitened by hoarfrost. Rocks that gave the impression of a face, rocks shaped like fingers, a calf, a foot.

Then like a puzzle it came together, and he saw the picture complete. Tante. One leg bent under her, the other foot bare. Her torso twisted. Her arm flung over her eyes so that he could not see if they were open. The sleeve of the nightgown drawn back, her arm exposed: the web of blue veins, the loose flesh, the bones of her arm from wrist to elbow, the hand with only four fingers. The nightgown clean and white against the ground. Like fresh snow with roses leaping red and vivid from it.

He sat on the ground next to her. Tried not to look at her. Took off a glove and reached toward her. Where his finger touched, an oval melted from her hand. But the flesh was cold, no warmer than the ground she lay on.

He wanted to take her into his arms then, hold her to him. Warm her. Breathe life back into her. But he couldn't.

When he felt his own hand freezing, he stood again, put his glove back on, and squatted to put his arms beneath her. It was like lifting firewood. She was a rigid, ungainly corpse.

He moved carefully to avoid trees, to keep from hitting her against them, her outstretched arm, her foot. More than once he slipped and nearly fell. He did not look down into her ancient face, afraid of what he might see.

He took her back up to the cabin, the nearer of two places; took her back to his bed. There, he removed the tarp and laid her head on the pillow where his own had rested, not an hour before.

The sheriff's office was in a new brick building, which it shared with the post office and a video store. A flag snapped against a flagpole planted in a concrete circle in the parking lot. Between two white lines, a black car gleamed. Otherwise the lot was empty.

Stepping into the glass entryway was like stepping into an airlock or one of those radiation baths in a science fiction movie. Somewhere a machine roared ferociously, filling the box with hot air, a buffer zone between the cold outside and the warm inside. A place to preheat visitors, so they would not bring the cold inside with them.

In this space, just opposite a handwritten sign that read NO SMOKING, stood a woman smoking a cigarette, wrapped up and slouching in a big winter coat, her hair and part of her face hidden by a hat. James spoke to her. "Cold out," he said. Two words together was all he could manage. She only nodded and took another deep drag, looking out into the parking lot as if she were expecting someone else.

He crossed the space in two steps. Opened the inner door. Stepped into the hallway with its shining linoleum floor. Found the door labeled COUNTY SHERIFF. Opened it. Stepped inside.

The sheriff's office had freshly painted green walls. There were no curtains on the broad windows that looked out on the parking lot; the blinds were raised up. Behind a long counter another woman sat at a desk, flipping the glossy pages of a magazine. She was not in uniform. He did not know her, but she looked familiar, about as familiar as the woman in the entryway.

It had been a long time since he had been to the sheriff's

office. Things had changed. The woman's desk was sleek and modern, U-shaped. Behind her glowed the blue screen of a computer, swimming with red and yellow fish. Or birds. He couldn't tell.

James cleared his throat; the woman flipped a page. James thought he saw lawn mowers, other bright red machinery. Tractors. He thought it must be a farm catalog. "May I help you?" she said, not looking up.

"Sheriff here?"

"No," she said, and now looked up. "Oh," she said, as if she knew him or as if the sight of him had startled her. "Can I help you?" She rephrased the question as if it meant something different.

He hesitated to speak, uncertain how to put it. "It's a death," he said.

The woman smiled. "Sure," she said. She kept smiling and looking at him, as if waiting for something. When he didn't say anything more, she gave a little laugh. "Murder, suicide, or accident? Hard to tell these days, isn't it? They just seem to throw themselves into the road. I hit two raccoons just the other day. And my uncle hit a moose, up there on the mainland. Totaled his truck."

James shook his head. "No," he said.

Keeping a finger at her place, the woman shut the catalog, swiveled her chair to the left, and stood. Her clothing struck him as peculiar for a woman who worked in a sheriff's office: a long white sweater over black pants, and shiny black shoes that clacked against the floor. Her blond hair was short enough to reveal her ears; her earrings were silver birds that hung down from chains and swung against her neck. She looked like someone who should be working in a department store. "What happened?" she asked, coming toward him, the catalog still in her hand, her expression curious.

"I'm not sure," he said.

She was standing arm's length from him now, only the counter between them. "Who died?" she said.

"Tante." He used the French word unself-consciously, not worried about whether she would uwnderstand. She did.

"Your aunt?"

"My guardian."

The woman's eyebrows rose and fell. James was too old to have a guardian. "She raised me," James said.

The woman nodded, understanding. "How old was she?" she asked.

He thought. "Ninety-four."

"Oh." The woman reached out to him, the gesture sympathetic, but he could not feel her hand through the sleeve of his jacket.

She leaned down behind the counter; he heard riffling noises; then she reappeared with a form in her hand and laid it on the counter, putting the catalog facedown next to it. From the collection of pens in a mug on the counter, she extracted one and held it over the form, as if about to write.

"I'm not sure," he said again.

"Not sure what?" she said. "Not sure she's dead?" She glanced away from him toward the telephone. "Should we . . . "

He shook his head. "Not sure what happened." He looked down at the top of the woman's head; the part in her hair was very straight, and as white as her sweater.

"It's all right," she said, her voice still kindly. "There's a place for that here." She clicked the point from the pen and pointed to a line on the form. "I'll fill it in," she said.

"No," he said. "Let me."

"Are you sure?" she said. He nodded, took the pen from her hand, and turned the form so that it faced him.

The first line asked for a name. Marguerite Anne Bernadette-

Marie Deo, he wrote. He read ahead. Date of birth. Address, occupation. Circumstances under which the body was discovered. He stopped reading and listened to what the woman was saying.

"The sheriff's out on a call, but you can wait here. As soon as he gets in, he'll call the coroner." She had her eyes on him and spoke in low tones, as if sharing a confidence. "They'll have to do an autopsy," she said. "Whenever the circumstances are uncertain . . ."

Women in bathing suits. The cover of the catalog showed women in bathing suits. Not lawn mowers, not tractors, but women with bare legs and arms, shoulders, bony chests, fleshy hips. Flesh and bone. Not machinery. How could he have made that mistake? Flesh and bone. The foot has twenty-seven bones, the hand twenty-eight, unless a finger is missing. Together the hands and feet constitute more than half the bones in the human body. A person's feet are as recognizable as her face, once you've come to know them.

When Tante was ill, the hospital sent home a bottle of milky lotion, the nurse telling him to massage her feet to keep the circulation going while she recuperated. The first time he held one of her long, bony feet in his hands, rubbing the lotion in, he thought: What kind of protection is this skin? So soft a fingernail could damage it. Like the petal of a flower, the skin of a ripe pear. He pressed his thumbs into the arch; he rubbed each toe between his fingers. Tante was silent, her eyes shut tight. Embarrassed, he thought. Ashamed. Or in pain. There were tears in the corners of her eyes. "Am I hurting you?" he said. She opened her eyes, smiled. "No," she said. "It's lovely."

Lovely. He couldn't remember her ever using the word before.

It felt strange to touch her. As a little boy, he'd clung to her, but growing up he'd pulled away, like a box elder leaning to get out of her shade and into the sunlight. It was only during that long period of her recuperation that he realized how infrequently, as adults, they had touched. During her sickness, he bathed her and dressed her, fed her, pulled the blanket up under her chin, tucked her in. Rubbed lotion into her feet, as solicitous as a lover, as careful as a parent.

He remembered what she'd said, the moment she woke up in the hospital, when she finally rose out of the hazy dementia that had accompanied her pneumonia. "How could you let them bring me here?" She'd had tears in her eyes then too. "I won't let them touch me. I won't."

He told her she had no choice, if she wanted to live.

Did he have a choice now?

Yes. He would do as she wished, as she had told him to do. One final obedient act.

James folded the form into halves, quarters, eighths; put it in his breast pocket. "I'll be back," he said, putting the pen in the mug. The woman looked startled. The silver birds flew at her neck. "Wait!" she said. She reached her hand out to him again. "Wait!" she repeated. She might have said his name; he wasn't sure.

But he was out the door and into the air lock, past the smoking woman. And then back in the truck and driving.

Earliest memory. He was walking along the road, his hand in his mother's. It was full summer. The woods were thick with leaves, dense with green. He must have been three. His mother's hand felt good around his. She kept herself between him and the road. When a car went by, she tightened her grip on him. Each car's passing made a little wind that eddied around him; dust stung his eyes.

When they rounded the bend, he wanted to run, but his mother's hand would not let him. On the porch of the big stone house sat Tante, rocking in the green chair, watching for him. She was old even then, but in memory now she seemed young. She did not get up when she saw him, but he saw her see him and he saw the smile she kept quiet on her familiar face. In a moment he and his mother had crossed the road and he was standing with his hands on Tante's knees as the women exchanged a few words. Then his mother kissed his head and was gone.

"I have a surprise for you," Tante said.

She took his hand then. Hers felt different from his mother's, larger and rougher and harder, yet the same in that he trusted it. They walked down the steps and around to the side yard, where the big trees grew. All summer he had been playing under those trees, looking up into their shining leaves. Tante called the trees "yolks," or so it sounded to him.

Now he saw what she had done. Up the trunk of one of the trees went a ladder, steps and rails, and in the tree was something to climb to. A place whose floor he looked up at and whose walls and roof he could glimpse among the leaves. "Go ahead, climb up," Tante told him. He ran to the tree and gripped the rail and put his foot on the first step, then looked back. Tante was right there behind him. He climbed.

They ate lunch together in the tree, high above the ground.

She was missing the little finger on her left hand. In the tree that day she told him a story about big lizards she called "gaters," in a wet place called a bayou in a place she called "Looziana." She told how she, a young and stupid girl, had wandered into the bayou one day, "trying to get lost," she said. How she had come upon a gater as big as a log—in fact, she had thought he was a log and had begun to step across him, when he twisted and snapped at her feet on his back. She fell into the water then and found herself eye to reptilian eye with him. "Please don't eat me," she said. "Hmmph," he said. "What kind of a gater would I be if I didn't eat you?" "But I am bitter inside," she said, "and not fit to eat." "Others have told that tale," the gater said, "but they were lying." He smiled broadly and his big teeth were white daggers in the sun. "Why should I believe you?" he asked. "Taste me," she said, and extended the littlest finger she could.

"Tante," he asked, when the story was done, "why are you bitter inside?"

"Can't say," she said.

"Did you get lost?" he asked.

She smiled then. "Eventually," she said, "but not that day."

James had made her tell the story many times after that, but the first time was his earliest clear memory of her. He brought it to mind now, as he drove the truck into the village.

It was a bright morning. There had been little snow since the January thaw, and what was left from December was either crusty and glinting where the sun hit it or black with soot, as if scorched. Strips of cloud moved through a milk-blue sky but did not interfere with the sun. In this light the town seemed shrunken, its buildings like knickknacks collected over the years, hodgepodge along the road. Nothing moved but a few cars and some chimney smoke, curling up seductively.

The woman in the sheriff's entranceway. If a woman smokes like a chimney, can a chimney smoke like a woman?

He was hungry. He had not eaten, he could not imagine eating, yet he knew he was going to. People said life went on; so it did. He pulled into the parking lot of the diner at the far end of the village. It was an old diner that had been bought and renovated from its derelict shell, transported here from its original location, somewhere south. Big news in the local paper half a dozen years before. How the owner had to get permits from every state he passed through. How wide the load had been, how long. The day the diner arrived, the locals had come out to watch it be set on its foundation. Once in place among the old maples, it seemed it had always been there, and summer filled it with gullible tourists seeking the flavor of authenticity, a taste of the past—flapjacks that they assumed were made from scratch, maple syrup that they assumed came from the big trees.

In winter, the locals made the diner theirs. This morning it was quiet and empty but for three customers, each alone. A man in farm overalls at the counter, a white-shirted man and a blond woman in separate booths. None of their faces visible. James slid into a red leatherette booth, and a waitress in a white uniform and a blue apron brought him a laminated menu. There was a full page of breakfast choices. "Coffee," James said, and she took the menu back, her face blank. "And toast," he said. "Lots of butter." She gave him a cramped little smile and made a note on her pad.

Yesterday it had been Tante who made his breakfast, stoked the fire, brewed the coffee, the transistor radio on the windowsill crackling with news and music. That's how it should have been today, too. When he came down from the cabin again and let himself in the back door, she should have been there to turn to him and say, "Seen the sunrise?" She should have been there to set his plate on the table, and when the toast came it should have been thick slices of her bread spread with butter melting fast, and beside it the mug of sweet coffee. Last night's argument forgiven, forgotten, without a word.

But instead this morning he had left her dead in the cabin. And when he came down to the house, he had found the outside door and the summer-kitchen door half open and the fire out, the house frost-cold and empty. He had closed the doors and stood for a moment, listening to the silent house, thinking of Tante lying in his cold bed up in the woods. By the sink sat their two mugs, washed by her hand and upside down on the drainboard. He had been five years old when she taught him to tear toast into pieces and dunk it into coffee. Morning had come to mean buttered toast and sweet coffee in the mug that fit his hand. Had his hand grown to fit the mug, or had the mug always fit? This was like asking if Tante had been born to take care of him or he to take care of her. The mug had always fit his hand. He took off a glove and touched the mug; it was icy.

Last night they had drunk tea and played rummy. Deuces wild. One-eyed jacks wild. Tante piled on the wilds when it was her turn to choose. Then she brought her cards close to her eyes, more to see them than to hide them from him. It was an old deck of poker cards they played with, the same cards they had played with when he was small. Through her fingers he could see the back of one, could see the blue etching of two bulldogs leaping at their chains, could almost read the caption under them: "There is a tie that binds us to our Homes." That *Homes,* with its capital *H,* turning a simple word into a castle with turrets. There is a tie that binds us, the way the two *I*s in the *H* were bound by the crossbar between them. As she had taught him to see.

On the mantel over the fireplace (they'd been in the front room, where they always played, at the big wooden table), the brass balls on the anniversary clock turned this way and that, mimicking and mocking the planets revolving about the sun, never finishing one revolution before they began another. Watching them, he thought of a woman's shoulders, the way a woman's bare, round shoulders could shift away, her eyes shifting with them. A glint reflected off the four balls as they turned, two pairs this way, two pairs that, sending fragments of lamplight sailing silently across the walls and back again. The fire was low but glowing and hot, and it and the pair of lamps that flanked the settee painted the room unevenly with light and shadow. The walls were murky with years of soot and resin.

"This place needs painting," he'd said to her, still waiting for her to play her turn.

"Do it when I'm dead and gone," she'd said back, not lifting her eyes from the cards.

She always said that. It meant only that she no longer liked the smell of paint, did not like the mess of it, did not like change, did not like disruption, did not want to waste her time that way. Nothing: it meant nothing. Remembering now, he had to believe that. She could not have known how close death was.

Unless that was why she had come after him.

Now in the diner the waitress brought him a cup and saucer. "Toast coming right up," she said, and dumped a handful of plastic creamers on the table. He stirred in two creams, two packets of sugar. He sipped. Coffee without Tante's chicory had no flavor for him, never had.

He tried to read the newspaper he found on his seat, but couldn't get past the headlines. He gazed out the window.

Across the street was the old Episcopal church. Two years before, it had been sold to a bank. Because the church was designated a historic landmark, the bank had been required to keep the steeple and the leaded-glass windows: a field of white lilies, a golden bridge over a blue river. Images of an earthly heaven that could be bought as easily as earned. Just right for a bank—no Jesus or Mary. The crosses they'd been allowed to take down.

Next door, in a new building built to look old, was an antique shop. Vinyl siding mimicked wood clapboards, the roof was pitched, the windowpanes falsely divided. As James watched, the front door opened and a woman in a hooded parka came out, walked to the edge of the road, and set up a sandwich-board sign, the capital A of its side toward him, the sign positioned so drivers could read it coming down the road. But he knew what it said. OPEN. ANTIQUES. SALE TODAY. Every day it was "sale today."

A car drove in front of the sign and pulled into the diner parking lot. James didn't so much look at it as turn his eyes on it. It was a blue-and-white car with some kind of emblem on its side. A man in a gray knit tuque and sunglasses emerged from it, gave James's truck a long look, and then came inside, cold air wafting around him.

"Morning, Mona," the man said to the waitress, nodding. "Hey, Sheriff," she said back to him. Then the sheriff came to James's booth, took off his gloves and put them in his pocket, took off his jacket and hung it on the rack, pulled his hat off and stuffed it in with the gloves, and slid into the seat opposite James, as if they had intended to meet there all along.

"Morning, James Jack," he said.

James nodded.

The waitress brought the sheriff a menu. He waved it away and said, "Coffee and a bran muffin," and she went off again.

The sheriff was wearing a nicely ironed navy-blue shirt with epaulets and pleated pockets and a navy-blue tie. Over his left breast was a badge. His face was still young except for the squint lines around his eyes; aside from the fact that the hair standing up from the static of his hat was white, he looked exactly as he had always looked. He had been sheriff a long time, and deputy before that. He had known James a long time, and James had known him. And the sheriff had known Tante. This was, more than anything else, why James had driven down to the sheriff's office. To tell someone else who knew her. To *see* someone who might care.

The sheriff folded his hands on the table. "I understand you visited the office this morning."

James nodded, sipped at his coffee.

"What's up?"

James shrugged. "Nothing." Nothing was what came to mind; nothing was all he could tell the sheriff, who would likely want to do the right thing, the legal thing. That was his job.

The sheriff sighed, and the waitress brought James's toast and the sheriff's muffin, balancing the plates on her forearm. She dumped another handful of creamers on the table, went away, and came back with the coffeepot and filled the sheriff's cup and refilled James's. James opened another creamer and dumped it in. The sheriff did the same, and took a sip.

"Everything all right up at the house?" the sheriff said.

James stirred in another packet of sugar, picked up one triangle of toast, and dunked it. Eyes closed, he took the first bite. Butter and sugar and coffee mixed in his mouth. For a moment, he heard Tante at the sink, washing the morning dishes. And when he opened his eyes, he thought he saw her there, standing across the room, watching. But no, it was the waitress—rag in her hand, wiping the counter clean, eyes on him.

"Death is a difficult thing," the sheriff said, tearing the paper from his muffin. "You knew that my wife died?"

James nodded and said, "I was sorry to hear that." Because it was the appropriate thing to say, and because the sheriff had often acted kindly to him, although sometimes that kindness did seem less than sincere.

The sheriff nodded. "More than a year ago." He sipped coffee. "It's particularly hard if you're alone, the way you are. Death, I mean. Do you want me to go back to the house with you?"

If you came to the house, James thought about saying, would you let me do what I have to do? But he knew what would happen if he asked.

So he didn't. He said nothing. The toast was cold, the coffee was getting cold; he felt ill, not hungry. The diner with its booths and stools and countertop felt small to him—close, hot. He felt like punching the sheriff, or crying. He had to get out, get away.

"Nobody's dead," he said suddenly, giving the sheriff what he hoped would look like a smirk. "It was a joke. Just a joke. Everyone's fine."

The sheriff gave him a long look. The expression on his face changed like weather, from compassion to confusion to anger. He stood up, brushed the crumbs from his fingers. "James Jack," he said, "if this is a joke, it's not funny, and if it's not a joke, it's serious. Very serious." He put on his hat and coat and gloves and stood so close that James had to crane his neck to look up at him. "I'll be coming by," the sheriff said. "You can count on it." Then he was gone.

The waitress came with the check. "I guess you'll pay for his?" she asked. James nodded, and handed her a five-dollar bill. "Keep the change," he said.

She hesitated, then folded the bill in half and slid it into her pocket. "Have a nice day," she said, and went back to wiping tables.

You were never afraid of thunder," Tante told him. "You were never afraid of anything."

"I wasn't?"

"No."

"But I am now."

"Yes. You learned it at school."

He did remember the day darkness filled the big windows, the trees danced, bright light scissored through the clouds. He had run to watch it through the glass. Some girls screamed behind him, but that wasn't what made him afraid. It was when the teacher grabbed his arm, dragged him away, her own eyes terri-fied, her voice angry and fearful at the same time. "Sit down!" she screamed above the din of children and storm, shoving him into his chair. Then she smacked him once, hard, on his left ear.

The next morning, Tante came to school with him. She stood in the doorway until the teacher saw her, rose from her desk, and came. Without a word Tante drew her into the hallway. He went to his seat, sat, pulled out his reading book, but his ears were tuned to the voices outside the door. Mostly he heard Tante's, as low and rumbling as thunder. When the teacher came back in, both her ears were red, as if Tante's talking-to had hurt them as much as the teacher's hand had hurt his.

That was his second memory.

He pulled the truck into Keller's Variety Store. It was as busy as usual—workmen buying their lunches, women picking up a few things they'd run out of or forgotten to buy at the big mar-ket on the mainland, an elderly man prowling the state liquor side of the store in search of something he could afford to drink. Some of their faces were pale shaded blue under the fluorescent fixtures, others were ruddy and dry with eyes bloodshot from exposure to winter sun and wind. Nobody there could have afforded to shop at Keller's in summer, when tourist prices took effect.

James picked up a bottle of red wine, put it down, picked it up again. Then he picked up a box of crackers and a wedge of cheese. At the checkout he bought two instant lottery tickets, scratched them both, won nothing. And then he went back out to the truck and drove toward home. Home. Tante's house would be his now. He had never thought about that before.

The metallic glint of the day had faded; the clouds were thick-ening. It had been so dry all winter that the possibility of snow seemed as remote as the mountains that appeared as he drove over the rise. But still—it might snow. It just might. Those looked like snow clouds coming down from the north: gray, shapeless, a herd of foggy elephants. Marching in over the flat, white lake and the fish shanties standing in loose groups here and there on the ice, like people gathered for a party. Or a funeral.

A little snow would be good, as long as it cleared off later.

He checked his mirror. No one behind him.

At the bottom of the hill he turned right and followed the lake. The road here was narrow, winding, and partly paved, partly not, depending on how close it came to the water. The town had learned the futility of fighting the lake for the right to have a road along its edge. Too many dollars had been spent paving a stretch only to have the lake steal the substrate from it. In places now, old tarmac had eroded into beach, so broken to bits that it seemed natural. In places now, after thaws and rains, or during a storm, the road disappeared under water. If you tried to drive through it, you might make it; if not, you could try to back out. At such places the woods and underbrush had been pushed back, driven back, to make room for three-point turns.

But this was winter and the road in winter was generally passable, and safe, if you watched for places where ice sat in the shade all day. This was not the way James usually came home from town; it was easier, and faster, to take the road that cut through the center of the island. But he wanted time to think, and he wanted to drive.

It was comforting to be in the truck. His hands fit the steering wheel, his body fit the seat; the truck sounded and felt familiar, normal, squeaking and groaning and jolting the way it always did. The truck felt like one right thing in the wrongness that the morning had become.

The thought occurred to him that he had ridden in trucks and almost nothing but trucks all his life. In fact, he could remember riding in only one car. And that was the sheriff's, although then it had been a different car, the sheriff had been a deputy, and James had been a little boy. He remembered how fancy the police car had seemed, the chrome instruments futuristic, the two-way radio keeping up a raspy, coded chatter like alien communication, like something out of his comic books.

The deputy had taken him from Tante's to his great-uncle's house, where he saw more cars and trucks and people than he had ever seen there before. Men and women alike wore heavy rubber boots; the ground was muddy with their prints. The day had been sunny and warm after the cold winter, and the people in the dooryard, like the geese in the bird yard, were gabbling and pointing their beaks, open jackets flapping. When the deputy pulled in and stopped the car and the people turned toward him, James felt a new importance. The deputy put his hand on James's shoulder and led him into the house. A peacock wailed.

In the kitchen sat his grandmother, her face sore with crying and two big, soft women in housedresses on either side of her. James did not know who they were, but he knew that they had made the cup of tea that steamed on the table, that they were there to minister to his grandmother. When James came in, they turned to him eyes brimming with tears. "Here's the little boy," one of them said, putting her ruddy hand on his grandmother's shoulder. His grandmother looked at him through red eyes as if looking at something she'd forgotten and didn't want to remember, and then she began to cry again.

That was a long time ago, the day his parents died.

He slowed for a patch of ice at the bottom of a blocked-off driveway. Summer places pocked this part of the lake road, big new houses sided with stained wood and fronted with windows facing the lake, looking west toward the mountains and the sunset. Summer homes for wealthy families, retirement homes for those still young enough to enjoy retirement. Set up off the road, just visible through the trees. Most of these people he knew by name. They were how he made a living: caretaking their places in winter, in summer doing the carpentry jobs too big for them to do themselves. But he didn't really know them, or they him; they weren't his friends. They pretended to be—waving in summer when they drove by in their air-conditioned cars, slapping him on the back in the hardware store or the market, joking with him while they paid for their birdseed or lightbulbs or toilet paper or beer. But their smiles said, "You're lucky to have been born here, just too dumb to know why," and their friendship was as superficial as their needs.

As the lake road wended east around the northern edge of the island, the houses got fewer and poorer. Here the location wasn't so good. You faced into the winter winds. You didn't get the sunset. The water was marshy at its edge, the bottom mucky; mosquitoes swarmed as soon as summer came. These latter were problems that could be overcome, but only by a lot of money, and the money hadn't gotten this far yet. Between the road and the lake grew some scrubby volunteer cedars; cattails stuck up out of the ice like quenched torches.

James slowed the truck and with a sharp turn of the wheel pulled into a driveway almost hidden by the cedars and scrub grown up around it. The trailer was set back in a clearing, rear end in the woods, nose toward the lake, the bow window on its front as dark as a pair of wraparound sunglasses. James stopped the truck behind the car parked there, got out, and went and knocked at the door. It opened, and he went inside.

Faith was so slight that, the first time he'd seen her, he'd thought she was a boy. She looked like a boy now, in T-shirt and jeans, her hair so short and red. But the big fuzzy slippers on her feet and her woman's mouth gave her away. Now she sat back down at the kitchen table, where cards were laid out in a game of solitaire. "Just let me finish this, will you?" she said, considering the cards.

James closed the door and went into the living room—which was really just the front end of the trailer, where carpet took over for the linoleum of the kitchen—and sat down where he could watch Faith in profile. She sat very straight, like a schoolgirl who had been chastised. On her face was an expression of calm but serious concentration, as if the game really mattered to her. With practiced motions, she peeled three cards at a time from the deck in her hand. When the sound of the cards changed, he knew she had begun to deal from the bottom, which she did whenever she was losing—she'd told him so. At the end of the game she swept the cards up into a loose pile and left them lying on the table like that.

She got up and walked toward him. She had a little bit of a bow to her legs; he noticed it now for the first time. For some reason it brought to his eyes the tears that had been waiting for something to set them off. He wanted his hand there, in the place where her legs did not touch one another. He wanted his hand there now.

When she got to him, she reached out as if to smooth his forehead, but didn't. "Hey," she said. "What's the matter?"

He put his arms out and she came into them and he pulled her to him, pressed his face into her bony chest. Her breasts were small through her T-shirt. She let him touch and nuzzle her, kept her chin on top of his head. "James," she said, about to ask a question. "Don't talk," he said.

He lifted her from his lap and laid her down on the carpet and came down on top of her. He ran his hand over her short hair and kissed her, first her forehead, then her lips. She kissed him back. Her taste was already familiar. In a minute, he said, "I want your clothes off."

She looked at him a long moment, then kicked off her slippers and helped him take off her T-shirt and her jeans and the underpants underneath them. Her body surprised him. It was as pale and new as a leaf that had been kept out of light.

The hair between her legs was dark, not red; he had expected that.

"You," she said, pulling at his shirt. But he just unzipped his pants and yanked them down, and in a moment was inside her.

How ready she was, and the smoothness of her—that was another surprise. It was like diving into summer water, the way the water closed around you, tight yet gentle, as warm as something alive. He felt the comfort of it, and the comfort of her skin under his hands, against his face. Concentrating on that, he thought he would be able to control himself. For a moment he wanted to. But when her legs closed around him, pulling him closer, something else took over, and he found himself pounding her into the floor.

When he opened his eyes in the middle of it to look at her, she was looking back at him with the same calm, serious look she wore when she played solitaire. It almost stopped him. But then he felt her hands at his back, pulling him toward her again, and he shut his eyes and forgot what he had seen.

When it was over, they lay on the floor.

"How long has it been?" she said.

He opened his eyes and gazed up at the ceiling. "Since what?"

"Since you were with a woman."

"Eight years," he said.

There was silence.

Then: "Why?" she said.

He thought for a moment. There was only one answer he could give, but he didn't want to give it. He closed his eyes again as he spoke, but the tears came anyway.

"Tante," he said.

It had been happening for a long time, and yet it seemed sudden. As if whatever kept me alive had released its grasp, a hand releasing a moth.

Everything so hard, resisting me. Gathering the cards one by one off the tabletop, my own hands worked against me, and then the cards would not, they absolutely would not square, though I tapped and tapped them. Even the rubber band fought me. The world rising against me, the world slowing me down.

Then each foot stepping into a hole, and never knowing whether or when it would touch bottom.

I reached out, but you were gone. I want you out of this house, I'd told you. Go.

I was being selfish then, thinking only of myself. I'm sorry for that, James. I have to ask your forgiveness for that. But I could not die with you there.

Two

I have heard it said that life occurs in cycles of seven years. It may be true: I had been alone on the island for seven years when I became your Tante and a new cycle began.

Seven years alone. To my ears now it sounds like a jail sentence, a punishment. But at the time it was a relief and a reward.

For decades I had tried to live among people. To be a worker in the beehive of human activity—to live in one cell among many, to fill my cell with honey, to do my duty by my fellow creatures. Had tried to have lovers and had tried to have friends. Had tried to love, both selfishly and selflessly, and had finally come to believe that one could love only oneself, and that not very much.

I left home when I was a girl, and returned only when my father died and left his property to me, the sole survivor of our family. As I read the letter conveying the news, sadness burned through me like a flame, then died, and I felt nothing. I had no desire to revisit the past. If I went home, it would be to sell the place for as much money as it would garner, and then travel or return to New Orleans, where I had long lived.

It was 1955. No one was there to meet me when I stepped off the ferry and onto Grain Island for the first time in almost forty years and found the general store gone from the ferry landing, replaced by a wood-paneled diner, the kind of diner where you give your order standing and take a seat to wait for it. It was midafternoon when I arrived, and the place was empty except for a woman behind the pine counter.

I asked if she could call me a taxi. "Taxi?" she said, her small eyes taking in my padded shoulders and heeled shoes, the cut of my hair and the matching luggage that flanked me.

"I need to get to the old Deo place," I said.

"How come?"

I didn't want to dignify her rudeness with an answer, but I was tired and it seemed the only way I might make progress toward a warm bath and bed.

"Because it's my home," I said, not thinking what I might be revealing.

"Marguerite Deo," the woman said, folding her arms across her considerable chest. For the first time I looked at her as you would someone you might know. The island was a small place, with a long and deep memory; it was possible she remembered me. But I did not recognize this heavy, coarse woman.

"Do you know me?" I said.

"Not really," she said. "Just knew your folks, like everyone did. Sad about your father dying like that, all alone. He was a good man."

"Yes," I said. "Well, that's why I've come home."

She squared a pile of penny newspapers on the counter. "Old as he was, even after your mother died, he took care of himself. Wouldn't leave, wouldn't sell the place for love nor money." Her eyes slipped over my clothes again. I could feel her judgment. "Guess he was saving it for you."

I saw there would be no rushing this conversation, so I nodded politely and waited.

"Just lucky someone found him before the coyotes did," she said. "Been dead there two days or more, out in the dooryard."

This was a detail I hadn't heard. Heat rose into my face. "I didn't know," I said.

"No, I suppose not," she said, and was quiet.

I saw that she was done shaming me, and asked again about the taxi.

She snorted in amusement. "No taxis here, Marguerite Deo," she said. "Not yet, anyway. We haven't got that far." I shrugged my shoulders and had turned to go when she stopped me. "But you can't walk all that way in them shoes," she said. "Nor with them bags. Let me get Billy to carry you over in the truck." She said this without a touch of kindness in her voice, just the weary island pragmatism I remembered well. But I smiled, grateful anyway.

The boy she called to, the boy who looked up from where he was coiling ropes dockside, couldn't have been more than fourteen. Yet there was already in his eyes the concentrated curiosity, the self-assurance, the righteousness that would come to mark him later, as deputy and then as sheriff. Without a word he listened to his mother and gazed at me, then picked up my bags and carried them to the truck parked nearby. I had to pull my narrow skirt above my knees to climb up and onto the seat, but he seemed not to notice or care, and continued his silence as he drove. I had questions I could have asked, he had answers he could have given, but somehow the etiquette of the moment did not allow conversation.

So I gazed out the window. When I'd left home the island had still been primitive—electricity had yet to arrive, motorcars were rare, the population was small and rural. Now cars and trucks traveled paved roads between clusters of new houses not quite organized into villages but nearly so, and electric signs buzzed above the doors of new businesses. Still, the island was poor as ever, the dwellings either neglected and ramshackle—unpainted farmhouses and sway-roofed barns—or cheap and new—house trailers and boxy one-story houses of the kind that had sprung up all across the country, to meet the needs of soldiers returning from the second war.

And then there was our house. Or rather, my father's house.

My father's father had been a fur trader when he was young—a savvy businessman, or so it came down to me. With the practicality of so many French traders, he took an Indian wife and settled down, claiming this big tract of lakeside land. His wife gave him twin daughters, who died as infants, and four sons; three went abroad and never returned, dying in foreign places, in foreign wars or of foreign disease. Only the oldest stayed on the island—my father, Marcel Deo.

He stayed to help my grandfather work the land, though the land wasn't very workable. They milked cows, grew potatoes, planted apple trees, worked around the clock, and still produced barely enough for survival. Then my grandfather became ill—from my father's descriptions, I would say it was tuberculosis—and he and my grandmother went off to take the cure. And did not return.

Now alone, my father took a wife. Anna LaRose was my mother's maiden name, and an apt one it was: she was a dusky rose, dark-haired and dark-eyed, her face heart-shaped and fair. Yet she had been born and raised on a farm, and so, despite her beauty, my father judged her a good mate, used to hard work and practiced in the arts of agriculture and animal husbandry. In him—who by any objective standard could not be called handsome—she saw "promise." Or so she was fond of saying. Looking back, I would say that what she saw was Papa's hundreds upon hundreds of acres of land. Her own family was land-poor and an embarrassment to her in every regard but one: that its French ancestry was pure—that is, untainted by native blood. This was the sum total of her dowry, and a fact in which she took great pride.

In any case, her ambition put under my father the fire that made him what he became. The story goes that, a year after their wedding, my father was walking the land with a sharp shovel, planting it every few feet or so, looking for what might pass as arable soil, when in frustration he thrust the shovel so hard into an exposed ledge that a piece of rock chipped upward. Always quick of hand, he caught it. It was gray and dusty on the outside, but inside, where freshly broken, it was black as coal. He'd found a rare, thick vein of what is known as Black River Limestone—that is, black marble.

Later, when my father became important in the community, people liked to talk about how strong he must have been, to break marble with a shovel. They liked to say he got rich by giving up on the soil and going straight for the rock. As my mother told it, it was she who pointed out the value of the rock, she who harnessed my father's anger and frustration to the yoke of ambition. He quarried the marble, found a market for it. They shipped it by barge to cities as far south as Baltimore. Polished up like glass, it made checkerboard floors, elegant architecture, posh fireplaces, even a cathedral. And it made them rich, at least by island standards.

On the foundation of the original farmhouse, they built the house I looked at now from the window of the boy's truck. Always frugal, they built it not from the valuable marble but from the plain gray granite that my father also quarried. Still, in its time it was a mansion. Now that the oak trees flanking it were massive, the house itself seemed small. And yet it was a solid presence, much as my father himself had been: built to survive.

The truck stopped at the summer-kitchen door, beside which I could see my mother's hollyhocks mounded green and already growing. *Alcea rosea*, I thought. I'd preferred the Latin name from the moment I learned it. A shovel stood there, too, propped against the wall, its blade rusting from the ground up. My father had died of heart failure, or so the lawyer's letter told me; he had died outdoors, I now knew. Had he been digging when it happened? Digging for what? I'd never be sure. But that would have been like him, for he had always loved physical work.

"Here you go," the boy said, as if to remind me that I had asked to come to this place and ought by rights to be getting out of his truck now. "Thank you," I said, and opened the door.

I'd left a Louisiana already humid with summer weather, but here the season was early spring, the maple leaves still reddish and hanging and small. A chill gust of wind ruffled my hair, and I was reminded that Grain Island was once called "Île de Grain," by which its first French inhabitants meant "Squall Island," an intention the officials who anglicized the name had failed to reflect. It was an island known for wind, not wheat. Winter nights when I was a child, the wind rumbled in the chimney like a freight train. In summer, wind and drought sometimes brought the fields to dangerous dryness, and wildfires burned so quickly that all was lost. Most often, the wind came with a hard, driving rain or worse. I remembered a summer storm that brought hail down on my five-year-old head as my mother and I ran from the orchard to the house. I remembered a winter night when ice-laden tree limbs snapped in a wind's angry mouth. I remembered a wagon ride home, my face buried in my hands against rain sharp as needles.

I fought a sudden urge to get back into the truck. If the boy had not already taken my bags into the house, I surely would have gone. Instead, I followed him. It was cold inside, with the kind of cold that comes of doors shut and not opened for some time. "Want me to start you a fire?" the boy said, lifting his chin toward the woodstove. I shook my head and fumbled in my bag for a dollar or two to give him. When he saw what I was doing, it was his turn to shake his head. "No need," he said, and I felt a little ashamed.

And then he was gone, and I began my seven years alone.

What made me stay?

Some thought it greed. That I was waiting for the property to grow in value—as indeed it eventually did—before I sold it to the highest bidder. Which I did not.

Others thought it pure contrariness. That since they expected me to leave, I defied them by staying. If so, I defied myself as well, since I had expected to go, having no more faith in my ability to survive here than anyone else did.

I learned what others thought only later, for at first I had no one who could tell me. Only the looks I got when I went for supplies, when I filled my father's old truck with gasoline, when I opened my wallet and pulled out a crisp hundred-dollar bill. I knew they were seeing me through a flawed lens, but I did not know what they saw. To tell the truth, I did not care, and made no effort to converse, to set the record straight. I cut myself off from communion, from community—telling myself I had no need of it.

No, I did not stay for the reasons they imagined, or even for reasons I could have imagined.

Why I stayed: First, I was fifty-two years old and happy to be alone. No, that's too strong. It was more that I knew *how* to be alone, and since being alone was less painful than not, I preferred it. And alone I was, in that house. Day in, day out.

Only myself to consider, myself to answer to, myself to entertain, myself to keep busy.

At first I had planned only to prepare the house for sale, to
clean it from top to bottom; to eradicate the old smells and
memories; to scrub floors, walls, and windows; to beat rugs; to
open windows and replace the dry air my parents had breathed
with the moist air of spring. I found clothes to wear in my
father's closet, work pants and flannel shirts. I rolled up cuffs and
set to work. I went at it systematically. Overnight my hands
became red, rough, callused. Light and air and the freshness of
various cleaning powders came into the house; the smells of
years of cooking, woodsmoke, and my father's cigars went out,
along with much of the furniture, most of which was new to
me and therefore uninteresting. I kept nothing but the few lost
toys I found, the furniture from my own childhood room,
and a trunkful of childhood memorabilia my mother had
accumulated—my confirmation dress and shoes, birth certificate, school papers.

But cleaning was not enough. I felt a strange desire to return
the house to the freshness it had had in my girlhood, when it was
new and every detail precise. I bought paint and brushes and a
ladder and began to paint woodwork, first inside and then out.
Then I stripped the paint from the kitchen cupboards, the wallpaper from the walls, the old linoleum from the floors. From
books and helpful clerks I learned or recalled the skills that I
needed to do what I wanted to do, from bricklaying to flower
gardening.

It became important to me that I do the job as well as I could,
but with my own hands. Besides the property, my father had left
me rather a large sum of money, stocks and bonds, other investments. I could easily have paid workers to complete the work in
jig time. But I did not. Home again, I found myself mimicking
my father, hunting the mainland for bargains but also going fur-

ther than need explicitly demanded, giving things a stronger foundation or a finer finish than required. Some choices—like the heavy brocade wallpaper I hung in my old bedroom—I imagined that my father would have blanched at. But otherwise, like any child, I also imagined he might have been proud.

The work kept me busy, made me forget everything else. And so a year passed, then two, three—seven. I gained scars and muscles, lost airs, I suppose; became self-sufficient in a new and deeper way, able not just to *be* alone but able also to shape that aloneness, to create a world of my own. I grew my own food, learned to fish summer and winter, cut my own wood. I needed no one, and no one needed me, and I felt satisfied.

And I fell in love, which was the second reason I stayed. Fell in love not only with the house, which despite its past had become my home again, but with the island itself, with the way the fields wove a green, swelling patchwork, with the way the lake turned to lead under stormy skies, with the way the wind scoured the air clean, with the light at dusk, even with the scruffy woods. Although I knew that love of a place was no substitute for the love of human beings, it was nonetheless a love of few risks. Fire, water, wind might threaten me, but the island could not be taken away, would never abandon me.

The third reason, of course, was you.

Your mother was still a girl. She looked like a woman, but she was a girl—transparent, luminous, a sapling with one root. She appeared at dusk one evening, emanating from nothing; was there when I looked up from the ground where on hands and knees I was planting beans, one by one. I knew instantly that she had come for a favor, although I did not know what shape the favor would take. I also knew that I would grant it, although certainly I had no reason to, and no one would have expected it of me. No, not the way I lived my life, a virtual hermit. Maybe that was why I granted the favor—to defy expectations? Or maybe it was only that she reminded me of myself: the clear hazel of her eyes, the way her hair hung over her bare shoulders, her slender arms, the milk-filled breasts that burdened her delicate frame.

I have always been a believer in signs. The circle around the moon that foretells snow. The pain in a joint that foretells rain. Simultaneity is never merely coincidence, serendipity never accident—cause *is* effect, effect cause. When I first looked up, I thought a door had opened up into the past to show me myself the way I had been, years before. When I first looked up, it was me as a girl I saw.

She showed me the baby—you—sleeping in a basket in the shade. She offered to let me hold you. I said no, thank you.

"Could you keep him," she said, "just a few evenings, till I find another sitter?"

So that was the favor. I stood up, brushing the dirt from my hands. "What makes you think I know how to take care of a baby?"

"You're a woman, aren't you?"

What made her think that was proof enough? I was fifty-nine then, more than three times her age; maybe she assumed some experience, some wisdom I didn't have. Or perhaps she thought only that if she could learn, so could I.

"Besides," she said, "you're so nearby." It was then I realized where I had glimpsed her before—sitting in the sun outside a trailer down the road.

I did not want money, did not need it, so we bartered. Her husband—your father—would split and stack my winter's wood in return for my keeping you evenings that summer, so she could wait tables in the bar at the inn, our one "resort." Her mother-in-law—your grandmother Caroline—had got her the job; they would be working side by side. Otherwise Caroline herself might have cared for you. And your father was working as a carpenter on the mainland, coming home a day here, a day there. (A gentle, clumsy, overgrown boy, voice still cracking but beard thick and arms powerful and hands large enough to make your head seem no bigger than an apple, when he came to collect you, your basket was light in his hand but he held it steady, and you never woke.)

She went off to work, and I carried you inside.

That first evening I had one goal: that you not wake. I protected your sleep like a lioness, as if I thought in sleep the growing happened and to disrupt it was to tempt death. In short, I was afraid. Afraid of a baby waking and of what it—what you—might ask of me.

That first evening. In the basket, sleeping in a pool of light, you were so small, your life measured in weeks. At my desk working, I felt miles and decades away from you, yet at first I was distracted by your presence, by your minute breath, moist and rhythmic across the room. Like the breath of a plant.

At first I listened to you; then I grew used to the sound; then, gradually, my work caught me up again and I was mesmerized by the motion of my own hand as it moved across the page, delineating in words and drawings the details of *Geranium robertianum*, Herb-Robert. I had set as my task the composition of a book about the more obscure wildflowers found on my land. I wanted to celebrate that myriad populace that is all but invisible, that requires a caring, attentive eye to see its beauty. Why? No doubt because by then I too felt invisible, a woman more than half a century old and as invisible to the people around me as a knotweed flower. As homely and common and small as the Marguerite my mother named me for, the pale yellow daisy she was unaccountably fond of.

On the desk before me that night sat a single Herb-Robert plant, uprooted and lamplit against a white leaf of paper, collected from the shady ridge behind my house. Its leaves gave off an angry smell. With a precise hand I drew their fine-cut silhouettes. I had to work fast, for the flower—pink, five-petaled, pure and small—would fade quickly. When I had the shape down and what details could be drawn in black ink, I paused to let it dry; next I would take the color to it, thin washes of green, of rose madder.

It was a late-spring evening, almost summer. As I worked, the sun sank behind the ridge; the room became cooler, darker. I hugged my shoulders. Through the open windows I heard the high-pitched chorus of tree frogs at the swampy edges of the lake, the crickets, the wind in the trees as the air cooled. The birds were quiet, but spring was out there, singing away. I let it wash over me. I felt completely content but at the same time only waiting, suspended for a moment before returning to my work, my attention dispersed just for that instant, resting before it gathered itself again to the task set on the desk before me. Yet into that openness came a reminder from some self I did not yet know. My ears, which had lost themselves in the cacophony of the evening, all at once attuned themselves to a closer sound. Where was it? Where was that tiny rhythm, that small breath?

The pool of light had long since disappeared; your basket sat in shadow, cooling. How could I have forgotten? I rushed to you, heart pounding in the cage of my ribs. Believing you had stopped breathing. Believing I had already failed.

You gazed up at me—silent, but awake and alert. I picked the basket up, brought it with me, set it close to my chair. Arranged the blanket more firmly. The whole time, your dark eyes were on me, watching. Nothing moved but your mouth, that voracious mouth with a mind of its own. "He's a hungry boy," your mother had said proudly. If that voracious mouth insisted, I would heat the bottle in my icebox and hope that it satisfied. "Hungry?" I asked. Of course you didn't answer. I wanted to interpret your look, to read that gaze, but I had not yet learned the language in which your eyes wrote their message.

I began to sing, the first song that came to mind. "It was just one of those things," I sang. "Just one of those crazy flings. A trip to the moon on gossamer wings. It was just one of those things. . . ." I made it a lullaby.

In a moment your eyes closed again, and the steady moist breathing resumed. I returned to my work, but never again would it absorb me as it had; in fact, gradually I abandoned it, or rather it abandoned me, having found my commitment lacking.

"Was he good?" your mother said when she came to take you back.

"As gold," I said, handing over the sleeping baby.

You.

Your parents loved you, but times were hard.

Of course, times have always been hard on Grain Island. It seems, in many ways, not a place intended to support life, or human life at least. Nothing but a big wind-blown boulder, poking up out of the lake like an iceberg. Nine places out of ten your shovel hits rock before its head is buried. Looking at the woods, you think the land must be good, must be rich. But notice how few truly large trees there are, how young the forest is, how young it stays. Cedar, box elder, maple: their seeds get here, take root, and grow, but before they can reach mature size, they run out of soil, sicken, and let the wind shove them over, roots and all. Only oaks can stay the course. Still, roots can break up rock, and one day centuries from now the island will have its soft deep cap of soil. For now it's only in places, a rich clay loam where you can find it.

It was not the soil, of course, that brought the first people here, but the water; and not just for fishing, but for transport, rivers and lakes being their highways. Like my grandfather, native people traveled for commerce, trading from village to village, not for wealth but to survive—trading fur for grain, grain for beans, beans for meat. New settlements piled up like barnacles on rock wherever traders stopped to rest or hunt. When the French traders came, native villages became towns and towns became cities, and cities forgot that what lay beneath them was native land, native bones.

Grain Island was a place where many had stopped but few stayed. It never grew enough to forget anything.

Your parents stayed, as I did, because they loved the island—your father because he grew up on it, your mother because she had not. They fought to stay here, they struggled against the place to make a place for themselves on it. Just to make enough money to live, to stay where they wanted to be. That is why your mother went to work, when in her heart she would rather have been with you.

The summer fell into a kind of rhythm. I found myself watching for your arrival each evening, planning ahead for us. At first you were an infant, not even able to turn from your front to your back, but I knew a child ought to be stimulated, could be taught, no matter how young. I brought you into the garden with me. I laid your blanket on the grass and showed you flowers and colors and told you their names. I warded off insects; I dandled you and talked to you and tickled you and played games with you. I listened as you learned to make sounds; I praised you as you learned to reach, to grasp, to bring my finger to your mouth. Fall came; I discovered how you loved to watch a fire burning, and we spent our evenings by the hearth. I watched as your eyes lightened to blue, as the coarse hair you were born with fell out and was replaced by a fine, dark fuzz. My days revolved around those hours you were with me, and the days your mother stayed home and kept you to herself felt empty in contrast.

When the inn shut down for the winter, your mother's job vanished, and she became free to care for you every night. It came up on me suddenly, that night in late October. "Well, Tante," she said to me—it was her nickname for me, pronounced "taun-tee," what she called the old aunts in her own family, in Canada—"Well, Tante, say good-bye to this boy. He won't be troubling you anymore."

I stepped outside to wave good-bye. The October wind battered the trees like surf. Even the great oaks swayed, their leaves clapping like children thrilled with a dangerous display. For some time your mother had been walking home in weather like this, had been walking *you* home in it, and I felt sorry that I hadn't been paying better attention. As she put you in the buggy she'd brought and started bumping you down the driveway toward the road, I shouted after her. She stopped and looked back. "It's turning cold," I said. "I'll take you in the truck."

It was the first time I had offered such a thing. She raised a brow but nodded, and I went into the barn and brought out my father's old truck. I rarely used it but always kept it running, at first because I thought I might need it to escape the island, and later because a truck is handy in rural life, something always needing to be hauled.

Your mother got in and I handed you up to her, then put the buggy in the back and got in myself. The truck had no dashboard lights, so I couldn't see you, couldn't see her, but I could hear her talking to you, low soft incomprehensible words, sweet words, loving words. Until that moment, my conscious thoughts of you had been not unfond, but I had pretended to myself that you were a bit of a nuisance, some extra trouble I had to go to. Now, as she spoke the feelings I could never speak to you and had not known I felt until that moment, my heart flooded with sadness at losing you.

She pointed me to her driveway. I knew it was there, but in the dark I did not know exactly where. In the truck's headlights the trailer looked drab and insubstantial. "Would you like to come in?" Helen said. "Have a cup of coffee?" I struggled against, then gave in to, the impulse to say yes.

The trailer was dark. "Jack's got a job down in Marlboro," your mother said. "He's coming home Fridays these days." She turned on the overhead light in the kitchen, and for a moment the place looked worse than I had feared—shabbier, poorer. But then she turned on a lamp or two, filled a pot with water and put it on the stove, brought out a plate of homemade cookies, and it began to feel like a home.

I stayed for more than an hour, listening to her talk. Helen told me the story of how she and your father met, skating on the canal in Ottawa when they were both fourteen, she visiting from Manitoba. How he had hitchhiked to Montreal to see her whenever she was there visiting her great-aunts, who lived in the old section of town, spoke nothing but French, and loved Jack as much as she did. How, after high school graduation, they had a wedding up in Montreal. How her parents hadn't made the trip, but the old aunts had thrown them a party, and Jack's family had been there, his mother, Caroline, and his uncle and his sisters, everyone except Jack's father, who had died two years before. She told how you had been born right in that trailer, on a winter night when the ferry wasn't running; how by the time Doc Hobbs, young then and the only doctor on the island, came stomping snow into the trailer, you were halfway born but blue in the face, the cord wrapped round your neck. "He was a blue baby," she said. "But he pinked right up."

I didn't say much, just listened. You were sleeping in her arms, and when she talked about you, she looked at you as if she still could not believe that you had come from her. "Isn't he something," she said.

Back home, nothing had changed. Yet everything had. As I lay in my bed, the silence I had once loved became oppressive. I found myself up and walking through the house. In the kitchen, I searched for something to eat or drink, although I did not want or need to eat or drink. Then I remembered the bottle I had found that first spring, hidden in a corner of the pantry behind moldy bags of rice and flour. Whose bottle had it been, I'd wondered then: Mother's or Papa's? Papa would have had no need to hide it, or, if he did, would have hidden it in the shed at the quarry. So—Mother's, then. My virtuous Catholic mother, with a bottle of vodka hidden in the pantry. Vodka because they say it leaves no odor on the breath, although I have never found that to be true.

I found the vodka and poured a bit of it into a mug. It burned my tongue, pure alcohol, and then lifted the weight bearing down on me so quickly that for a moment I seemed to float above myself.

I filled the mug and took it with me to my bedroom, where it helped me sleep in my empty house.

A week passed. Your mother had invited me to come and visit "anytime." But a certain stoicism infected me. I had become accustomed to a solitary life; the yearning I felt for you made me feel sick with loneliness. I wanted to wean myself of you, rid myself of the weight of our connection. But at odd times of day I would find myself thinking of you. An internal clock reminded me that it was time for your bottle, time to change your diaper, time to rock you to sleep in my arms. And suddenly I remembered the sensation of your fingers closing around one of mine, the calm, curious look in your eyes, the smell of your skin. Those last few days, you had sometimes got up on hands and knees, sometimes made sounds that sounded like words. And I was so proud. Now when those moments came back to me, and I found myself smiling, I tried to shunt them aside, to think of other things, jerking the steering wheel of my mind to the left or right as if a deer had stumbled into the road ahead.

And every night I drank a little. Just enough to help myself sleep.

Then the vodka was gone. I made a trip to the village, to the relocated general store. To make the vodka seem less the purpose of my trip, I bought several things, things I did not really want or need, including a small box of the zwieback cookies you gummed when you were teething. I watched the clerk's eyes to see if she would stand in judgment of me, or wonder at this odd collection of purchases. But to her I was no different from any other customer. Tourism had changed the island; to the young clerk I was just another unfamiliar face in a sea of many.

Outside, a big-flaked snow was just beginning, the first of the season. I drove slowly over the slippery roads, but passed the turnoff for the center island road and instead drove down and along the lake road, toward your parents' trailer. I was like a woman in love with a married man, drawn to you but at the same time wishing I were not. I thought at first I would just drive past, would not stop, but I could not fight the urge, and found myself turning the truck into the driveway again. The zwieback would be my excuse.

In the daylight and the snow, the trailer was not so bad. I could see flowered curtains in the windows, potted plants; I could see how the sun would shine in on a clear morning. "Tante! It's good to see you," said your mother when she opened the door to me.

You were there, sitting in a new contraption: a seat in a ring with wheels. You bounced in this thing, laughing; then, when you saw me, you pushed yourself across the floor toward me, rolling. "It's called a walker," Helen said. "Jack brought it home last week. Look how he took to it!"

I heard her but saw only you. You put your arms out to me and made the sounds that I had come to recognize as your way of calling me. I bent to you, took you up. "Big boy!" I said, pressing my face to your warm, sweet neck.

"He misses you," Helen said, smiling.

My throat swelled at her words. I handed her the box of cookies. She opened them, and, still holding you, I took one and put it into your fist. You smiled at it.

We all sat down at the table. Helen leaned back, folded her arms, cocked her head and looked at me—at us. "You know," she said. "I've been thinking about getting another job. A day job . . ."

I saw the query in her eyes. "I could watch him for you," I said. My voice quavered, but only a little.

"I wouldn't want to be a bother. I could pay you."

"No," I said. I had my hands under your arms; I felt your strong legs straightening, your feet pushing against my lap. "That won't be necessary."

And so I became your tante, for real and for good.

The next years passed so quickly for me, like frames of a movie flashing by. But I took solace in knowing how slow it must have seemed for you. You grew; how you grew! Overnight, or so it seemed, you were a boy, not a baby anymore.

I cared for you while your parents worked. When you were

with them, I missed you, but always with the certainty that you would be with me again. You were four when Helen confided that she was trying to have another baby. I tried to imagine caring for two of you. It was not beyond imagining. I had changed that much.

People still talk about the winter of '66–'67. The winter of the big fish, they call it. Not because the fish were large, but because there were so many of them. Who knows what causes these occasional felicities of nature, or even if, in nature's terms, they are felicities? The lake froze over early, froze deep and quick and never thawed till spring; the fish must have been frantic for food. The fishing shanties went up as quick as the ice froze, and quick grew into a ragtag village sprawled across the ice. Like short, faded strokes of paint on a white canvas. We could see it from the ridge above the quarries, you and I. We could look down and see it.

By then you were four, and I was sixty-three, and it had been more than a decade since I came back to Grain Island. By then the life I had lived in New Orleans seemed like an intermission, a long vacation, a dream. This house, this island, this life was reality, and I was happy in it.

But that winter a melancholy stole into me. Maybe it was the weather. As everyone knows, water warms an island, but that winter, the snug of warmth went early and stayed gone too long. The wind got caught in the trees, growled and wrestled among the branches. Dead branches brittled and snapped off from where they met the trunk, clean as if they had been cut. The days were endlessly sunny, but whatever heat the day accumulated, the night sucked away into an unlimited sky, clear and starry, no clouds to stop it.

The only happy note was that it did not snow. Oh, a thin crust persisted, replenished now and then by a lazy flurry, but the snows of normal years—hip-deep and then some—never came.

The cold kept it away, kept moisture out of the air. Instead, hoar-frost gathered an inch deep on the insides of the windows, a fili-gree of white plumes preventing us from looking out. It was like living in a tomb of white crystals.

Each night after you had gone, I drank, even though it only took me deeper and deeper into the sadness that infected me like a virus. I could not understand why the past had come back to me just then, or why it would not leave, but I dwelled in a private hell, memories swirling around me like a play watched through a scrim.

This is how I felt that night, the night before the Ides of March, the year of the big fish. And so I drank more than I ever had before, drank until I had blotted out all sensibility, until I entered that dark timeless space I both cherished and feared.

I woke cold, head on the table. The coals almost out, the woodbox empty. Roused myself to stoke the fire. Went outside, into the dark.

My steps echoed like a giant's in the silence. I felt swollen, leaden. It was still winter, still so cold that my breath froze into snowflakes that rose strangely up from my nostrils and fell again to melt on my eyelids. For a moment I considered lying down right there, right then, and giving myself up to the cold, taking that last step into oblivion. I looked up at the stars pricking the sky, and thought how pleasant it would be, to die under the con-stellations. But then I remembered that you would be coming in the morning, that you and your mother would find me, and I carried wood into the house, an idiotic two sticks at a time, one in each hand, taking each pair all the way into the house, leaving the doors wide open behind me and letting the cold bully its way inside. The wood cart stood idle. I was oblivious to everything but my objective: to fill the woodbox.

At last it was full. I chucked a few sticks onto the barely glow-ing coals, watching until they caught fire. Then I shut the doors and went into the front room and curled up on the settee, pulling the quilt around me.

My own coughing woke me at dawn. The scrim of the night before had become real; smoke was everywhere. My body conscious but mind still sleeping, I opened the doors, front and back, let the cold sweep inside again. I checked the stove. Shut tight. The smoke was not coming from the fire. I stepped out into the frozen air and craned my neck up to the chimney. Nothing there. Sometimes birds build nests in chimneys, but no bird builds a nest in midwinter. No bird can descend into a hot chimney.

I went back into the house. The smoke was curling about my things, caressing the wing-back chair, pausing over the open book on the table, sending a sidelong glance at the garden plans laid out there. Everything seemed gray and distant. I picked up a sheaf of drawing paper and waved it at the smoke, coaxed and cajoled it out the front door and out the back. Slowly the air cleared and the colors returned. I stood for a moment, sniffing the air, surveying the damage, asking myself what the smoke had wanted with me. It must have had a powerful desire to stay inside, when it loved nothing more than to rise straight up to the moon.

By the time you came, only a wisp or two of smoke remained, wandering about the house in a forlorn and desultory fashion, as if it had lost all ambition and didn't know what to do with itself. It would be some time before I would recognize this for the sign it was, would be able to read the message the smoke brought to me, the way it foretold that day's events.

According to your grandmother Caroline, who told me this story so that I could tell you, your father came of a good family with bad luck.

It is hard, in this scientific age, to believe in luck, to believe in curses or blessings given without reason. A good family's good fortune can be explained by hard work, honesty, and perseverance; a bad family's bad fortune by sloth and weak character. But only luck seems to explain how the slothful succeed, how the hardworking fail, why life seems like a lottery in which some people are born winners, others losers. A good family with bad luck; a bad family with good luck.

What could it be but bad luck, that a man like James Wright Sr., your grandfather, a football star in high school and as strong and healthy a man as anyone could imagine—hardworking, honest, and willing—would die of a heart attack at thirty-five? Leaving your grandmother with three children to care for and no insurance policy, his only legacy to your father—the oldest, at sixteen—the rickety fish shanty he'd built with his own two hands.

It seemed at first like good luck that your grandfather had an older, unmarried brother who could take care of the abandoned family. Homer had always worked the family farm, a going concern with fifty milking cows and a stand of sugar maples and the sugar house to go with it. After the war, he'd also begun what many people saw as a strange business: raising ornamental fowl. He'd done it more out of curiosity and a love of birds than ambition; still, before he knew it, he was, in relative terms, successful. People from as far away as Japan would come to buy from him—birds, chicks, eggs; his swans and ducks swam in ponds all over the globe, his chickens and geese populated lawns in England and France. In summer, the bird yard was like something out of a dream, peacocks dragging their tails, shiny black roosters, ducks with bejeweled eyes—all manner of rare and surprising creatures, the ground littered with their feathers and the air full of their calls.

If you went to visit, it was best to stay out of the house. The bird yard, the barn, the sugar shack were as neat as a pin, well cared for. It was the inside of the house that smelled like a barn. The kitchen seemed, at first, to have a dirt floor, but in fact it was linoleum that had not been swept or mopped for years; dirty dishes crowded the countertops and sink; the living room was mounded with old mail, newspapers, tin cans, milk cartons, jars—things Homer could not bear to throw away for fear of wastefulness—clean and dirty laundry mixing together freely (when he needed a clean shirt, a rare event, he sniffed until he found one). Having given up on the kitchen, Homer ate standing up and out of cans, washing the fork after each meal and keeping it in his breast pocket like a pen till the next.

It was not that he was an uncaring man. He was simply a man who cared less for himself than for other things: the land, the barns, the animals, the trees, his family—and Caroline, his brother's wife.

Homer loved Caroline. She knew this. He did not know she knew this, but she did. And it became clear, after his brother died, that he wanted to marry her. He was so different from his brother, though, so different from the man she had married, that it was hard for her to consider the notion of him as a second husband.

Jimmy had been popular and handsome; he's who gave you your dark hair and light eyes. He and Caroline were teenage sweethearts, married straight out of high school. They'd never had much, but it hadn't seemed to matter. Caroline was happy with him because he was a happy man, an open man, the kind of man who cried when his babies were born and walked the floor with them when they cried, the kind of man who let you know his feelings straight out. Honest as the day was long, and free with his affections.

Homer had always been a quiet one. Not just quieter than his brother: *quiet*. It was rare for him to say more than a few words in sequence to anyone. I met him once myself, and can testify to this, but I cannot tell you whether it was because he was shy or because he had nothing to say. He was a hunter and fisherman who liked to go off by himself. Caroline said he could rarely tolerate a room that contained more than two other people. When he visited her house—to bring the weekly eggs and milk, say— he stood awkward in the kitchen while the daughter who had opened the door fetched her mother. Yet when Caroline came in, something happened to his face. You couldn't call it a smile, she said, but it had a smile's effect. And so she would invite him to sit down for a cup of coffee and he, awkward as he so obviously felt, would sit with her and listen and nod and pay attention as if he were distilling every word she had to say, boiling it down from sap to precious syrup to store away in memory.

And so, despite his silence on the matter, Caroline never doubted his love for her, never doubted that it was a pure, generous love, a rare love. And she knew he would have made a decent father: steady, reliable, capable. And she knew that when enough time had passed, he would ask her to marry him. She thought long and hard about what she would do—for her family, for herself. She didn't love him, would never love him as she had Jimmy. And, in many ways, her life was already ideal—all needs met, except those most intimate. So she waited, hoping that the answer would come to her, that she could avoid hurting him, that time would somehow take care of things.

The winter of the big fish, it had been seven years since your grandfather's death. Only the girls, eight and twelve, were left with Caroline; your father had married when he was eighteen and moved out and into the trailer down the road from me; you had been born. I had been caring for you for four years.

Something happened to islanders that winter. When the ice-boxes were full but the fish kept coming, people saw a chance to make money, and when the smell of money got in the air, people couldn't help but inhale it. Some got together and began to truck their fish north to Montreal and inland to the landlocked cities, to sell to fish markets and restaurants. A kind of fever developed, something like gold fever. Fish fever. Those who were turning a profit showed it by spending the money in visible and frivolous ways: a new television set, for instance, or a new CB for the truck. Fancy winter boots, a new parka. Alcohol. Meat. It was not enough money to bother saving; not enough to put toward a new roof for the barn or a new truck. Just enough to make everyone feel greedy.

Soon the ice was cluttered with more than shanties. Feuds broke out when some people accused others of moving their shanties during the night; there were theories that shanties ought to be twenty feet apart, or thirty, or forty, but not everyone thought that, and there was only so much room where the fishing was best. Not wanting to share the bounty, men broke up with longtime fishing partners and brought their wives out instead. Fishing became a livelihood, a job—not a bonus, but something you counted on, something you had to do. Out before dawn and gone till after dark, parents neglected their children, who went wild with the freedom, grew surly when reined in. Sometimes a wife would make the long trip to take the fish to market while her husband stayed to fish alone. When profits dropped, mistrust developed. Was this all you could get? Where did you spend our money? Who'd you spend it with? You knew which women couldn't answer by the port-wine bruises on their cheeks.

As tempers grew short, so did the season; as the season grew short, so did tempers. Now, men got up long before dawn to listen to the radio. Would today be the day the great thaw began? Tomorrow? Next week? And slowly, slowly, fish numbers diminished. Exhausted, angry, disappointed with themselves—the money gone, always, as soon as it appeared—the men kept pushing themselves, their wives, even their children. Lines had to be kept in the water at all times. Health didn't matter, nor school, nor love; nothing mattered but fish. Even in the bitterest cold.

It hit your mother and father, too. Work was scarcer than usual that winter, housing starts being down; fishing seemed easier than scrabbling for jobs. And so Helen and Jack fished, and left you with me long hours every day while they went out on the ice in your grandfather's shanty. "One more day," your mother would say when she got you in the evening. "Jack says one more day." She loved your father, Jack loved her; they were in this together. "We want to buy the trailer and the land it's on. We want to build something together," Helen told me, her face with a new, adult determination on it. "We want to have another baby." Another night your father came to pick you up, his eyes bloodshot but blazing blue in a sunburned, smiling face. He held up a bucket of gutted fish. "Nest egg for the new baby, Tante!" he said, triumphant. And I knew then that their efforts had succeeded.

Your grandmother told me the fever was on Homer too, but for him it was different, she said. She got the feeling that, this winter more than any other, being on the ice was Homer's way to get off to himself, to get away from people, including her. He set his red shanty far from either shore, where it sat by itself like a bishop's miter, and he faced it north, up the middle of the lake, which must have made the wind bitter but kept the other shanties out of sight. And he went out as soon as chores were done and didn't come back till sundown. But Homer didn't care about the fish, or the money; in fact, most of what he caught he gave to Helen and Jack to sell, and the rest he gave to Caroline, stopping by almost every other night with a pailful, his face also reddened by the wind and sun and cold, and his own eyes like lights burning.

You know the ice can do strange things to a man, especially a man alone. Many a solitary man has walked off the ice and into his solitary home—his rented cabin, a trailer on a bit of owned land, the old farmhouse his daddy left him—and taken out the gun he inevitably has, and put it to his head. My father called it "ice sorrow." Like lightning, it only needs to strike once.

That winter, Homer was a more solitary man than ever before. Caroline worried about him, out there day after day, speaking hardly a word to anyone, and no one to speak a word to. She asked Jack and Helen to keep an eye on him, which they were glad to do, and did, putting their shack as close to his as he'd allow. ("Don't crowd me," he told them when they wanted to come closer.) Still, Caroline was glad as the season drew to a close. State law said that by March fifteenth, the shanties had to come off the ice, for nights at least—too many shanties already littered the lake bottom from unexpected thaws. Although the more ambitious could drag them back on for the day if the ice held, March fifteenth was at least a kind of harbinger, a warning that spring would come and the ice would go. Caroline thought that once the brighter season of birds hatching and sap running began, Homer would come back from whatever dark country he had been visiting, the dark country she'd glimpsed in him now and then that winter when he'd come to visit her.

By the fourteenth of March, most everyone felt as Caroline did. Glad for winter to be ending. Ready for spring. Twilight time that day, Caroline was outside hanging wet clothes on the line, knowing they would freeze by morning, but also knowing that in freezing they would dry. Still, for the first time since November, the air was warm enough that it did not pinch your nostrils when you took a breath. Things looked softer, too, moister, as if some small, unmeasurable thawing had already begun. The sunset was generous, good cheer in its colors.

When the truck pulled into the driveway, Caroline knew it was Homer by the careful way he took the turn, by the unhurried way he shut off the engine and opened the door. He carried a box containing eggs and milk and the pail of fresh perch. "Hello, Homer," she said, nodding, smiling at him, and he looked at her with his gray-blue eyes. "A bit warmer today, eh?" He nodded, still carrying the box. "Why don't you set those inside? I'll be in shortly." He put the box under one arm as he opened the door and let himself into the kitchen.

I can picture it so clearly, the gray-haired, gray-eyed man, his large hands, his stooped shoulders, his whole being poured into that moment of providing sustenance to the woman he loved. Standing there in her dim kitchen, waiting for her. His ears tuned to her movements. When at last she comes inside, he sees her the way any man sees the object of his love, with eyes softened by longing. She takes off her coat. She's still in her dirty waitress's uniform, still smells of fried food and bacon grease, but when she thanks him, touches his hand, reaches up to kiss his cheek, then, at last, after seven years of longing—or more, for who knows how long he has felt this way—he is overcome. And for the first time he reaches his hand out to her, touches her shoulder, turns her toward him. It is a tentative moment, a dangerous moment; everything rests on this moment. But she kisses him—or does she let him kiss her? It is an awkward kiss, he knows it, an unpracticed kiss. But a kiss that changes everything. No turning back. So he asks her, his face in her hair so that he cannot see hers. At last he asks her, as if asking for release. "Marry me, Caroline," he says.

"Oh, Homer," she says, pulling away, turning her back, attending to the food he's brought her. "Don't let's be silly."

Why? Why did she treat his offer so lightly, dismissing it without hesitation? The proposal had not surprised her. Why not just ask for time to think? Why?

This is what she asked herself later, what she could not explain. She had humiliated the man who loved her. And whom she loved—as a brother, at least, and as a friend—although she let him leave believing she did not.

I never really knew your father except for what I saw of him and what your mother told me, but your mother and I became something like friends. Maybe because she was an outsider too, or maybe because she felt grateful to me, or maybe—who knows—because she thought by ingratiating herself to me she might benefit you financially. Whatever the reason, Helen treated me with respect and honesty. Often, when she came to drop you off or pick you up, I offered her coffee or tea, and we sat together and watched you, just watched you, sharing the wordless pleasure that only two mothers can share.

That winter, I'd taught you to play cards with me. And, using the cards, I also began to teach you to count, to add, to subtract—even to read, writing the words out next to the numbers and pictures. We told no one; it was our secret. When we were ready, we decided to show your mother first. That morning Helen kept her coat on while she listened to you read from the child-sized book I'd given you, shaking her head in amazement. "I thought he was too little to learn," she said.

You went off to play. Helen turned to me with that sly look she sometimes got when she was amused. "Tante, you know, at first people said I was crazy to let you keep him."

I dreaded the answer, but asked the question anyway. "What else did they say?"

She hesitated, gazing at the floor for a moment, and I knew

she didn't want to tell me. Finally, she spoke. "They said you didn't belong here," she said. "That you broke your parents' hearts. That you were stuck-up and spoiled." She paused again. "That you let your father die alone."

"So why did you leave the boy with me, then?" This question was out before I thought about the danger of asking it.

"Because they were wrong," she said, and I could see in her smile that she believed it.

Most days my house fairly glowed with heat, even early in the morning, because when the fire died down in the night, the chill nudged me awake to stoke it, and though made of stone and very old, the house was well insulated. I had seen to that in my renovations, and over the years I had found the gaps and holes and filled them. When mice and sometimes birds came and pulled bits of insulation out for their own nests, I merely filled it in again. "You've got to let creatures do what they will," I told you. "They've got as much right as we do."

The morning of March the fifteenth, the morning after I let the fire go out and the house grow cold, the morning the smoke filled my rooms, your mother let you in the front door and was gone before I could speak to her. The air still smelled like something burning, and the gray haze still wandered about the front room. I called to you from the kitchen, and you came, your cheeks red from the cold and eyes bright as always. "Wet log," I said, explaining the smoke as I spooned coffee into the boiling pot. "Wet log, and I left the stove door open a minute, and I think someone was sitting up on the chimney top, keeping warm or cleaning his feathers." A bit of smoke moved around the kitchen; some of it found the lamp on the table and went up through the shade and out its top. I watched you watch it.

"Smoke loves a chimney," I said. "It does?" you said. I nodded. "Smoke is the soul of the tree," I said. "Fire sets it free, and a chimney helps it find its way heavenward." You nodded, understanding.

When I had the coffee ready—mine hot and black, yours halved with cream and sweetened with sugar—I put it on a little tray with a plate of buttered toast and brought it out to the table in the front room. The smoke was almost gone, and the sun shone through the frosted windows, a pale but diffuse light. "What kind of tea is this?" you asked as you tasted yours. "Not tea but coffee," I said. It was the first time I had made for you the chicory coffee I loved so much in my New Orleans days; my supply was shipped to me, and I considered it too precious to consume daily. "A very special kind of coffee, from far away." "It's delicious," you said, the big word rolling around in your mouth like a marble. I showed you the treat of dunking buttered toast in the sweet coffee—my father's treat—and you drank the coffee all up and asked for more.

The table was spread with our garden plans. We were working on a means to defeat the raccoons that had raided my corn the summer before. Coons like corn, so we would give them corn—some. I showed you the map I had finished the previous evening. "Here, by the woods, I'll plant six rows of corn. All the way around." I pointed. "And then here, I'll plant the squash. All the way around." My finger made a circle inside the corn. "Coons hate squash—it has those tangled, prickly stems, and they're conservative about where they put their feet. So here, in the center, the good corn. The coons'll eat the outside corn and leave the middle alone because of the squash." I sat back in my chair, sipping. "What do you think?" You nodded approval like a wise old man.

After lunch that day, it was warm enough for a walk in the

woods. We put on our wool jackets and went out with our hands bare for the first time in months, yours small in mine. I sniffed the air. "Smell that?" I said.

"Smell what, Tante?"

We stopped walking and raised our noses up, sniffed together. "That," I said. "A little sharp, a little wet. Not a smell, really. More like a mood." You nodded. "The ice is melting," I said. "Mark my words, it'll be out before the week is over." We walked on, following the road up to the quarry, and then the path up to the ridge, where we could look down at the lake where your parents were ice fishing.

When we reached the top that afternoon, what we saw confused us. Smoke rising from a red shanty; a truck, nose down in open water and sinking; people clustered and scurrying; the huge arc of water spraying. We didn't see what had happened, what calamity had caused all this. By the time we climbed the rocks to the view, it had already happened and the fire truck was there, and the ambulance was on its way, though they would not find the bodies, then or ever. But we knew it was Homer's red shanty smoking, half sunk in the open wound in the ice, the blue of water as shocking against the white ice as blood on a sheet. And we knew it was your parents' truck, too, nose down in the wound. We could not tell what had happened, but we recognized the shanty, we recognized the truck. We stood there, the two of us, silent, looking, knowing but not comprehending. How could this have happened? What, exactly, had happened?

I don't think anyone ever knew. Your grandmother Caroline thought she knew, thought it was her fault. Thought Homer had done it to himself, set his rejected soul on fire. But it could have been an accident. Homer'd had a gas heater in the shanty. Perhaps he'd fallen asleep. Maybe he'd fallen down, knocked it over.

People had watched your parents see the fire, had seen them rush to their truck, drive out to him, jump out of the truck and slide and fumble toward the burning shanty. People say Jack got the shanty door open and was inside when the ice gave way. The ice would have been weakest there—it was where the current ran. "Homer knew that. Homer knew the ice, and he would have known it was weak," Caroline told me. Helen's scream echoed across the lake. No one could tell if she rushed in after Jack, or if the ice took her down with the truck. It happened too fast. And then it was over, and quiet, and for a moment of sheer disbelief no one could move. Then everyone was moving. Somebody got on the CB, and the fire truck came, and the ambulance was on its way. And just then you and I topped the view, and looked down, hand in hand.

I knew they would come for you.

You had recognized your parents' truck, so there was no pretending, and I'm not sure I would have pretended in any case. So when you asked me, "What happened, Tante?" I told you what I knew for a fact and nothing more: that it looked like an accident had happened. What I knew in my heart I kept to myself. What was in your heart, I'm not sure even you knew. You were only four.

We walked home. We went inside and had a cup of cocoa. Neither of us spoke much. We were waiting. For me it was one of those moments when everything around you seems at odds with what you know. The day shining, sun streaming through the front windows, the hoarfrost almost gone from the glass. Spring on its way.

And yet disaster was everywhere. For you, I'm sure, it felt unreal—a bad dream. For me, a dream recurring.

We went out and sat on the front stoop. By now the intimation of melting had become a reality of faint gurglings. Shady places would be frozen for months yet, but wherever the sun touched, the world was melting. I found a piece of yarn in my pocket, tied the two ends, and taught you to play cat's cradle. Your small hands found the movements difficult, but you concentrated intensely, the distraction welcome. To teach you a new move, I shifted the strings from my hands to yours and demonstrated. Over and over we began again, our hands diving under the yarn and through, fingers plucking and pulling and weaving.

And so we were occupied when the car pulled into the driveway. "Afternoon, Miss Deo," the deputy said, standing by the steps, hat in hands.

I nodded.

"There's been an accident," he began. I could see how hard it was for him. He was still a boy himself, really—only twenty-five. I stopped him.

"We saw," I said.

This information lifted his head and opened his mouth. "You saw," he repeated, shifting his eyes to you.

I nodded again.

"Well," he said. And explained that you were wanted at Homer's house and that he had come to fetch you.

We put you in the car and shut the door. He faced me. "They're all gone," he said. "All three."

"I thought so."

He turned to go. I put my hand on his arm. He stopped and looked at me.

"The boy," I said.

He put his hand over my hand. "We'll take care of him," he said.

I watched the car pull out and move slowly down the road. You were so small in the seat that I couldn't even see you to wave good-bye. And then you were gone.

I went inside. I sat down in a chair by the window. I folded my hands in my lap. As the light dimmed, I let the day and what it meant seep into me. Your parents were gone. I could see their young faces before me, but knew I never would again. Not Helen's tender gaze, nor Jack's strong one. Nor would you. My heart contracted at the thought of your loss—poor motherless, fatherless boy!

Most likely, you would go live with your grandmother now. It was only the other side of the island—certainly I could see you, could visit if I wanted. But I would no longer be your tante. For me, it was as if you had died, and with you, my own reason for living. I berated myself for not loving you more, for not loving our time more. For ever being impatient with you, or angry. For wasting any of it.

Four years had slipped through my hands like sand, like water. Gone. All we ever had was time, and that time had ended.

I drank myself into another stupor that night. Normally alcohol inhibits my dreams, or at least blackens them from memory. But I remember that night's dream well. I did not dream, as you might think, of the horror of the accident, the fire, the ice giving way, the chill of the water enveloping your parents' shoulders. I dreamed instead that I heard a sound like crying, like the mewling of an infant. I followed the sound, searching that house of the unconscious where rooms are too numerous to count and no hallway leads to the same place twice. Finally I found the source: a black kitten so small it fit into the palm of my hand. By now its cries were such torture to my heart and ears, I thought I might have to drown the thing to end our suffering. But instead I took it in my hand, stroked its head, put the tip of my pinky into its small, pink-tongued, voracious mouth and let it suck, as I had done for you when you were small and needed a nipple. The crying stopped; the kitten relaxed in my hand and shut its eyes in contentment. In contentment too, I then slept till morning, when I woke and set about getting you back.

Caroline Wright's house had begun its existence as a horse stable. No one knew how old it was, but on the walls of the original room you could still see where the stalls had been. Over the years additions had sprouted in a hodgepodge, so that you had to go through one bedroom to reach another. A house making room for change, growing as a family grew.

I had seen the house in summer, and I knew Caroline had a talent for flowers. The land there was almost all rock, but that didn't stop her: she simply planted rock gardens. The one that fronted the road flashed such color from May till October that you hardly noticed the house.

In winter, though, nothing kept you from seeing the aluminum siding, faded yellow; the patched window screens; the plastic stapled to keep the wind from penetrating the exposed foundation; the doorless shed, a drift of dirty snow in its entry. All this I noticed for the first time when I came to see her that day.

I half expected not to find her home. But a girl opened the door for me, nodded when I asked, and let me come in, abandoning me for the television set. I glanced at her and her sister, their eyes fixed on the grainy picture. I didn't see you, though, and that worried me.

An archway led into the kitchen, which was lit up, and there I found Caroline, sitting at the table, smoking. When she saw who

I was, for a moment she looked angry. But then our eyes met and her mouth crumpled; tears began to slide down her cheeks, and I saw she had just been keeping her sorrow at bay.

I bent and put my arms around her. It was not something I would normally do. She was a stranger. But she was also Jack's mother, Helen's mother-in-law, your grandmother, and I felt her sorrow as deeply as I felt my own. We stayed like that for a while, and then, slowly, we began to talk.

At some point, we opened a bottle of whiskey. Caroline was less accustomed to drinking than I was, I saw that quickly, so I kept a careful eye on her glass. But the liquor enabled her to open her heart to me as a young woman would to an older friend. And I listened to her as a friend would. We were not friends, but it seemed she had no one else to talk to, and I needed to listen.

We talked into the middle of the afternoon. I found myself unable to ask the question I had come to ask, unable to turn the conversation from her grief, her problems and guilt, to mine. For a long time she did not mention you, as if it were almost too much to bear, the thought of your loss on top of hers. A parent-less child, an orphan. It was only when the topic shifted from the past to the future that you came up.

"I'll get Homer's farm," she said. "I know he intended that." At this point her eyes were dry, her tone resigned. "James Jack will come live with us," she said.

"Where is he?" I asked, as matter-of-factly as I could.

"With the deputy and his wife," she said. "I thought he'd be in the way—I need to clean the house, get ready for the crowd. . . ." Her eyes shifted toward the front room, where the television set talked to itself. "The girls can be helpful," she said. "They're old enough. But he's only four."

The tears began again. I would have cried for you too, and for myself, but I had not cried in many years and tears did not come now. I can watch him for you, I wanted to say. Let me watch him for you, let me bring him up for you. But I didn't say what I knew would be fruitless. Caroline was not about to give up another member of her dwindling clan.

She kept the aluminum storm door open as I walked out to the truck. "Thank you for coming," she called. I waved her off, promised to come back the next day, got in the truck and drove, not knowing what more I could do.

That afternoon, the deputy appeared at my door. "James Jack wants his truck," he said, avoiding my eyes. I knew immediately which truck he meant—the big red one I'd bought you for Christmas that year, the toy you loved to play with more than any other. I left the deputy standing in the cold and went to the summer kitchen, where we kept your toys when you were not here. I put the truck and a few other things in a box. I did it mechanically. I took the box to the door. "Tell James the rest will be here when he comes back," I said, shoving it out.

The deputy paused, as if considering whether to speak again, then said, "I guess it's okay to tell you—my wife and I are thinking about keeping him," he said. "Adopting him." He shuffled his feet. A knife twisted in my heart. "Alma can't have children," he said, lowering his voice.

"I'm sorry," I said. I didn't know what else to say.

"Well, thanks for these," he said, lifting the box.

Tell James I love him, an inner voice said. Tell him that for me, will you?

I did not speak. I shut the door.

I did not sleep that night, did not dream. I lay awake in the darkness of my bed and listened to the wind roaring through the trees, whistling like a hooligan determined to keep me awake and ill at ease. But I needed no help for that.

Things were stacked against me. The deputy and his wife were young, respectable, churchgoing, and infertile. I was old, disliked, mistrusted, and a lapsed Catholic, something not easily forgiven in these parts. The only thing I had was money, but money would mean nothing to the court, much less the town. If the deputy and his wife got to Caroline first, it was hopeless.

I decided to pray. It had been a long time since I had been to church, and longer still since I'd believed in God. But I did believe in that thing in the universe, something—not a being or a force, but a thing—that for lack of a better name could only be called luck. It was luck, I decided, that had brought your mother to me in the first place; luck that had brought me back here so that she could find me. Now I prayed for luck to bring you back to me again.

As soon as the sun rose, so did I. A restless energy motivated me. I was not sure what to do with it, but I had to do something, so, in the half-light of early morning, I made my bed, filled my wood bin and swept my house, scrubbed the kitchen and bathroom clean, and otherwise imposed order on my small world. Then I loaded the winter's accumulation of trash bags into the truck and got in to take them to the dump.

The day was clear and springlike again. A line of vehicles waited for the gates to open. Inside, we parked and began to unload, like ants carrying giant crumbs to the hill. In summer the dump was a chaos of nauseating odors; in winter, smells frozen, it was almost pleasant. This morning it had not yet begun to thaw. People gossiped as they passed one another or walked together to and fro. Usually I would have ignored them, but that day I thought I heard Homer's name, and tuned my ears to listen. The smattering of words I put together made me more curious, and I stopped a man on his way back to his car. "What's this about Homer Wright?" I asked.

"Died intestate," he said. He was a stubby, dark-bearded man who looked surprised to be asked a question by me.

"Intestate?" I said.

He nodded. "Owing back taxes, too," he said, and moved on.

I rushed to empty my truck and drove straight to Caroline's house. An unfamiliar car sat in her driveway; when I knocked, the door was opened by an older woman I assumed to be one of those plump busybodies who show up after a tragedy—in this case, a financial one. She eyed me warily. "I heard the news," I said.

"Poor Caroline," she said.

"How is she?" I said.

"Holding up."

She blocked the doorway with her sizable body.

"May I see her?"

"Not now."

"Tell her Marguerite was here, will you?"

A nod, and the door shut.

The nervous energy I'd awakened with shifted to a strange sort of optimism. I felt sorry for Caroline, who had after all trusted me, and who had suffered more than most people could stand—but somehow this seemed the answer to my midnight prayer. If that sounds selfish, what can I say? I was fighting for my life then, and for yours too.

It was Monday before I could do anything. I spent the waiting time drafting a document, researching what I could by telephoning a lawyer who had not heard from me since I'd left New Orleans. First thing Monday morning, I was sitting in the truck outside the town clerk's office, waiting to do one last bit of research. In the books there I found the figures I needed, and I was ready.

This time when I arrived at Caroline's, she was alone.

The girls were staying with friends, she told me; she herself, dressed in black, was waiting to be taken to the memorial, which would begin that afternoon at one. For a moment, seeing her ashen face and the resigned slump of her shoulders, I hesitated. But I'd become a predator by then, and in her weakness I saw opportunity.

"What will you do now?" I asked her.

She shrugged. "Stay here," she said. "What can I do? They're going to take the farm for taxes. This place is all I have." She sighed. "Oh, Homer," she said.

I took a breath and began. "I'll pay the back taxes for you, Caroline," I said.

She looked up sharply. "You?"

"Yes," I said.

"Why?"

"So that you can inherit the farm, sell it, and go away. Start a new life."

She looked at me with a gratitude that turned, in an instant, to doubt and suspicion. "And what do you want?" she said, her eyes clear and steady.

I told her.

In a matter of fifteen minutes it was decided. She was surprisingly sharp-minded, surprisingly good at bargaining. I would not only pay the taxes, but buy the farm myself. I was happy to do so. I knew it would sell eventually and I would recoup the cost, or most of it—but even had that not been the case, I would have been willing. It was only money, and my father's money at that. I would have given it all for you.

I don't want you to think that she gave you up without pain or consideration. Perhaps if I had been kinder, if I had approached her at another moment, at a later time—if I had waited until she had time to recover from the devastation laid to her life—she would have refused. I admit I preyed on her at the moment when her future seemed bleakest. But she knew you would have a good life with me; she knew I loved you; she knew you loved me. Helen had told her all that, and Jack too. If they had thought to make a will, I felt certain they would have named me guardian. Besides, Caroline had her own daughters to worry about. She wanted to leave the island, to go away, to start over while she was still young enough. To find love again if she could. So, though she cried, she did what she thought was the right thing.

A day later, the notary public witnessed our signatures, and it was all but done.

I stood at a distance from the church, watching you arrive in the deputy's car. His wife held your hand and led you to Caroline, who knelt and put her arms around you. How handsome you were, how grown-up in the suit they found for you, your dark hair wet-combed back. But I worried that you weren't warm enough. I worried that no one would console you if you cried.

You didn't.

You stood quite still and held your grandmother's hand, but you did not cry. Three dead, but no casket to be buried. They would search for the bodies—not now, but when the ice went out. They would never find them.

I worried that you would not understand, and that you would.

It was a damp-cold day, and you wore nothing but a cheap suit, a white shirt, a black bow tie, thin leather shoes. I watched you go into the church, and then waited for you to come back out.

My sweet little bird.

You never cried.

Three

By the time James drove home from Faith's trailer, dry snow was sifting down from thick yellow clouds. He felt as if years had passed since he had come down from the cabin at dawn. But the clock said it was only midmorning, so he also felt as if time were slowly coming to a halt.

At the house, he sat outside for a moment, looking. The windows were flat and dark, set deep into gray stone, the slate roof a heavy brow above them, the porch rails like gapped teeth below. Yet it was a handsome house, even stately.

On the porch was the wicker rocker Tante'd had him paint green again this past summer. Left out in the weather, the paint had already begun to chip; he could see it even from this distance. The chair was motionless, the wind calm, as if quieted by the solemnity of the day, or as if its past restlessness had been a product of some human turmoil now ended. Tante's death had stopped time and stilled the wind.

In Faith's arms he had cried like a child. It had felt good to cry, it had felt right. He had cried because Tante had died alone; he had cried because he had not said good-bye to her; he had cried because their last words had been angry. He had not been able to explain any of this to Faith—the words would not come—but she had not asked him to. When he'd gotten up to go, she'd just sat there on the floor, pale legs folded under her, the look on her face sad but unquestioning.

He decided to hide the truck behind the barn, drove it there, got out, started toward the house, went back for the bag from Keller's store, started toward the house again. On the stoop, he stood and angled his face toward the falling snow, letting it settle on him. It melted on his skin, made his cheeks wet, and he felt the tears come again, shamelessly warm, and let them come until they stopped of their own accord.

Once inside, he made the decision to go about business as usual. He stamped the snow from his feet, took off his outdoor clothes, hung them on their hooks. He took the wine from the bag and set it on the counter. He put the cheese into the refrigerator and the crackers into the pantry. He squatted by the woodstove and shoveled ashes out, knotted newspaper, shoved it in with kindling and a few sticks of wood, struck a match on the stone hearth. With the stove lit, the kitchen felt more like home.

He moved into the front room and lit another fire in the fireplace there. The simple thing would have been to turn up the thermostat, start the oil furnace—a convenience he'd insisted on only a few years before—but he didn't feel like doing the simple thing; he felt that the complicated thing was right and proper. A fire warms a house in a different way. He wanted light and motion as much as heat.

So from there he went up to his room. It had been a long time since a fire had been lit in his fireplace, and at first it seemed as if the chimney wouldn't draw, but then it warmed and up the smoke went. Smoke loves a chimney. Tante told him that.

He went back downstairs. In the front room he turned on the lamps. More light. He saw the deck of cards, loosely squared on the table where they had been played the night before. He found the rubber band for them and put it around them and put the deck into Tante's drawer. He folded her old silk quilt and put it on the arm of the couch where she liked to keep it. He straightened the twin petit point pillows so that the houses on them stood upright. Then, for a moment, he stopped, stood still. And then he went back through the kitchen toward the back bedroom.

Tante had been eighty-five when they moved her down, next to the kitchen and the bathroom so she wouldn't have to climb stairs. They had brought down her things, too, all of them. They crowded the smaller room, each piece of heavy old furniture elbowing the next, but that only made it "cozy," Tante'd said.

He paused with his hand on the knob of her door. It had been a while since he'd entered her room. It felt odd to consider going in without her there to answer his knock. He had no idea what he would find, or even why he felt compelled to see it. But he turned the knob and pulled the door open.

A tall mirror blocked the bottom of the only window, and dark drapery blocked the top, so he had to turn on the light to see anything. The room was little more than a large closet; in fact, it had originally been a second pantry. Where the walls were visible, he could still see the horizontal lines of paint that had accumulated around the pantry shelves, long since removed. Tante's small, plain bed was directly in front of the door, foot toward him and a highboy towering by the head of it. Next to that, a vanity table with a small, straight-backed chair, then the mirrored lowboy in front of the window, a trunk, a standing wardrobe that she used as a closet (she called it a "chifforobe"), one small cushioned rocker, and the door itself, tucked into the final corner. There was just enough room to step inside. He did.

Not a thing was out of place. The bed was made, white che-
nille spread pulled tight and exact over the corners. Tante's
heavy, laced orthopedic shoes sat side by side under the bed (her
feet the only thing she ever complained of). On the vanity table,
her old tortoiseshell brush held its matching comb. A little vial of
perfume he'd given her long, long ago was the only other item of
toiletry.

Framed photographs crowded both dresser tops. Some were
of family or friends from her distant past, people he knew only
by the names she gave them, names he'd mostly forgotten by
now. The rest were pictures of him as a baby, child, boy. He
did not remember the camera snapping, the flash in his eyes,
but here was evidence, pictures like stills from a film he had
seen so many times that he could reconstruct the gaps between
them.

The pictures stopped when he was thirteen or fourteen, when
the camera shifted from her hand to his and became an adolescent enthusiasm. In boxes in a closet upstairs were sunsets and
water, trees and animals (a deer caught nibbling on the corn in
the garden), the house and barn from many angles, his projects
(a hand-built go-cart, for one). And a few portraits of Tante, the
few she would allow: Tante cooking, big wooden spoon in a pot
of steaming black raspberry jam; Tante in the garden, mud to
her elbows; Tante rising wet from the quarry swimming hole,
gray hair streaming, grinning at the camera and at him. As she
aged, she liked herself less and less in pictures, although—this
was his opinion—she had aged well, had been one of those
women whose characters give their faces an interest better than
mere beauty. "Indian bones," she said. "From my grandmother."

Finally photography had gone the way of other early hobbies.
In recent years he'd taken pictures only on her birthday, sneaking
the camera into the room behind his back and snapping just as

she blew out the candles, or rather trying to as she ducked her head. Sentimentality neither of them liked, though they kept many traditions.

He had reached a hand to pull open the top dresser drawer when in the mirror he thought he saw her face behind him, her eyes. He turned. Nothing, no one. She was everywhere with him but not there at all. He shook his head and opened the drawer. Underneath some correspondence, he found the envelope with his name on it. She'd gone over it with him when they took the document to the notary: her will, her wishes. It wouldn't make anything he did legal, but it would give him a defense. He thought he remembered the details, but wanted to be sure. He slipped a thumb under the flap to rip it open, stopped. It was too soon. There would be time later. He had nothing but time from now on. He put the envelope back where he'd found it, left and shut the door behind him.

The kitchen clock said eleven when he heard a car in the drive-way. He opened the door to the summer kitchen and looked out. The snow was coming faster now, still fine as sugar. Through it he saw Faith's car come to a stop.

He met her at the door. "I postponed my flight till tomorrow," she said. He let her in. She wore the black tuque he'd lent her, pulled down to her eyes; beneath it, her face was like a child's, small and pointed. "James," she said. They put their arms around each other. "James," she said again, this time her voice muffled in his shirt. "What's going on? What happened?"

He found it too hard to say. "I'll show you," he said.

In a moment he was dressed again and they were on their way past the barn and up the hill, climbing into the woods, the only sounds their steps, their breath, and the hiss of the snow through the air. As the path narrowed, he let her go ahead of him so that if she fell, he'd be able to catch her. Snow accumulated on her hat and the shoulders of her jacket, a jacket too light for this kind of winter, although she insisted it was fine, "rated to twenty below." He didn't know anything about ratings; he only knew what common sense told him, that she needed more between her small self and the winter.

He'd been walking in the woods, too, when he'd come upon Faith the first time, only the week before. Not these woods, but the woods down and across the road.

The wind had been playing games that day. One minute it'd be roaring through the upper limbs of the trees; the next it would die down so quiet he could hear the twigs cracking under his feet. Then it would gust at him, pulling at his scarf this way and that, buffeting one side of his face, then the other, like two bullies teasing a weak kid, never quite hurting him but never quite leaving him alone. Not the kind of fierce squall the island was named for—just a playful wind, a bored wind, an afternoon wind.

He'd just come up over a ridge when he spotted her. Of course, he didn't know who she was. Didn't guess even that it was a woman hidden in that winter gear, until she turned toward him and put her finger to her lips and pointed down toward the lake. He stopped and looked where she was looking and saw what she was seeing: a good-sized flock of turkeys, walking in line the way they did, tallest first and smallest last, coming up to an old piece of split-rail fence and hopping over it, one by one. And then taking off on short flights through the trees, unhindered by the wind.

She was breathless when she got to him. "I thought they were garbage bags," she said, still watching the birds. "When I first saw them. And I thought, why would someone be out here throwing garbage bags over that fence? And then I realized what they were."

"Turkeys," he said.

She turned those eyes on him for the first of many times. "I know," she said.

He took in the flush on her pale skin, her shiny red hair, the expensive—but too thin—parka with fur on the hood, and figured she was a wandering tourist. Although why she would be here, and be here now, he couldn't imagine. "This is private property," he said.

"I know," she said, looking him square in the eye.

"Doc Milton owns it," he said.

"So what are you doing here?" He couldn't tell if it was a smile or a smirk on her lips. He felt himself smiling back.

"I'm his friend," he said.

"Well," she said, "I'm his daughter."

He hid his surprise, he thought, by nodding. He knew Doc had a daughter, of course; he just hadn't seen her in years or expected to see her now. "How is Doc?" he said.

"You knew he was sick?"

He nodded.

"Well, he died," she said. "Just a few days after he left here in August."

The wind quieted for a second, as if listening to what they were saying. "The cancer," James said.

It was her turn to nod.

"I'm sorry," James said, and he was. Doc had been different from other summer people; he never had pretensions, always liked the island for what it was, never wanted to change things. Never even built on his land, this hundred acres; just lived in the old trailer already on it. "I'm only here two weeks a year," Doc used to say. "I don't need anything fancy." He'd been a good neighbor, too, there for James Jack and Tante whenever he could be. He was an ophthalmologist and, knowing how Tante hated doctors, always came prepared, took a look at her when she had a chest cold, checked her eyes and blood pressure, wrote her prescriptions. So James had been happy to help him out, fix this or that when it was needed, as strange as it was to see someone else living in the trailer where his parents had lived, where he had lived when he was small.

"He was a good man," James said.

"Yes, he was."

James put out his hand. "I'm James," he said.

"Faith," she said. They shook gloved hands.

He nodded. "I remember now."

"Remember?"

"From when you were little," he said. "Your dad brought you by Tante's house."

"James Jack." She shook her head.

"What?" James said.

"I always thought you were a product of my imagination," she said. "I had this vague memory of playing with a little boy, but I thought I invented him—you know, the way kids do when they're bored or lonely."

"Maybe you did invent me," James said, feeling himself smile. "I don't remember us playing together. I never liked girls much."

She grinned at him. "If I made you up then, how do I know you're real now?" she said.

He took his glove off and put his hand out again. "See for yourself," he said. And she'd taken off her right glove and reached out, their bare hands touching warm in the cold.

It was only later that he saw her other hand and the ring on it, and realized she was married. "Where's your husband?" he'd asked. "Elsewhere," she'd said, with a little twist to her mouth.

Now here she was with him, climbing up to the cabin where Tante lay. As the hill grew steep, he heard her breath catch. She was a smoker. He'd been surprised by that, given what had happened to her father, given that her father had been a doctor. "I've got a strong self-destructive instinct," she'd said, looking at the cigarette in her hand. "But I'd quit if you asked me to." *If you asked me to.* It was the second time they'd met. "What if your husband asked you to?" James said. "Definitely not," she said.

When the cabin came into view, they paused, and Faith looked at him, inquiry in her eyes. "*My* getaway," he said, and she nodded, understanding. She'd called her father's place her "get-away," and what she said she was getting away from was her husband.

He led her up to the cabin, opened the door for her. Showed her the bed where Tante lay, uncovered, her face showing no pain, no surprise, no regret. Only the strange posture of her body—the arm still up, the leg twisted under—made it seem as if she had fought death. James explained how he had found her. "What happened?" Faith asked, differently this time. "I don't know," he said.

They descended the slope side by side, talking about Tante's wishes, James's plan, how Faith could help. "She wants stars," James said. Faith looked up. "It'll clear," she said, gazing at the opaque white sky.

When the going got slippery, he took her arm, and he held it until they came to the quarry road and the going got easier; then he held her hand. The barn and house reappeared, blurred silhouettes at first, and then more and more solid. The snow showed no signs of letting up. "If this keeps on too long," he said, "it'll make things harder tonight." She squeezed his hand, and he squeezed back through the thick gloves.

They were drinking tea at the kitchen table when the sheriff's car pulled up. James stepped into Tante's room, pulled the door shut behind him, peered through a crack in it that let him see nothing. "Hello, Mrs. Grayson," the sheriff's voice said when Faith opened the door.

"You know who I am." Her voice, light.

"Small place, this island," the sheriff said. "I was sorry to hear about your father."

"You knew him?"

"Some. He was a good man."

"Yes," she said. Then, "Thank you."

"So," the sheriff said. James imagined him looking around, casual. "James Jack here?"

"No," Faith said. "He and Marguerite went to the mainland for the day."

"Funny," the sheriff said. "He didn't mention that when I saw him this morning."

Their dialogue seemed stilted, canned—each of them playing a role.

"No?" she said. "Well, they left just before lunch. Invited me to use the house, keep the fire going."

"Surprised they didn't just use the backup furnace. That's what most folks have it for."

"I wouldn't know anything about that," Faith said. "I just thought it would be nice to spend the day here."

"Come to think of it," the sheriff said, "maybe they don't have a backup."

"Maybe not."

"Well," the sheriff said, "if you see James, you tell him I've got some business to discuss with him. Could be serious."

Nice touch, James thought: *serious*.

"What about?" Faith said. "So I can tell him."

"Just tell him," the sheriff said, "that there are laws that govern these things. Laws he shouldn't break."

"Okay." James liked Faith's tone—almost flippant. He pictured the sheriff like a sheriff in a movie, reaching a hand up to tap the brim of his hat. But of course the sheriff didn't wear a hat like that, not in winter. "Have a nice day," the sheriff said; then came the sound of the kitchen door opening and closing, then the summer-kitchen door, then the car starting. Then the engine just running. James imagined the sheriff looking up toward the barn, seeing the faint outlines of the footprints and truck tracks the snow had begun to fill. The sound of the engine in reverse, then drive. James stepped out.

Faith pointed to their two mugs, still hot on the table. "I don't think we fooled him for a moment," she said.

"No," James said, "we didn't." He shook his head. " 'Have a nice day,' " he said, mimicking the sheriff's tone. Faith laughed.

"What did he mean about laws?" she said.

"Don't know," James said, although he did. "Doesn't matter."

"No," Faith said, "I don't suppose it does." She paused. "Well," she said, "we have some time to kill, don't we?" She opened her arms, and James went to her.

Holding her hand, he led her up the unlit back stairs. Took her to his warm room, where the fire had burned down to coals. Put another log on, crossed over and pulled down the green shade. In the false twilight, he turned to see her standing outside the door looking in, as if surveying the future before stepping into it. He held out his hands, and she came to him this time.

They undressed, each of them helping the other with buttons, zippers. They took their time. There was no hurry. He wondered what she felt now, what she was thinking. He wondered if the first time had pleased her at all—if not, he wondered whether she had forgiven the way he had done it, the lack of tenderness. He had needed to get it over then, to get past it fast, but now he was sorry and wanted to make it up to her. When the clothes were gone and they were all flesh, nothing between them, he opened his mouth to say he was sorry, to apologize, but she kissed him and it began again.

Afterward, as they lay deep under the covers in each other's arms, she said, "This is too easy."

"What do you mean?" he said.

"I mean," she said, and sat up, the covers falling away from her small frame, "that I've been married to the same man for the last fourteen years. It ought to be hard to make love to someone else, don't you think? But it isn't."

She climbed out of the bed and found her shirt, the pack of cigarettes in the pocket, the matches.

"Don't," he said.

She gave him a new look, mouth small, eyes large, as if she were about to laugh at him. But she didn't. "Say please," she said, and he said, "Please," and she put the cigarettes down and climbed back into bed.

"Poor Marguerite," she said, laying her head on his shoulder. He felt ashamed then, to have forgotten for a moment, when even Faith had not, that Tante had died. His throat swelled; he swallowed hard, not ready to cry again.

"Tell me the story," Faith said.

"What story?"

"The one about the last eight years."

"All right," he said.

On his twenty-seventh birthday, James got shit-faced drunk. He admitted it freely: he'd been feeling sorry for himself, sad about his life. Any normal day, he felt okay about things, but for some reason, that birthday got to him. Worse yet, though, he'd come home in that state and said things to Tante, things he shouldn't have said. The problem wasn't that he hurt her feelings; the problem was he'd opened a can of worms that just wouldn't shut.

Tante got on his case. "You need to do something with your life," she'd say. "I am," he'd say. "Something else," she'd say. "Like what?" he'd say. Once a week they had the same argument, although she liked to call it a discussion. Once a week she came up with something new he could do: go to forestry school; join a singles club on the mainland; start his own business with her seed money. "What kind of business?" he said. She rolled her eyes. "Do I have to do all the thinking?" she said.

It was Tante who saw the ad in the paper, brought it to him. "It's what you always wanted to be," she said. He shrugged it off. He'd been a kid when he said that; what kid didn't say he wanted to be a fireman? "I just wanted to wear a shiny hat," he said, which was a truth, although not the only truth. "Well," she said, "now's your chance."

So he had called for an application, filled it in, gone for an interview, been accepted. The training program was eight weeks. Six in the morning till five at night, six days a week. Too hard a commute from the island. So he rented an apartment on the mainland, lived on his own for the first time in his life. Went home on the ferry every Sunday to check on Tante. She was eighty-six then, still able to take care of herself.

Most of the trainees were a little younger than he, but they'd all been out in the world. Some had been to college. Like him, others had worked—as carpenters, truck drivers, linemen in one of the local furniture factories. There were two women, too. They'd all looked awkward, crammed into old school desks in their winter parkas and boots, like a bunch of working-class parents called in for a talk with the school principal. James had come in late and sat toward the back, near the door, the way he always did in school, staring at his hands, waiting for the teacher to arrive, feeling foolish and trying to fade into the walls. But the guy across from him wouldn't permit it. "I'm Perry," he said, sticking out his hand, and James had to shake it and look into the guy's face. Milk-white skin, hair, eyebrows. Pink eyes with fire-red pupils. "I'm albino," Perry said, grinning. "An albino fireman. Unique, don't you think?" He grabbed the sleeve of the person sitting in front of him, and she turned around. "And this here's Marion," he said. "She's Abnaki. What do you think of that? An albino and an Indian in the same class. I hear you Indians got special talent for fighting fires. Is that right, Marion?"

The woman rolled her eyes and shook her head. "No more than you albiny-o's," she said. She stuck her hand out to James. "So, who are you?" she said.

"James," he said.

"James," she repeated. "That's formal enough, I guess."

"Formal enough for what?" he said.

She rolled her eyes again. "For the debutante ball," she said. "For anything."

Perry laughed. "Sharp as vinegar, ain't she?" he said, nodding to James. "We'll have to watch out for her." James liked them both.

The days were long, the training hard. Most of it was drills. Learning SOPs: Standard Operating Procedures. Sprints carrying a hundred pounds of hose, up and down stairs. Dressing hydrants, dragging dummies. Getting the routines. Responding to the call, prepping equipment, carrying and climbing ladders. Getting, as the instructor said, to the point of "automatization." They had to be able to do the right thing, always, automatically, without thinking. But they had to be able to think, too, in case things didn't seem to be going according to Hoyle. "Don't shut your brains down, boys," the instructor said at least twelve times a day. "Keep those brains up and running."

The first few days, both Marion and the other woman took a lot of ribbing. But then the other woman found out she was pregnant and quit, and when it was just Marion, the ribbing stopped. She was as strong as any man, and built solid, and she talked tougher than most. James and Marion and Perry became a trio. Teamed up for drills, studied together. Each of them with different reasons for being there. Perry was a dreamer: he wanted to work for the national park system, he wanted to be the guy dropping tons of water on the trees, he wanted to be a hero, saving the forests. He already had his pilot's license. Marion wanted to do anything other than the waitressing she'd been doing since she was sixteen, to make more money than she could any other way, as a woman with a high school education. And James—he couldn't tell them why he was there, wasn't sure he knew, so he just said he wanted to join the volunteer fire department on the island. Do some good. Save some lives and property. "Saint James," Perry called him.

Saturday nights, before he went home, they went out drinking. It felt good to be with people close to his age. He liked the camaraderie, the talk, the laughing. Perry and Marion would get so drunk sometimes that he'd have to call a cab to take them home. They were three friends—just friends. It was the first time in his life he really felt he could call a woman his friend, or a man for that matter. He felt he could talk about anything with them, although of course he didn't. It wasn't his way. Marion would lean across the table, her breath sweet from the Amaretto she liked to drink, and say, "Loosen up, James! Don't be such a wooden Indian." And Perry would shake his head and say, "Marion, you may as well ask a tree to do a cartwheel."

The last week of training was test week. The test was a real fire, if there was any, or a set one, if there wasn't. You never knew when your test was going to come. Trainees were on call twenty-four hours a day, living at the station, playing cards and polishing chrome if there was nothing else to do. If you passed your test, you got the certificate, and you could pretty much write your own ticket from there: any fire department in the state would take you, soon as there was an opening. Perry pumped himself up. "I'm gonna ace it," he kept saying. "I am *ready*." Marion just smiled and kept to herself. James swam through the days and nights, nerves dancing.

The call came in late Tuesday night. A real fire. This time when they suited up, it felt different; reality had a different flavor, made things sharp.

The house was an old Victorian broken up into apartments, on a narrow street just a block long. At one time it might have been a farmhouse or even the center of an estate, acres of prime land around it. But now it was just an old building wedged between newer buildings, head and shoulders above them like a peacock among chickens. Like most old buildings its wood was dry, its wiring deteriorating, its structure open. Balloon construction. A fire that started in the basement could be in the attic within minutes without touching another floor.

By the time they arrived—minutes after the call—flames licked out every window. The instructor took James aside. "This isn't your test," he said. James nodded. He and Marion were to take care of the tenants, who stood clustered on the sidewalk in their pajamas and robes, some of them with bare feet. The chief was asking them, "Is everyone out? Are you sure?" and they were all nodding: a couple of college-age women, a guy in his thirties, an Asian man and his wife and two kids. James and Marion wrapped them in blankets, put thermal slippers on their feet, encouraged them to climb into the back of the ambulance, where there was a heater and coffee.

Perry was right in there, handling the hose that fought his

hands like a giant snake, his face grim but also, somehow, happy. He loved it, loved fighting fire; anyone could see that in the red center of his eyes, hot despite the ice that coated him quickly from the back-drifting mist.

But the fire kept on. It was cold that night. Well below zero. The wind was not strong, but it was cutting, and that took the temperature down another notch. The water steamed at first, then froze on the building before it could do much good. The Victorian was lost; now the main worry was protecting the exposures—the adjacent buildings, the garage and the house next door. The fire was loud, popping and roaring and strangely alive in the rigid cold, the darkness of the dead of night. Fireballs shot into the air, seemed to hang there and drip sparks for a moment before they fell, as if the cold made the fire thick as jelly.

Despite their efforts, the garage caught fire as they watched. The garage was actually an old barn, separated from the house by a narrow alleyway. A single tongue of flame flashed out of the vent in its peak, and then the roof was aflame.

Marion and James were standing with the two men who had lived in the building, the four of them gazing mesmerized at the new fire as it was born. "Any cars in the barn?" James asked the men, but they shook their heads. Then one of the college girls came rushing up, her blanket trailing behind her. "Florence!" she screamed, and they looked at her, not understanding.

Shouts came from the direction of the barn. When James turned his head, the doors were just swinging open, seemingly by themselves. Perry, who'd had his hose trained on the doors, shut the flow off for a moment and stared. Through the opening came a walking column of fire—a woman, fire wrapped around her like the petals of a glowing flower. For a moment, she stood there, her face lost in her burning hair, only her mouth visible, gaping as if she were screaming silently to Perry, who stood before her slack-jawed and stunned, letting the moment lengthen beyond tolerance.

It was Marion who rushed forward, wrenched the hose from Perry's hands, opened the nozzle to a fog stream and trained it on the burning woman. The woman fell; the flames went out. But it was too late.

James stared at the charred heap that had, moments before, been a human being. But in his mind he was seeing the water arcing through the air, the truck nose down in the lake, the smoke, the red fish shanty burning—and then inside the shanty, bodies writhing in the flames. His legs gave way beneath him, his mind left its bony shell, and he passed out, right there on the icy sidewalk, in front of friends, in front of everyone.

Later the story came out that Florence had been old, homeless, a bit crazy, alone. The college girls had given her blankets, food, and shelter, befriending her the way they would a stray animal. Making her feel safe and welcome. But the horror of the fire had made them forget her until it was too late.

When the sun came up, James and Perry were sitting in the pumper truck, watching some of the other men wrap orange tape around the Victorian's lot, using the shrubs and lampposts for support since stakes wouldn't drive into the frozen ground. In the morning light, Perry's face looked even more ghostly than usual; he seemed older than his twenty-three years. He nodded when James asked him if he had passed his test. "Marion, too," Perry said. "It wasn't her test, but she passed too."

James found her back at the station, stowing gear. He stood in the door and watched her for a moment, letting her be unaware of him. When she looked his way, her face was grim. "Congratulations," he said.

"For what?"

"I hear you passed."

She clambered up the side of the truck and began to unwind the flat hose from its reel; after a fire, you always had to check to make sure it wasn't tangled or twisted, so it would spool off clean the next time you needed it. "When's yours?" she said.

He made the decision at that moment. "I'm not taking it," he said.

She stopped what she was doing to look at him. "Why? Not because you passed out?"

He shrugged. "I guess I'm just not cut out for it," he said. He waited for her arguments, but they didn't come—just the long look, reading him. "Guess you're right," she finally said, and kept working while he watched.

When the hose was cleanly spooled, she came down and stood before him. "Well, James," she said, "I guess this is good-bye." She put her arms out and he came to her. She was so small he had to bow to touch his chin to her crown. Her skin was warm through the T-shirt she wore; her shoulders were solid under his palms. "Good-bye," he said, breathing the smoky scent of her hair.

He was at the door when Marion called out. "Hey," she said. "Maybe I'll come see you?"

"Sure," he said, and went home.

When he returned to the island, he decided to fix up the cabin on the ridge.

He'd gathered from Tante that it'd been built when she was just a girl, when the farm was still a working farm. A place for hired help to stay in the summertime. One room with a hole for a stovepipe. No running water, no electricity. He gave it a sink, a cupboard, a countertop; filled in the chinks, replaced the broken windows; hauled up a woodstove, two rocking chairs, a table, a cot, a few dishes. He never intended to live in it. He just wanted a place of his own, a place to go. A place to bring Marion when she came.

She showed up unannounced, as he had suspected she would.

The first night, they opened the woodstove door and watched the fire as if it were a television set. Rocked, drank wine chilled in the snow, and talked. Then they stood up, undressed one another, and got into bed. He loved that. How direct it was, how simple, even that first time. She had round breasts with large nipples, and the wine made her mouth taste like apples. In the darkness when he closed his eyes, she seemed to be all hands and mouth and skin.

Lying in bed, she told him about her difficult parents, her wayward brother, the big sister she depended on; the men in her past; her childhood hurts. He told her how his parents had died, how Tante had taken him in, and what it had been like, growing up on the island. Compared to her, he had few stories to tell. Maybe because he hadn't had much practice. He'd had girlfriends, of course; he'd even thought he'd been in love, once or twice. But nothing had lasted, and he never knew why, for sure, except maybe it was that he had been unwilling to change his life.

With Marion he was comfortable, too comfortable to think about that.

The cot in the cabin was narrow, so when they slept, they slept touching. His chin on Marion's shoulder. His knees against Marion's thigh. One hand on her belly, feeling her breath come and go. Sometimes one of them would wake up in the night and start things again. Usually it was him, the dream of sex so strong that it blurred the line between sleeping and waking, and suddenly he would find himself inside her, not sure who had put him there. Sometimes they stayed like that a long time, not moving. Two I's bound by him between them. The tie that binds.

They kept each other warm, even on the coldest nights. In the cave beneath the blankets. Like children they would pull the covers over their heads to warm their noses, giggle and grope under there till they came up gasping for air. In the morning he would jump from the bed to put more logs on the fire, then jump back in till the fire warmed the room. Sometimes it was warm enough then that they could move about without clothes, putting together a breakfast of coffee made with bottled water and store-bought doughnuts served on his cracked plates. Hair in her sleepy eyes. Two fleshy creatures doing ordinary things. He liked to see her naked body, to see the way her muscles and bones worked together, to see her whole that way. The unbroken line of flesh, pink here, brown there, almost white in places: downy, smooth. The slope of her back above her buttocks. Her torso narrowing in the middle, but not a lot; a gentle curve inward, that's all. She had strong legs and a strong back and strong shoulders—her own kind of beauty.

They were together always those weeks. She didn't have work yet; she was waiting for a spot to open up at a station in the city, where they paid more. Every day she used Tante's phone to call her sister's house, to check if there'd been any news; every day that there wasn't, he was grateful.

She hadn't brought anything with her, hadn't planned to stay, so she wore his jeans cinched in with her belt, his flannel shirts with the tails skimming her knees. They walked in the woods, came back to the cabin, ate, made love. Once a day they went down to Tante's, took wood in, stoked her fire, used the phone, got supplies, took baths—the two of them facing each other in the tub, dovetailing their legs.

He worried about Tante, so old and alone most of that winter, but she said it was fine, she was fine; go ahead and enjoy himself. When she developed a cough, she told him she had a little cold, that's all. She promised to get up only to use the bathroom and fix herself tea and toast. "I'm fine," she said, waving him off, her voice like gravel sifting from a hand. She had a cough, that was all; she had her herbal teas, thank you very much. She hadn't come more than eighty years without learning to take care of herself. "Why don't you take one of those nice steaks from the freezer?" she said. That was how she let him know that Marion was all right with her, that it was *all* all right. She seemed pleased as punch, as pleased as if this had been her plan all along: for him to meet someone and be happy. He was grateful, and took the steak. They cooked it in a frying pan over the woodstove and ate it rare with potatoes fire-roasted in tin foil, and rum and cola to drink.

Nearly four weeks had passed when the job offer came in. "I have to take it," Marion said. "It's not every station that's willing to hire a woman." He nodded. "It's a chance to prove myself," she said. "From there, anything can happen." He nodded again.

The next morning, she got up first and put her own clothes back on. "I'll be staying at my sister's," she said. "Call me tomorrow night, and I'll tell you how my first day went."

He nodded, they kissed, and she went, leaving behind his shirts with their sleeves rolled up.

That morning, he came down to Tante's house with a pillowcase full of laundry. She wasn't up yet, so he took it straight down to the cellar and started the wash. The sheets had in them the smell of this last month, the smell of him, of Marion, the two of them together. All his clothes smelled of her. He pressed to his nose the crotch of the jeans she had worn and felt no shame in doing so. It was a salty scent that filled him with nostalgia.

They had reached a crossroads, he and Marion; he felt them standing at it. Did he want to marry her? Did he love her? He was comfortable with her. That was enough. He couldn't let her go, and he couldn't hold her back either.

Marion was what was on his mind when he came up the stairs

and stepped into the kitchen. The fire was almost out; he stirred the coals and stoked it up, and the noise of this kept him from hearing Tante. But as he finally closed the stove, he heard the rasping cough behind her door.

She was lying on one side, curled up on the narrow bed, the blankets on the floor. Breathing hard. Face gray, lips blue. Eyes rolling in her head. This is what he told the doctor, after he covered her and went to the phone. They sent an ambulance, which took her to the island clinic, where they pumped her full of penicillin while he filled out forms and signed papers. Then the helicopter came, and flew her to the mainland hospital. He could not ride along, they said, so he drove the truck to the ferry and waited there, as patiently as he could. He called Marion then, from the pay phone, wanting to let her know what was happening. But no one answered.

Tante's lungs were so filled with fluid, the doctor said, that she had come close to drowning in it. Yet she fought the nurses so, they had to tranquilize her—dangerous at her age, but what choice did they have? James stayed by her side, day and night, listening to the gurgling wheeze that was her breath, and holding her hand that was like a bundle of twigs in his. In those long, quiet, nighttime hours, he wondered at her strength, her will to live. It would have been so easy for her to give up, and watching her pain, he sometimes thought it would have been best.

But the penicillin worked its wonders, and one day she woke, scowled at him, berated him for keeping her alive. "What are you doing here?" she finally said, when he made it clear she had no choice in the matter. "Get home and make sure my house is all right."

Sitting in the truck on the ferry crossing, he thought of Marion again. She must have wondered why he'd never called, why no one answered when she called him. He promised himself he would call her, as soon as he got back to the house.

Then the island loomed up out of the cold mist before him, and he forgot again. Tante's pipes had frozen and burst, and it took days to repair the damage. Then he brought Tante home, and he had her to tend to. He called Marion one evening, but again there was no answer. Spring, he had to plant the garden. When that was done, he called again, but this time a voice said her sister's number had been disconnected. He went to the mainland and drove by the house where her sister had lived; a FOR RENT sign sat in the curtainless window. He went to the fire station where she'd gotten her first job and found that she'd moved on already, no one knew just where. "Somewhere out west," one guy said. "Chicago, maybe?" Someone else said it was downstate. He had no way of finding her.

For a long while he lived with the feeling that something valuable had slipped through his fingers. Gradually, that went away, and his memories became more objective. What had there been between him and her, anyway, except sex? Lonely people came together all the time, and sex had a way of connecting them. But a real connection was something more than that, something more like what he had with Tante. He could not leave her, would not risk her dying alone. Not the way she depended on him, needed him. Not after all she had done for him.

And it had seemed, for a long while, as if she would die. And then he would be free. He could wait till then.

But the bird that fluttered in Tante's chest was as resilient as the chickadee that foraged all winter long, close to starvation but never starving. She lived, and they wove their lives together more tightly than ever, wove them into a single life, bound together by habits and rituals and debts.

It was nearly a year before he visited the cabin again. He went one morning in early spring, intending only to check on it, to make sure it was still standing, whole. It was dank and cold inside. The fire would not draw because birds had roosted in the chimney. Mice had made a nest of cardboard and paper in the cupboard; they squeaked when he opened the door, were quiet when he closed it again. The mattress on the cot was black with mildew.

He pulled one of the rocking chairs into the open front door, and sat. With the leaves not yet out, across the lake he could almost see the mountains, blue and snow-covered. One day, he and Marion had stopped on the top of the ridge to look at those mountains, barely visible through the haze. "How can something so far off be real?" she had said. "They're probably saying the same thing about us," he said, grinning, and she punched his arm, and he ran, and she chased him, and caught him, finally, only when they had reached the cot, still warm from that morning.

He found that each time he came back to the cabin, he could recall some other thing, some other moment, sensation, or image, that took him back to that time. And then he could close his eyes, feel the wind, and imagine it was her touching him. For eight years, that was all he had. All he dared to have.

As long as Tante needed him, it didn't matter what he needed.

"And now she's gone," Faith said.

His throat swelled again; he could only nod. They sat silent for a moment. Then he said, "Your turn."

Faith rolled away from him, sat up, the bones of her shoulders catching the light. "Too boring," she said. "Besides, you already know as much as you need to know." Then she turned back with a grin, grabbed his hand. "I'm hungry; let's make lunch," she said, and pulled, trying to get him out of bed.

He pulled back. "No," he said. "Tell me about your marriage."

Her face shifted. "My marriage," she said finally, "is much, much farther away than the mountains, and not nearly as real." She reached for her cigarettes; when he saw the bitterness on her face, he didn't try to stop her.

There was a time I wanted to be alone.

It was winter. Penniless, fifteen, I rode the rails, not knowing where I was going, not caring so long as it was away. In empty freight cars I often thought how pleasant it would be to let the cold hold me in its arms until the shivering stopped, but my body was young and would not surrender to such a chilly lover.

Then one morning there came a terrible clattering. Through the wooden slats I saw sunshine and a great swampy lake. My lungs sucked in the steamy air, my heart beat fast. And when the train stopped, my feet brought me out and down and plunged me straight into the current of a teeming city, and once again into the heat and complication of love, of life.

Four

I married but once.

It was New Orleans. I was only sixteen but, thanks to the Great War that had just ended, gainfully employed as a clerk for one of the great shipping lines on the Mississippi River. At my desk I labored over bills of lading, inventories, and accounts, familiar to me from my father's business. Here, mine was one desk in a row of desks, each occupied by a young lady like me, all of us in white cotton gloves to keep the ink off our hands. Down below our offices, the wide and muddy river lay like a sleeping alligator; when we stood to stretch, we could look out at it, at the steamboats with their paddle wheels, at the crowds of men and wooden towers of crates, and know we were contributing to all that. I don't know about the other girls, for I never became real friends with any of them, but I felt a small thrill to be close to the center of such commerce. It was a bustling, alive place where a great deal of money changed hands. A place of power. A masculine place.

At noon we were allowed to leave the building. I most often brought my lunch wrapped in paper and ate it on a bench near the wharf. But sometimes I wandered the French Market instead, and ate fried oysters on bread, or coffee and hot, sweet beignets, sitting at an open-air table like a lady of leisure. So I was doing that day.

All the other tables were full; I had an extra chair at mine. The man who was to become my husband smiled at me from beneath the thick hank of blond hair that fell into his eyes, and I knew, as women do, that for some time at least our destinies were to be linked.

He was an actor, a writer, a schoolteacher, and a student—all at once. He'd come home from the war early—he didn't say, but I assumed he'd been wounded. His name was William. He gave me tickets to the vaudeville show in which he was to appear that night. I went, drawn by curiosity to this handsome young man who had asked so politely if he could share my table and then, once he sat down, had brazenly taken my hand and kissed it and said, "Thank God not every woman has eyes like yours."

I took my hand back and put it on my lap. "And why is that?" I said. I could not help but smile a little; he looked such a monkey.

"Because the world would come to a stop."

"And why is *that*?" Letting him play out his joke.

"Because we men would be smitten at every turn," he said, "and none of us could get a thing done."

You have to understand that no one had ever flirted with me before. You have to understand that despite the steamy New Orleans air, inside I was frozen but longing to melt. Maybe this explains why I let him sweep me away. Or perhaps I was just in need of a friend.

The theater was both elaborate and small, like a velvet-lined jewel box trimmed with gold. When the lights went down, I saw that the ceiling was a night sky in which starry constellations moved about magically. The crowd, which had been chattering away, became strangely subdued under this nighttime illusion, and then the show began, a series of skits and moral tales interspersed with songs that ranged from melancholy to winsome and bawdy. William had warned me that he played several parts throughout the evening, but at first I did not see him at all, because he played them in women's clothes. It was only during a quiet moment in the second skit—about the evils of alcohol, I think—that his eyes came to rest on me in the audience and I recognized their impish glee. Thereafter I was fascinated to watch him act like a woman, at which he was entirely convincing, his expressive mouth dressed in red, his cheeks rosied, his lashes curled and darkened. In black wig and with shadowed eyes he played a woman of the Far East; in white curls and hoop skirt a lady of the royal court. His voice was similarly malleable, piping high for this role, low and sultry off his tongue for that.

I suppose I ought to have been put off by this ability, if only because it showed what a chameleon he could be. Instead, I thought: a man who understands women this well . . .

An usher brought me a perfumed envelope, in which was an invitation to come backstage at the evening's end. But, not yet ready for such an encounter, I penned my regrets—and then, on impulse, an invitation to meet again, lunch hour next day.

Despite my youth, I had come to New Orleans with a past—a past that William dismissed as easily as he dismissed my missing finger, my apparent lack of family, my apparent poverty. "You are beautiful, smart, hardworking, and kind," he said. "What more could I want?" I suppose I had as much to overlook as he; his own family, back in Arkansas, had disowned him; he had little money; much of his past was a mystery to me. But, having never been courted before, I was so warmed by his attentions and so astounded when he asked me to marry him that I hesitated only a moment before agreeing. I wrote my father with the news of our engagement; by the time he responded with a generous wedding gift, we were already married.

We could not afford a honeymoon, so planned instead to spend the first night of our married life together in the house we had rented, a long, narrow house in Faubourg Marigny, a neighborhood of long and low and narrow houses, pinched fronts facing the street. At that time in New Orleans, property taxes were charged by street footage, and thus many houses were built as ours was, the rooms like railroad cars, one after another with a corridor of doors through the center, so that you could have shot a rifle straight through the house and out the back door without hitting a thing.

But if it was not the house of my dreams, it was, at least, not the rooming house in which I had been living till then, sharing a single toilet with twelve other young women and a bed with two of them. And it was well located: within walking distance to the French Quarter and a short streetcar ride to William's employment, just on the other side of Canal Street. Unfortunately, across the street too was a saloon frequented by boatmen whose boozy voices traveled easily into our little home.

So it was that first night. Both exhausted, we moved about our new rooms as if in a daze, rearranging the few sticks of furniture William had brought with him. And then it was time to retire. "I'll step outside for a smoke," he said, which I recognized as his gracious way of letting me disrobe in privacy, which I did, putting on my nightgown, but nothing underneath. Then I was faced with a dilemma. William had owned one small bed already, and it had been cheapest to buy another for me, so there were two beds in our room, a small lamp table between them. Was it appropriate for me to slip into his bed, or my own? Should I come to him, or him to me? Feeling shy and uncertain, I slipped into my own bed and turned out the light.

For a while I lay there in the dark, listening to rats scratching in the attic and to the sounds of our neighborhood: music, men arguing, someone calling someone's name over and over: *Mally, Mally, Mally.* . . . I listened hard, waiting for William to come in. But he took so long that I fell asleep.

When I felt him on me, I thought at first it was a dream, a dream I'd had before on those cold nights of my journey. A dream of warmth and security. I welcomed it. I wanted to reach up, to put my arms around him and hold him. But I couldn't.

I opened my eyes and saw, in the dim light that came through our window, my new husband above me. His eyes were closed; he was still clothed, but I felt him moving in me, a distant sensation of short jabs. I tried to move too, but his hands on my arms discouraged me, and then as quickly as it had begun, it stopped. William sighed, released my arms, and was gone.

I listened to him undress and climb into his own bed, and then I lay there in the dark again. Perhaps, I thought, this was the way of respectable Catholic husbands and wives. Maybe this was why I had hardly ever been aware of my parents' own couplings. It made sense: if the purpose of sex was procreation, why indulge excessively? I wished it weren't so pleasureless; felt, even knew it didn't have to be so. But if this was sex without sin, then I ought to feel lucky to have such a chaste and thoughtful husband.

Thereafter, William came to me once a week, always when I was sleeping, always quick, always without a word.

Still, I was happy to be married, even though it soon became clear that ours was to be no ordinary marriage. If I had left my job to stay at home, as did most wives those days, we would soon have landed in debtors' prison. William was a man of many talents, but none particularly lucrative. His acting brought in nothing, really; I did not realize this at first, but his professional performances were intermittent at best. To keep bread in mouth, he had turned to teaching, for which he had an equal talent. He taught at a private school for boys, where his manic manner and glib tongue made him popular, if not well paid. Literature was his subject, and theater, of course; he directed the fall musical and the spring drama, for which the boys played all the parts, male and female, and in which he sometimes gave himself a small role, so as better to model for them the skills of performance.

William's third vocation—and, unfortunately, lesser talent—was for the writing of drama itself. This he loved above all, studying the craft with a great and formerly well-known playwright whose wisdom was imparted by weekly mail for a sum that William considered a pittance and I considered a small fortune, given our circumstances. But even I had to admit that, with both our salaries, we could afford the expense.

Then, when we had been married just over a year, William announced that, with the advice and encouragement of his mentor, he had resigned his teaching position. Of course I supported his decision; as a good wife, I believed in his talent even though I'd never read any of his work, which he felt was unready for public consumption. I agreed to draw on my father's wedding gift, which till then we had saved, to pay for his "sabbatical."

Our story, then, might well seem the familiar one, of misdirected ambitions and the failure of love. For no matter how much I loved him, no matter what I did for him, he could not become what he was not. He disdained the real talents he had—acting and teaching, those sister abilities—for one that would always remain just beyond his grasp. He had neither the temperament for lonely work nor the patience for delayed rewards that writing requires. What he loved was an audience, and the only audience his writing brought was his mentor, who praised him with all the objectivity one might expect from an old man struggling to make a living.

But here we diverge from that more familiar plot. It was neither William's failure at writing nor the lack of money that destroyed our marriage. By dint of my native frugality we maintained a stable household economy, and William was ever hopeful, keeping at his craft day in and day out, and acting in local performances just often enough to feed his craving for applause. At odd moments those first years, William would take my hand and look into my eyes and tell me, "Marguerite, you give me joy." And I could, with all honesty, say in reply, "And you me." We were happy.

It was in the fourth year that William changed. He began to have trouble sleeping, long nights of insomnia followed by fretful days. I thought the moodiness might be due to exhaustion and encouraged him to seek a doctor's help. He did, but the strange territory of sleeplessness persisted, and I began to feel from him a bottomless anger, as if I had done something wrong, something quite particular for which I ought by rights to apologize or make amends—what, I could not imagine. Meanwhile, any increased kindness to him from me seemed only to fuel his animosity, and his eyes grew more and more weary, like those of someone who has lost all hope.

When the weekly nighttime visits stopped entirely, I became even more worried. Perhaps, I thought, his deep sadness came from my failure to fulfill his needs. I would have sought the counsel of an older woman had I known any, but at that time I did not. So I did what I did without advice or counsel, relying on my instincts not as a wife but as a woman.

The best feature of our house was the neglected garden onto which our bedroom windows opened. Gardenias were in bloom that night, their scent sweet and almost cloying. Above us in the attic the rats still scrabbled. William always claimed they were river rats that come in through the vents in the roof. I had tried to close off those avenues—stuffing them with steel wool—but to no avail. At times I wondered if instead the house were haunted by some murdered soul.

This night, after we had retired to our beds and turned out the lights, I took a deep breath of gardenia scent and arose. Nervous, I dropped my nightdress to the floor and slipped in beside William where he lay. I slid my hand inside his nightshirt, stroked his chest; touched his face with my lips. The past had taught me that men could be aroused easily, but there my husband lay, awake but motionless and stony, as if my touching him were something to tolerate, something offensive but necessary. I brought my hand lower, lower still, to touch what he had never permitted me to touch, my hand reaching the hair low on his belly; a moan escaped his lips, and I felt encouraged.

But then he gripped my hand in his, clamped it tight. "Don't" was all he said, as if his anger wouldn't permit him to go on.

"William," I said, my voice soft, my mouth next to his ear.

The next moment I found myself shoved from the bed to the floor, where I sat, stunned, for a long moment before I managed to speak. "William," I said, keeping my voice low, "I am your wife. Can't you tell me what the matter is? Why can't we—"

"What's the good of it," he muttered into the darkness, "if there are to be no children?"

"No children." With those words, the truth I had long been avoiding gripped my heart and squeezed it, and I knew that the past I had run away from had come back to haunt me. I cried then, cried for myself and for the babies that would not be, cried for William. Then, as best I could, I explained what had happened and begged forgiveness for not telling him sooner.

He could not forgive me.

Instead, over the next months, his despondency turned again to anger, and this time the anger came at me. My bruises pained me less than the knowledge that our marriage had brought a gentle, funny, cheerful man to such a pass. For I was certain that if I had loved him enough, or differently, or if he had loved me enough, or differently, he would have had the strength to face reality, give up chasing hopeless dreams, and love the life he had, rich in its own right, if childless. And we would have been happy again.

The more he hurt me, the more I blamed myself. Until I too became despondent beyond my control. Days I was able to tolerate: I kept busy with work. But nights grew unbearable. We continued to sleep in the same room, except that I could barely sleep; the very sound of his breathing in the bed so close and yet so far away kept me awake, listless. Green nets of thought trolled my mind. I loved and could not leave him, yet I could not stay.

I was trapped.

So I began to drink, just a little at bedtime, to help me sleep. Then a little more, and more, until I opened a cheap bottle of wine at dinner and nursed it to emptiness through the evening, and fell into bed only at the moment of passing out.

Prohibition was by then in full effect. But this being New Orleans—in many ways, a country and a law unto itself—alcohol's availability was unaltered; only its price was almost out of reach. I began to cut back on other essentials so as to have enough for my evening wine. I bought day-old, then two-day-old bread. Fewer fruits and vegetables. We ate cheese instead of meat. I repaired my old clothes to make them last longer, until even my undergarments were brailled with small stitchings. We fell into a life poor in every way: poor in daily sustenance, poor in prospect, poor in love.

Don't think I didn't realize what I was doing. In the clear light of a Monday morning, dressing myself for work, I would swear to change, promise myself that things would be better. But as the end of the day approached, I could not return home without knowing a bottle awaited me, something to get me through the night.

Serendipity saved me.

One evening, rushing to get home, I stumbled through the

open door of my most recent purveyor of wine to discover that he had changed locations, as these fly-by-night operations were wont to do. Before me instead was a forest of artists' easels, each with a stool before it, only one of them currently occupied. "May I help you?" asked the man sitting there in paint-stained shirt. "Are you interested in painting lessons?" The smells of paint and turpentine filled my nostrils; I shook my light head. The man looked at me quizzically, then smiled. "Drawing, then? Drawing lessons?"

I found myself, almost against my will, nodding. And that was the beginning of a new life for me.

That first night in the drawing studio, learning to see with my eyes and not with my brain, I fell in love with this simple art for which, if I could believe my instructor (I did not always), I seemed to have a natural talent. To afford it took every penny I could scrape together—I even gave up drinking for it. At first that was hard, but after a day's work and an evening's drawing, I found I fell asleep easily and no longer needed drink. Once a week I attended class, where my teacher pressed me to experiment with various media: gouache, India ink, pastels, silverpoint, watercolor. On my way home from work and on Sundays, my one day off, I roamed the city in search of drawing subjects. New Orleans was home to so many sorts of people, people that had fascinated me when I first came to the city, so unfamiliar were they to me: jazz musicians, the black men who swept the walkways and streets, exotic dancers scurrying from cab to nightclub. But I found that, for drawing, I preferred things to people, and certain kinds of things to others, certain textures and shapes and patterns: a pile of dishes for sale at the flea market, an old felt hat on a table. I could not name what these objects had in common, but they compelled me in a way faces did not.

I was wandering around like this after work one late-spring day when I discovered one of those side *rues* so narrow that it is dark even at noon, a slit between buildings hardly worthy of the term "alley," much less "street." In the dim light one window gleamed cleanly, drawing me to it. A small white sign— *Quiltmaker* was all it said, in fine script—stood propped inside the window, against a quilt that glimmered unlike anything I had ever seen before.

I stepped through the open door. Inside was brighter than outside, freely lit with electric lamps. From wooden frames hung more quilts like the one in the window. They were made of fabrics rich in texture and finish and pattern and, most of all, color: the greens and blacks of olives, the purple of eggplant, the red of blood on a platter, the blue of juniper berries. And the diamonds, triangles, squares, and octagons of these fabrics were themselves arranged in elaborate patterns—swirling out of the center like a whirlwind, or marching across the quilt first this way, then that, like wheat blown in different directions by a fickle wind.

My mother had made quilts. Growing up, I had taken them for granted, had slept under one as if it were any blanket, worthy of no more respect than a piece of scratchy wool. Her quilts, I realized now, had been well enough sewn but unimaginative. She had made them from remnants of old dresses—hers and mine—and used techniques passed on to her by her grandmother, no patterns except those created by the accidental repetition of fabric across the field of large, plain squares. Her quilts had been warm, durable, not unpleasing to the eye, but mainly frugal. Made for the body, not for the soul.

In contrast, these quilts were works of art. I stood gazing at them, one after the other, and felt myself drawn into them. I began to see in them tableaux, stories that could not be put into words or pictures, but that nonetheless conveyed great emotional depth—much in the way music can. I wanted to take one home with me and wrap myself in it.

No one else was in the shop. I reached a hand out and touched one of the quilts. Its surface was cooler than the air, as cool as its colors: so many shades of blue, all taken directly from nature, from the sky, from lakes, oceans, ponds, and from blue blossoms—bachelor's button and larkspur and monkshood. I lifted the folded quilt from its rack. It was heavier than I expected. It occurred to me that I could take it with me; simply walk out of the door with it in my arms. It would be mine, and that would be that. The blue coolness in my arms.

A voice said, "Blue suits you."

The speaker stepped out from behind some racks at the back of the room. It was a tall woman with a face younger than the nearly white, bobbed hair that surrounded it. White was also what she wore: a long narrow white skirt topped by a white linen shirt, collar open and sleeves rolled to elbows. Her dark eyes passed over me quickly, as if appraising my ability to pay; then she launched into a kind of a sales pitch. "We make them from silk," she said in the gravelly voice of so many Southern women, and came forward and ran her hand over the blue quilt in my arms. "From the remnants of men's ties. Based on Quaker patterns." I looked again, and could see the familiar designs: the paisleys, the jacquards, the stripes of men's ties. "We buy the silk from local haberdashers. Would you like to see how it's done?"

She gestured toward the back of the room, where I saw, nearly concealed, an open doorway. I nodded, replaced the quilt, and followed her into a studio lit by skylights. There, half a dozen young women were at work, leaning over huge frames, taking stitches with minuscule needles. I was surprised to see brown and yellow women working beside white women, all clothed like the proprietress, which is to say they looked rather more comfortable than I felt, in my hot layers of petticoats and undergarments and stockings. They were barefoot, too, their shoes in a neat row to the right of the entranceway.

I watched them stitch a quilt of reds and golds for a long time before I realized that the white-haired woman was watching me watch. "I'm Judith," she said, extending a hand.

"Marguerite," I said, taking hers.

She took a silver case from a slit at her hip, opened it, and offered me a cigarette. I shook my head. She fingered one loose for herself, replaced the case, lit the cigarette with a match, and eyed me through the smoke. I thought I had never seen a woman so elegant, the long white cigarette between long fingers not quite so white. "You're not here to buy, are you, Marguerite?" Her eyes appraised me again, as if in the sunlight my circumstances were revealed.

Embarrassed by the evident shabbiness of my own clothing, I shook my head and began to explain, fumbling for words. I hadn't yet revealed my new hobby to anyone except William; it was hard to express to her how important drawing was to me, why I had been wandering around, pad under arm. But she simply smiled and nodded, peering into my eyes and saying, "Yes, I see."

She invited me to have coffee in her courtyard. There, over the next hour or so, her interested gaze and gentle questioning made it so easy to talk that it wasn't until I left that I reflected with surprise on the intimacy of our conversation, my own candor. I had even told her—although not in much detail—about William, our situation, my unhappiness. She told me that she had been married too, and had divorced. And despite the regret in her voice, I could see that she had survived, had even thrived, and took solace in that.

But the real surprise was the joy I took in our discussion of art and artists. My enthusiasm must have seemed naive; what was so new to me was familiar territory to her. There was no name I could mention of which she had not heard; she had been to Paris, to London, to New York; had visited the great galleries, had bought great works. "I can introduce you to some people," she said, "who might take an interest in your work," and I knew then that she intended to become my friend.

Most important, by the end of that day, I had the impression that if she liked my drawings, she might let me display them in the shop, and this thought—the thought of my work being seen and sold—gave me incredible pleasure. I was to bring my best work to her the next morning. As I hurried home at sunset, my mind raced. I wanted to bring her something fresh, something that would show the best of what I could do. I wanted to produce something that would have on her the same kind of effect her quilts had had on me.

I searched my options for an appropriate subject, but none came to me. Everything seemed hackneyed, used up.

By the time I got home, I had fallen into something like despair. Instead of going inside, where William would certainly be slouched in his own moody funk, I stepped through the gate and into our garden. Decaying and neglected, the garden had come for me to be a symbol of our marriage, and so I usually avoided it. Two broken rattan chairs leaned on one another in a corner; the brickwork floor had come loose in places, exposing soil that had invited weeds to take root. The only clues to former glory were a dark-leafed magnolia whose white blossoms still filled the air with the scent of citronelle in early spring, the camellia's faded blooms, and a dead rosebush's thorny, leafless stems. But these were strangled by a wild growth of vine and native weeds, some large as trees.

I gazed mindlessly at these plants, these weeds, and gazed at them some more. And slowly their seeming disorganization gave way, and I began to be able to distinguish among them. At the time I could not identify them—that came later. Then, I only saw, in the tangle of their leaves and flowers, the shapes and colors I had been searching for. Here was my subject for drawing.

I worked through sunset and beyond. Sometime long after midnight, William came to stand in the doorway, gaping at me at work in the dark, with kerosene lamps all around and drawing board propped on the rattan chairs. We had long since reached a wordless plateau. I looked up at him but did not speak; he disappeared.

In the morning, exhausted, I covered the drawing carefully and took it inside, where, trying not to wake him, I bathed and dressed and ate and waited till the hour Judith had said she would expect me.

Sunday morning in the French Quarter was quiet, save for the sound of mops as black menservants swabbed doorsteps after Saturday night's revel. Like most businesses, the quiltmaker's shop was closed. But when I arrived the door was open. I made my way inside, wove through the racks of quilts and into the studio at the back. It was empty, but the door to the sunny courtyard was open. And there was Judith, in nightgown and striped satin robe, sitting at the ironwork table that was set with coffee and croissants for two. She was reading a paper, her feet up on the other chair. "You're here!" she said and, giving me a delighted smile, took her feet down and gestured at the chair with her cigarette, inviting me to sit.

I shook my head. "If I don't show you the drawings right now, I am going to die of anticipation," I told her.

"Then show me," she said.

I showed her the things in the portfolio first. Bowls of fruit, stacks of dishes, old hats. She nodded and made small, pleased sounds, but said nothing. Then I showed her the new one, still tacked to my drawing board, lifting the tissue from it for her to see. She gave a low whistle. "When did you do this?" she asked.

"Last night."

I looked at it with her. It was a drawing, primarily, of what I later learned was the blossom of an Angel Trumpet, *Datura wrightii*. Huge, white, unfurled like a narrow umbrella—a horn, a trumpet, with sharp tips that marked where its petals would have been divided, had God chosen to divide them. I had drawn it largely by negation—by inking the leaves around it in black, as they had looked to me in the strange light of my lamps. The flower itself I had detailed in pastels—its pale shadows faintly lavender and yellow, and, at its center, the glowing orange pistil and anthers. As I looked at it, its musty, sour smell came back to me. It was a plant both beautiful and evil—being, as I later discovered, quite poisonous, a member of the nightshade family.

Judith said nothing more. But when I turned to look at her, she was smiling at me, and I knew she liked it. "May I buy it?" she said, quite suddenly.

My response surprised even me. "You may have it," I said to her. "A gift."

She gave me a long, quiet look. For the first time, I noticed the color of her eyes—a deep hazel, combining the warmth of brown and the coolness of green. "What can I give you in return?" she asked, but it was not a real question; we both knew. Her friendship, her patronage, would be my reward.

The exhibit was to be called "Floralius"—festival of flowers. It was Judith's idea. Among her books she discovered one, quite old, that listed native flowers and gave their Latin names, genus and species, with descriptions but no illustrations. "Imagine this book with your drawings," she said, and I immediately could.

For two months I drew like a demon whenever I could steal a moment: early mornings, late evenings, even lunch hours. On Sundays I sought the flowers out in vacant and overgrown lots, among the rocks along the Mississippi, in the swamps, studying their names and descriptions in the book, bringing back specimen after specimen and storing them in Judith's icebox, wrapped in tissue. For these outings, I took Judith's advice and wore men's pants and shirts and heavy shoes, with my hair stuffed under a hat—in part because my own dresses and shoes were inappropriate to the kind of walking and climbing I had to do, and in part to make myself less vulnerable to unwelcome approach from the vagabonds who also wandered such places. Soon I began to feel as though I lived life on a mirror with two sides, one side reflecting a wife and diligent clerk, the other an independent woman and artist, a wanderer across southern wastes. This disjuncture caused no discomfort, however; I was quite happy with the balance it granted me.

The exhibit opened. We had hung it in Judith's courtyard, where my flowers looked as if they had grown there. I had told no one else I knew about the exhibit, not even William—if I was going to fail, I wanted to fail as discreetly as possible. But, to my amazement, dozens of people came; a few were friends of Judith's, but the rest were strangers drawn by her advertisements, bills pasted on lampposts and fences and walls in the neighborhood. Several drawings sold, for more money than I could have imagined possible; Judith oversaw the sales, playing one collector against another to raise the prices. She was an avid agent for me, driven, she said, by her genuine belief in my talent and potential.

As twilight came on, the drawings faded into the walls and our guests left us standing in the courtyard. "You are a wonderful artist," Judith said. I hugged her. "You are a wonderful friend," I told her. "How can I ever thank you?"

She stepped back from me. "You can't," she said with a casual shrug of her shoulders. "Nor do you need to."

Judith was my first real friend, accepting me completely as I was. While William had overlooked my faults, she embraced them. "Everything that has happened to you," she told me, raising my hand up so that we both could see the scar where my finger had been, "has made you what you are today. There is no shame in that, only pride."

We shared secrets. I learned that Judith's husband had been wealthy but cruel. Still, she took the blame for the end of their marriage: her personality, she said, was "too willful." She was a firm believer in divorce. Of course, she was not Catholic.

One day, as we were lunching, she wiped her mouth, put down her napkin, and made a pronouncement: "You should divorce William," she said, as if after long consideration. "He is a parasite on you. He sucks your money away for those self-indulgent 'lessons.' He sucks your pride away. He sucks the joy from your eyes—I see it every time you leave here."

I knew what she said was true, but some part of me, some remnant of childhood religiosity, would not accept the notion of divorce. It seemed a failure of profound proportions, a denial of solemn vows. It would vanquish me from the Church forever. I could never tell my parents.

I had not told Judith everything, though, and when I did, at last, admit that there was no longer a physical aspect to our union, this only made her more determined in her arguments. At last I was persuaded to broach the subject with William, to let him decide for himself. "I'll invite him to dinner," Judith said, sensing my reluctance. "We'll talk to him together."

Surprised to be invited, William surprised me even more by accepting the invitation.

It was the first evening of gaiety I had shared with him in a very long time. Judith poured bottle after bottle of wine. I abstained, having sworn off alcohol, but William was seduced not only by the luxury of the meal—three kinds of meats, a table set with linens and real silver—but also by Judith, by her charm and, I imagine, her throaty Southern laugh. Over chocolate torte and cherries poached in burgundy, Judith leaned across the table and fixed her eyes on William's flushed face. "William," she said, "will you give Marguerite a divorce?"

William turned to me a shocked face. "Would you divorce me?" he said. "Could you?" He took my hands in his. "I thought . . . "

It took a moment for me to understand that he was *not* refusing me.

"Yes," I said. "If it's what you want."

His gaze seemed to turn inward for a moment, as if he were consulting his heart. "Yes," he said finally, and a great smile filled his face. I had not seen him so happy—well, since the day we married. "Yes," he said again, and squeezed my hands with the love I had thought long since dead.

I was surprised by the happiness of my own response. It was as if some dark and heavy spirit had exited my body. I was free again.

W hen the divorce was final, it seemed natural to move in with Judith. She was my friend; she had a spare room. As she put it, "We divorced spinsters can grow old taking care of one another. Who needs husbands?" She was forty, and joking. Fifteen years her junior, I did not imagine either of us a spinster, or growing old, but I was happy to have such an elegant place to live—the quarters above her shop were spacious—and happy to have such a friend to live with.

In preparation for my arrival, Judith refurbished what she called "the ballroom," her top story, an attic unlike any attic I had ever seen. High ceilings and shining floors, huge windows at either end, it was hard to imagine what its original purpose could have been, although Judith insisted it was for dancing. As we walked up the steps that day, she confessed to me that she was nervous. "I tried to imagine what you would like," she said. "You and I are so different." She was right: her taste ran to brilliant colors, and she was a collector—her spaces were so full of objects that one's eye could never rest. As much as I enjoyed that, it wasn't for me.

But when I opened the door of my room that first day, my eye met a most pleasing room; a better combination of simplicity and luxury I could not have imagined, and still cannot. The walls had been painted an astounding shade, not white but not quite another color, either; depending on the light that hit them, they glowed yellow, pink, or bluish, and the effect was soothing, almost as if they changed color to suit—or counteract—one's mood. Under one window sat a round table with straight legs and two matching chairs, all in dark wood; on the table, atop a piece of starched linen, sat a vase filled with blue larkspur. Against a wall was a couch upholstered in rose brocade, with a table and lamp on one side of it and a small shelf for books on the other. In the center of the floor was a round rug braided in shades of blue and red. Under the window stood a four-poster bed dressed in white linens—and folded at its foot, the beautiful blue silk quilt I had once coveted.

"Oh, Judith" was all I could manage to say.

"It's all right?" she said.

To answer, I could do nothing but embrace her.

Judith seemed a little embarrassed as she pulled away, but pleased. She went to the bedside table, where she had champagne on ice for us, twin glasses.

I stood speechless for another minute, gazing at my beautiful room, the impeccable furnishings, the loving touches. Finally, I spoke—a bit rudely, I'm afraid. "Judith, you spent too much," I said.

"Money's meant to be spent," she said, and poured champagne. "To your happiness, my dear."

In Judith's courtyard grew an avocado tree whose fruits fell to the ground and lay there till we needed them. There was a fig arbor, too, figs hanging like little brown sacks, resistant to the teeth but sweet and gritty, and a lemon tree, the lemons almost too sour to eat, but good for lemonade on a hot day. It was like Eden, and the next few years were as close to bliss as I ever came. I left my job and spent my time drawing and designing quilts for Judith. We displayed the drawings next to the quilts and sold as much of one as the other. We changed the sign in the window: HAND-SOME ARTS, it read, DRAWINGS AND QUILTS FOR THE DISCERNING COLLECTOR. It was a brief but prosperous time for us both, those years between my divorce and the Great Depression.

This bliss was domestic, as well. Judith and I fell into happy routines. We rose early, ate breakfast together, either in the courtyard or in her room, fresh croissants or muffins and chicory coffee and fruit. Then we worked till about eleven, when we sent everyone home for lunch and siesta, then made ourselves a luscious lunch of one sort or another. At two we resumed work, at six o'clock stopped again. Dinner we cooked slowly, sherry in hand, talking and laughing in the kitchen. We grew a little plump, I admit, from the pleasure we took in food and its preparation, but what matter?

Evenings found us reading, Judith in her easy chair and I on the settee in the room she called her study. She introduced me to what I had missed as a child, extending my education into new areas of literature, art, philosophy, history. I found myself able to think more clearly, able to consider the past in a new light, even able to see my parents as they really were, and to forgive them at least for those things over which they had had no control. My love of learning rekindled, I enrolled in classes at the women's college, and eventually got my degree, yet another thing for which I owe Judith, who paid the tuition and gave me the time to study.

I felt myself maturing into a woman—not a woman as worldly and wise as Judith, but a woman in charge of her own destiny nonetheless. It was in this state of mind—full, you might say, of myself—that I met Charles.

He came into the shop late on an afternoon when Judith was away buying silk. He wasn't the usual sort of customer we had; he wore rather rough trousers and a pair of suspenders over a collarless shirt, and on his feet were dirty brogans. But one look at his face and I knew he was a "discerning collector," quite possibly a man richer than his clothing suggested. Smooth-skinned and fine-featured, he had intelligent eyes and a strong jaw and mouth.

The combination of roughness and refinement attracted me. When I introduced myself, hand out, and he took my hand and shook it as he would a man's, I felt an instant liking. He explained why he had come: his mother's birthday. "She's a hard woman to please," he said.

"We can please anyone," I said, flushing when I realized the double entendre.

He smiled but ignored the opportunity to make fun of me. "I like your confidence," he said, and I could tell he meant it sincerely.

I sold him a fine quilt that day, an elaborate design of geometric roses. On his way out the door, he paused before one of my drawings, itself a wild rose, *Rosa rugosa*. "What's this flower?" he asked. "I've never seen it."

I confessed that it did not grow in Louisiana; I had drawn it from memory.

"You drew this?" he asked. I only nodded. "Let me have that too, then," he said.

"Your mother will be well pleased," I said, taking the drawing down to wrap it.

"Oh," he said, with another smile, "but the drawing is for me."

That evening as I told Judith about the quilt and the drawing, she gave me a long look, then finally said, "You're leaving something out."

"No," I said, shaking my head but avoiding her look by peering into the pot I was stirring.

"Yes," she said.

"All right," I said, putting the spoon down. "Yes. It's the man who bought them."

"Name?"

"Charles Morley."

"Morley," she said. She took a cigarette from her case, lit it, drew in, gave a cough. "Morley. A very good family hereabouts," she said, her voice raspy from the smoke. "A very good family. And this Charles?" she said, giving me an opening.

"He's taking me to the theater," I said.

Judith seemed pleased. "That's lovely," she said. "Lovely."

Charles and I began to spend time together. Once, at most twice a week. At first I was not certain it was a romance at all, so slowly did it begin. But gradually I recognized it for the genteel kind of courtship it was. We were getting to know one another—really getting to know one another, in a way which I had never done with a man. And I found it endearing, the way this man methodically went about teaching me about himself, and himself about me. Each outing was to someplace new, but always somewhere that ensured talk. After the theater, walking home; over the table in a quiet restaurant; in a carriage touring the city; a waterfront picnic. One Saturday morning he took me to see his family's business, a shipping enterprise not far from where I had once worked, and there he took the time to show me everything, bales of cotton yet to be ginned and tobacco leaves wrapped in paper and wooden crates filled with machine parts. It was straight from this work that he had come the day we met, and as we traveled the docks, he wore those same dirty brogans—but a clean, white, collared shirt, clearly in honor of me.

Finally, he invited me to meet his family—his mother and sisters, his father having long since died. When I told Judith, "I'm happy for you, Marguerite" was all she said.

The night before this momentous occasion, I could not sleep. I suppose it was because I had not yet been completely honest with Charles. As kind as he was, I was afraid that he, like William, wanted children and would reject me when he knew I could not have any; it seemed dishonest to visit his family without telling, but I lacked the courage to do so. So I lay there, eyes burning in the still, hot, wet night. Finally I got up, changed into a dry nightgown, and descended to the second-floor kitchen to get a drink of water.

Judith's room was on my way, her door closed as it usually was. As I passed, I thought I heard her coughing. I put my hand on the knob, hesitated. I knew she hated me to dote on her; should I go in? But just then the sound grew worse, became an awful gagging. I knocked, loudly. No reply; the noise continued. I burst in. "I'm sorry—" I said. In the light of her bed lamp I saw Judith, tears streaming from her eyes. "Oh my god, Judith," I said, going to her. She put her hands over her face, tried to turn from me.

I put my arms around her. "What's the matter?" I said. "Tell me, you can tell me."

"You know," she said, her face still buried.

I couldn't imagine what she meant. I shook my head, stroked her hair. "Tell me," I said again.

She pulled away from me, looked at me with red-rimmed eyes. "Well," she said finally, sitting up straighter, squaring her shoulders. "Well," she said again, clearing her throat. "It seems that I love you."

I let go of her, sat down, averted my own eyes—not so much as not to see her as to give myself a moment to think. When I looked up again, she was gazing at me, her eyes full of such sorrow that I went and put my arms around her again, consoling her with the only words that would: "I love you too, of course I love you too."

When she was finally sleeping, I returned to my room, shaken—yes, disturbed—but uncertain why. I was not unhappy to know that Judith loved me. But I did not know what meaning to make of it. I wanted to be friends with her always; I could not imagine a life without her in it. Yet at the same time I had not imagined a life with her. I knew, of course, that some women loved each other, even physically; I was naive but not ignorant. But I did not feel that attraction for Judith. For her I felt something more abiding, less transitory. Yes, I admitted to myself, I loved her; not as one does a friend, nor quite as one does a wife, or a husband, but I loved her nonetheless, and more than I had ever loved anyone.

For a long while I lay awake in the bed Judith had given me, lay with my head at its foot so that I could stare out into the night sky. I watched as it grew light, black shading to blue much as the quilt under my head did. And as the palest shade signaled morning, I thought to myself: Does anything matter but love? And I told myself: No.

The next morning, I went to see Charles. He took the news with the kindness and understanding I had come to expect from him. I told him our time together had been wonderful, glorious. But it did not match, nor did it promise to match, the times I had with Judith. We were the same species, she and I; we knew each other as only members of the same species can, understood each other more than any man and woman ever could. We loved each other as only true friends can: unconditionally, sweetly, without demands or expectations. And we had built a life together that neither of us could imagine giving up. I knew what choice I had to make.

Did Judith and I become lovers? We were intimate in every way—intellectually, emotionally. We gave each other the solace of affection when it was needed; we lay down together when we were cold or lonely. We loved each other; therefore, we were lovers. Whether we crossed that final boundary or not is irrelevant, and no one's business but our own.

The Great Depression struck New Orleans as hard as it struck anywhere else in the country. When the market crashed, people we knew did what so many other people did, taking their own lives in moments of deep despair. In the city it was a time of great sorrow and fear, and it was one time when I wished we were back on Grain Island, where poverty was a natural state, survival a way of life, and money the least useful commodity.

As soon as it became clear that the hard times would last a while, we shut down the shop. Throughout that horrible decade, though, we never stopped designing and planning for the future. And I kept drawing as long as my supplies lasted.

We settled down to a frugal, quiet life, our main consolation that we had not invested in stocks, and that the bank in which we kept our money had—miraculously—not collapsed. Our nest egg was intact, although we worked to preserve it, to save as much of it as we could, not knowing how long the lean times would continue. We gave to others as much as we could; the women in our neighborhood knew that they could come to us for food when their children were hungry, and as long as she could afford it, Judith saw that her former workers received a small monthly stipend to help them survive. We had a strong roof over our heads; in the courtyard we had the vegetable garden, which provided most of our food; we counted every penny, rose and retired early to save light, mended our old clothes. And so we weathered the Depression together, one year after another, until it was over.

Then came the war. All the silk went to parachutes then. Judith surprised me with her patriotism, going to work at a factory that produced boots for soldiers. I went back to work at the docks and collected old shoes for refugees. The war rose and fell like a wave, and we rose and fell with it.

After the war ended, I convinced Judith, despite her claims that she was too old, to reopen the shop. We had preserved my drawings and the remaining quilts in moisture-proof boxes in the cool air of the root cellar; now we took them out and aired them in the courtyard. They were as beautiful as ever. We painted and redecorated the shop, and placed advertisements in the *Times-Picayune,* and soon we were rediscovered. After nearly two decades of frugality, people were hungry for beauty, for luxury. Money flowed again. Judith was happy. So was I.

Judith cut her white hair short, so that it framed her face like an aura. She had changed, of course; she had begun to show her age. Yet, though she was older than I, I had always expected I would die before she did; she seemed stronger, indomitable.

And I think she would have outlived me, if not for the cigarettes. For years her coughing had kept her from sleeping well; now she became so short of breath that conversation was a challenge. She laughed at what she called her "furry" voice. I begged her to see a doctor.

The winter that year was unusually cold. In January, temperatures began to slide below freezing with alarming regularity, and sometimes at night fell to the single digits. The green of the city faded, turned brown; it was like living in a sepia-toned photograph. Until then, we had always gotten through the winters with nothing but an occasional fire to take the chill off; now we had to keep a fire going at all times. Still, pipes froze and burst.

The shop had no fireplace, so I convinced Judith to buy a small kerosene heater, reasoning that customers stayed longer if it was warm, and the longer they stayed, the more the quilts could work their magic. Judith didn't like the smell, and worried about the quilts taking it on. I worried about her health. I knew that sitting day after day in that cold, damp shop would not be good for her.

One night I discovered a handkerchief spotted with blood. Judith tried to dismiss it, pretended it was from the meat she'd been making for dinner, but I didn't believe her. Finally I managed to get her to a doctor. Within a week or two, we learned what was happening. The doctor told us he'd seen this in other smokers; he admonished Judith to quit. She only raised her silver case up and removed another cigarette, the elegance of the gesture canceled by the coughing that ensued.

For the next year I did the best I could to nurse her. I knew she would not get better; I only hoped to prolong her life, and thus ours together. The doctor advised us to leave New Orleans, leave its damp heat and mildew, which only irritated her symptoms, but Judith would not, and I didn't want to either. I wanted nothing but to stay home, home with her.

As she grew worse, I spent many hours by her bedside, reading to her. When she slept, I looked at her face and thought of all the reasons I loved her, not least of which was how, even as she lay dying, she continued to love me.

One day we had a terrible argument. She had continued to smoke for a long time, but now that she was no longer able to leave her bed unassisted, I had begun to mete out the cigarettes, saving them for the times of day when I knew she most needed them: with her morning coffee and just after supper. But that day the supply had run out after breakfast, and I suggested that this would be a good time to stop altogether. "Do you have no understanding," she said, "of how few pleasures remain to me?"

I was tired; I was tense. Still I have no excuse; I ought not to have responded as I did. "Put someone else ahead of yourself for once," I told her. "Think about me, for once."

The hurt on her face was almost more than I could bear. "*All* I think about is you," she said.

Within the hour, I was walking home from the store, another pack of cigarettes in hand. It was a crystalline day in February 1950, the week after Mardi Gras, the gutters still glittering with beads and coins here and there. As I walked, a strange, acrid smell filled the bright air. But I made nothing of it, till I came to find our little alley clogged with smoke.

The firemen were still there, the ambulance gone. The upper stories, they told me, had suffered only smoke damage. The shop, meanwhile, was a total loss. "Silk doesn't burn easily," the fire chief told me. "The fire must have been pretty hot." I remember his sooty face, white teeth, blistered lips. And the bitter, bitter smell of burnt silk.

Someone must have taken me to the hospital, but I do not remember the ride. I remember only the dingy room where I waited alone. The sky outside was still bright and clear, but the grim filter of an unclean window dirtied it. I sat there for hours, vaguely aware that time was passing and that somehow I was being ill-treated, ignored, but lacking the will or courage to rise from my chair and ask questions. I did not think; I could not think. I could only listen to the thoughts my mind produced of its own accord, random and furious and incoherent as a bee trapped in an airless jar.

Finally, a nurse came in and took me to Judith. She was inside an oxygen tent, her face so bandaged that her eyes were all I could see. At my insistence, the nurse let me inside the tent. I put my mouth to Judith's ear and said her name. The hazel eyes fluttered open. She couldn't speak. I took her bandaged hand in mine.

We had only a few moments before they sent me back to the waiting room. In a while a man came in. I watched his mouth move. A pair of liver-colored lips in a sallow face. I heard what he was saying. He was explaining to me that there would be an autopsy. An autopsy was standard in such cases, he said. Whenever foul play might be suspected. In this case, luckily (he actually used that word—*luckily*) there had been no foul play. However, there was some chance it was suicide. After all, she had been dying, she had access to laudanum. In such a case, suicide was hard to prove, of course. She might simply have fallen, knocked the heater over, and been unable to rise. In any case, most certainly the insurance company would pay . . .

I believe he was still talking as I left the room.

Judith had been dying, that last moment we spent. I had not known this until the man began to speak. I had, without realizing it, assumed that she would somehow recover, if she received the care she needed. But she had been dying, and I realized suddenly, with certainty, that she had wanted to die; that, even if she had not started the fire herself, she had let it burn.

And now she was to be dismembered. Cut up. Her body violated by this man whose only purpose was to give her death a name. I thought of Judith, her skin flayed away from her, pulled back to reveal the blackness in her lungs, her unmoving heart. My beautiful Judith. Dead, and now to be destroyed.

I turned back. I found the man with the gray lips. "No," I told him. "No autopsy. I won't allow it."

He asked what gave me the right to stop it.

I am her lover, I wanted to say, might have said—maybe even did say, given the expression on the man's face.

"I'm sorry," he said. "But only a family member has the right . . . "

At the funeral I insisted that the coffin remain closed. No one questioned my right to do so.

I paid someone to demolish the shop and studio, to empty them of everything but the timbers that supported the rest of the house. The weather warmed. I stayed home and sat in the cool sun in our courtyard. I felt hollowed out, haunted.

Judith's lawyer came to see me. I had not thought about her will; we had never talked of it; there had seemed time, she'd been only sixty when she died. She'd left me everything, of course—the house, her savings, her investments. But, the lawyer said, there were complications. A challenge to the will from her son.

Her son. I heard the story at last. How she had divorced her husband, how he had paid her handsomely to leave the boy with him. How badly she must have wanted to get away, I thought. Then the boy came to me, now a man, seeking his birthright. Like his mother, he was tall, but there the resemblance ended, for he was selfish, with the oily skin and desperate eyes of a man who has reached the middle of his life without a thing to show for it, and he let me know in no uncertain terms that he would fight me as long as it took to take my inheritance away. Seeing the father reflected in the son, I thought I knew why Judith had left.

I did not have the strength to fight him, and did not want to. I could not live in a house so full of my own sorrow, and I would not sell the memories it bore. Judith's house was a burden to me that I could neither shirk or discard. So I gave it to him.

I moved into a hotel. Temporarily, or so I told myself. My life became a series of moments that piled up into hours, days, months. With nothing but the storefronts to remind me, I lost track of seasons and years. I woke only when I learned of my parents' deaths: first my mother's, then my father's, in the winter of 1955. It had been so long since I had seen them, I didn't so much mourn as add them to the catalog of my losses. Still, settling their estate gave me something to do—gave me a purpose, if only temporarily. So I left the city at last, and came home to the island, bringing with me only one thing to remind me of the past.

How you loved Judith's quilt.

When you were a baby, I would lay you on it to change your diaper, and sometimes leave you there, naked, to roll about on the slippery silk. Like a little eel you were, squirming there, squeaking, singing. So hard to imagine you now, ever that small. The little arc of your pee when I didn't get the diaper on soon enough.

And later, when you were older, on rainy days the quilt became our blue sky, a tent over our heads as we played games: cards, Indians, house. And when you were sick with fever, it was the blue quilt that calmed you, that cooled you down, as it did me.

Two days after Caroline signed the papers that gave you to me, I went to the deputy's house to bring you home. You can't imagine the sinking fear in my heart when I knocked and no one came. Through a window I could see his wife—Alma was her name—sitting at the kitchen table, her back to me. I rapped on the pane. She did not turn, but I could hear what she said. "Go away, old woman," she said. "He's mine. You'll never get him." Like a witch in a fairy tale. To this day, I don't know whether she truly said those words or I only thought she did. But I know she felt them.

I pitied Alma, I truly did. She must have wanted a child very badly. And I knew how easy it was to love you. But you were my boy, mine, and I would not give you up.

Sense told me to wait for the deputy. I stood in the dooryard there, under the leafless trees, watching the road for him. The thaw that had begun a few days before had continued; what snow remained lay in shrunken heaps where it had been plowed. If I had been a smoker, I would have smoked; this was the kind of moment cigarettes were made to fill. But nothing filled my moment but restlessness and an increasing fear of what she might do to you, what she might already have done.

I walked around to the back of the house, looking for something to use. Evidently the deputy had been building a barbecue the summer before; here was a handy pile of leftover bricks. I took one and went back to a front window and broke a pane— only a small pane. Quietly, carefully, so that she did not hear me and so that the glass would not hurt you if you were nearby. I reached in a hand, unlocked the window, slid it up, and climbed in. Once inside, I was a little surprised at myself. Standing in their living room, heart racing, I wished it had not been necessary to take such a risk. But it was what any mother would have done, her son in danger.

It was, I suppose, the kind of home you should have had. Small, cozy, immaculate. Warm, even cheerful. Afghan on the back of the couch. Overstuffed chairs. Ruffles at the windows. Even a television set, something I would never have in my house. A few of your toys sat piled in a corner, but no sign of you. So I listened harder, and heard your small movements, your voice, behind a door.

Opened it. Steps led down. It was a cellar. Was she keeping you in the cellar? You looked up at me without surprise. "Hello, Tante," you said. You were playing on the cold dirt floor, toy soldiers arrayed in rows. "James," I said, "time to go home."

You stood up without question, came to me and took my hand. We went up the stairs. But when we stepped back through the door, there she was. What came out of her mouth was more a wail than a word, a sound more sorrowful than any sound I had ever heard: "No!"

"Come on, James," I said, putting my arm around you, my hand gripping your shoulder, keeping myself between you and her.

"No!" she wailed again, coming for you, her hands reaching like claws.

I pushed her away. She stumbled back, nearly fell. Instantly I wished you'd never seen that, but it couldn't be helped. I moved us toward the door, which opened as if by miracle as we reached it. The deputy stepped back and let us through.

"She's there," I said, pointing behind me, moving us toward the truck.

He only nodded and went inside.

The next day I sent him a check for the window. We never spoke of it again.

I had a room ready for you. Your toys in it, your clothes, all your things from the trailer. On your bed, the blue silk quilt. The first night, I asked if you wanted to sleep with me. No, you said. You wanted to sleep in your new room; you were excited to sleep in it. I started a fire there, made sure it was safe, and went away. But I could not leave you alone, so I slept just outside your open door. Every sound I heard I thought was you. But you did not stir. You slept well.

I knew what people would say. About what I did to the deputy's wife. About how I paid Caroline to get you. People would say terrible things; some might even want to go to court, to have you taken away. But somehow I knew that the deputy would stop all that. I thought he understood, and I was right.

Aside from your staying with me at night, our life was substantially the same. On the surface, you scarcely seemed to notice that your parents were gone. When you asked me about them, I reminded you of the simple fact—that they had died with your uncle Homer—and you nodded solemnly and went back to your clay or blocks or truck. So I thought you understood it, accepted it, would come to love me as you had loved them. I was glad when spring came and then summer. The further we were from those events, the more secure I felt.

You had always loved strawberries. So, the year before, I had planted a strawberry patch in the sandy soil to the south of the house, where the morning sun shone longest. Your summer living with me would be our first crop. You turned five that June, old enough to help. I had grand plans for us to make jar after jar of delicious jam, and to sell what we did not need at the farmers' market. I thought it would be good for you to see how labor produced income. I pictured you on a stool by the stove, stirring the pot of steaming jam; I pictured you counting out change of a dollar for customer after smiling customer.

As soon as the snow melted and the three-leafed plants appeared, you began to make daily trips to check their progress. They grew fast, bright green and bushy from the manure I added to the soil. On the day the first flowers budded out, you came to me flushed with excitement. Then the white petals fell and the green nubs swelled with spring rain. How slowly they ripened! First the faintest pink, then deeper and deeper. Then one day you came and took my hand and dragged me from where I was hanging clothes on the line. "Is it ripe, Tante?" you asked, pointing, and yes, there it was, the first red strawberry. "May I eat it?" you asked, and of course I said yes.

They came on fast after that. A pint the first day, two the next, and then the deluge. Every morning before the heat of the day, the two of us crouched in the rows, picking, filling buckets and pails. Then into the house to clean them. I gave you a sharp knife and taught you how to use it, and you cut off the stems and sliced up the berries, and I put them into pots with sugar and pectin, and we cooked them. The steaming jars and lids ready to be pulled with tongs from their bath. The glistening dark jars lining the countertop as we finished them. Jar after jar of delicious jam. You ate strawberries fresh, you licked the pots before I washed them. We scarcely ate anything but strawberries for two entire weeks.

It was at the first farmers' market that we noticed it. Or rather, that it was noticed. We set ourselves up in the shade, displayed our jars on the tailgate of the truck. Fifty cents each was what we asked. The customers did not flock as I had imagined, but we had some, we had a few. One of them smiled down on you and said, "What a lovely boy you are." And when you handed her the two quarters in change for her dollar, it was she who said, "My, child, what's that on your finger?"

Dark red, the growth was, the size of a pea; no surprise, really, that it had gone unnoticed till then. You washed your own hands, took your own baths; you were quite a boy already. But now as I took your hand in mine and looked at it, I tried to shrug it off. "Oh," I said, "just a mole. Nothing to worry about." The woman smiled through her grimace and went off; since you seemed unperturbed, I soon forgot it.

A week or two later you came to me. "Tante," you said, holding out your hand. The mole had grown; it was the width of your index finger now, and when I pressed on it, it bled. "It's like a strawberry," you said, and it did look like a small, ripening berry. I smiled, tried to make light of the coincidence. "Maybe we ate too many," I said, "and this is what we get."

But I was frightened.

Doc Milton was new to the neighborhood then. He had bought the land across our road and brought his little girl, Faith, to vacation in the trailer where your parents had lived. I'd spoken to him once or twice, but that was all; I knew he was a doctor, but not what kind or how he would receive us. But I put you in the truck that very minute and drove you to the trailer.

We were lucky to find him home. "Yes?" he said, coming to the door. I showed him your hand. "Miss Deo," he said, "I'm an ophthalmologist. An eye doctor. I have some instruments here, but this kind of surgery takes a delicate hand, precise control. The boy's finger is small, the nerves close to the surface. And there ought to be a biopsy. This kind of cancer can come back. You understand that?"

I hadn't understood that. Cancer. That's what it was, then, this strawberry growth. The word scared me, scared me more than I had ever been scared. But only made me more determined. I had already let it grow too long; I would not wait. And besides, I felt certain that, if I took you to anyone else, you would never come home again. To go to the village doctor, to go to the mainland would be to reveal to everyone that I was failing, failing in my role as your guardian, your mother. It would be proof to them that they were right about me. It might cost me you. "If you can operate on an eye," I said, "a finger should be no problem."

"I can't in good conscience . . . "

"Please," I said.

He must have seen the fear in my eyes, the determination. With a sharpened and disinfected scalpel and two careful incisions, he removed the growth. You did not cry, I remember that. But that is all I remember, so caught up in my own distress was I. The girl was there then, she must have been; the two of you must have met then, for the first time. But she would have been small, and I don't remember seeing her; I was too focused on you, I suppose. I was so worried about your finger, I didn't think of anything else. I had even forgotten one thing more important: that this was your first visit back to the trailer where you had been born.

On the ride home you held your bandaged hand high, as the doctor instructed. Your silence then seemed natural to me—it was a frightening thing, to have a man slice into you with a knife. It wasn't till that night that I began to worry. You could not eat your supper, even though I made your favorite, ham steak and potato pancakes. You started to, but after a bite, stopped. I could not tempt you, even with ice cream. I thought that you'd wake hungry during the night, but it never happened. And the next morning your eggs and sausage grew cold. "James Jack," I said, using my angry voice. "You eat now. Don't waste your food." You looked up at me then. I expected to see rebellion, but there was none in your eyes. "I can't," you said. "I can't." You took a forkful of eggs into your mouth but couldn't swallow; you had to spit it out. And I realized you were telling the truth.

I thought and hoped it was a reaction to the surgery. I feared it meant something more, something worse. Another day went by, then two. "Do you want something to eat, James Jack?" I said periodically. You shook your head. You were hungry, I knew, but could not eat.

You lay about on the settee, weak and pale. Outside, summer was in its glory, hot and green during the day, cool and breezy at night, but you stayed indoors. You wanted the shades pulled. Even in midafternoon, you slept under Judith's quilt, as if you were cold. I took your temperature; it was normal. We discovered that you could sip a bit of water, but that was all. We tried every kind of food I could imagine. You could not eat. I asked you why. "Everything tastes bad to me," you said. "Bad how, baby?" I asked. You grimaced at me; you hated when I called you baby. "Dead," you said. "Everything tastes dead."

On the fourth day, I drove to the doctor's again, thinking to ask his advice. But he had gone home. I sat there in the truck, my view of the closed-up trailer blurring through tears. As I sat, I remembered the day I had come there with the zwieback cookies, the fat little baby you had been, bouncing in your walker, smiling at me and at your mother. It dawned on me then: this had been *your* home only months before, until one morning you had left it, never to return. And when you returned, your parents were gone, replaced by a strange man with a knife. Their things gone, everything changed. I had told you many times that your parents had died, that they were dead. Could it be that until that moment, you hadn't understood? "Dead," you said. "Everything tastes dead."

I came back to the house without a plan, not knowing what I could do, but at least now believing I knew what was wrong. Sitting in the cooling truck, I made up my mind to call the mainland, to take you to the hospital there, to the emergency room. I had to do it, no matter what it might mean. I could not let you starve.

I got out of the truck. All around the house, flowers were in bloom. Glorious flowers, fragrant flowers. July's end was the best time for my garden, the fullest time, the most promiscuous. As I passed by the bank of daylilies that ran alongside the house, I smelled their spicy scent and plucked a petal from one and put it in my mouth. It tasted clean and crisp, alive. It gave me an idea.

I pulled my shirttails into a pouch and began to gather petals. Daylily, nasturtium, violets, even rose petals. A beautiful, glorious salad of flowers, caught in the net of my shirt like sleeping butterflies.

I rushed into the house. Found a bowl and filled it. Brought it to you where you lay, eyes half closed, on the settee. "James Jack," I said to you. "Here's something alive to eat."

You opened your eyes, sat up a little. "Flowers?" you said.

"Flowers," I said. "Just picked."

You reached into the bowl, pulled a purple petal from it, placed it cautiously on your tongue. I imagined it there, all but melting. I watched, waiting to see if it would make you gag. "Spicy," you said. You swallowed it, took another from the bowl, the golden-yellow petal of a daylily, so big it required you to bite it in half. You did so, chewed and swallowed one half, then the other. "Oh," you said. "Sweet," you said. You ate another, a nasturtium this time. "Bitter, like pepper. But I like it." And on you ate, until they were gone.

Afterward, you slept. I sat by your side and watched you sleep, as I had done when you were very small. When you opened your eyes again, I was still there. "Tante," you said. "I'm hungry."

Later that night we sat on the porch, looking out into the darkness, listening to the summer sounds, smelling the evening-blooming flowers. I explained to you that not all flowers could be eaten; I promised to show you which next day. You came to me and sat on my lap then, as you still did sometimes, although more and more rarely, when you were afraid or unhappy. For a long time you didn't say a word, but just clung to me there. Then you spoke, in a voice so small I thought at first I imagined it. "Tante," you said, "you'll never die, will you?"

I held your small face in my hands, looked you in the eye. "No, I won't," I promised.

And so I kept my promise, and grew very old, after all.

Your first shoes. Soft white leather, soles thin as paper. Learning to walk, you held on to my fingers, first with both hands, then with one. We went everywhere together for three months. When finally you walked alone, one hand remained in the air, holding on to my invisible finger.

You outgrew the shoes before they wore out, so I sent them off and they came back bronzed. Creases, scuffs, the little convexities of your toes, all preserved, sweet record of the baby you were. I cannot look at them without remembering, without feeling the love I felt, then and now. This is the love I want you to have; this is the love you have to find.

Five

Lunch was strange without Tante. It was strange to be in the kitchen without her, knowing her room was empty, knowing she was nowhere in the house—nowhere at all, really. Strange to be alone with Faith because it was only Tante's absence that made them alone. Yet they weren't alone; Tante was everywhere, and not just in what she'd left behind. Every time he came into the kitchen, he saw her stooped shape bent over the sink or rounding the corner into the bathroom. In the crackling of the fire he heard her calling him, the bedsprings creaking as she rose, her shuffling gait as she walked. Once, looking out the window, he thought he saw someone passing by, shadowy in the snow, going up toward the barn, but when he went to look, there were no tracks and nothing else to see except the dark empty rectangle of the open barn door.

James had to get away from the house. They had a few more hours of daylight. He wanted to go fishing.

"Fishing?" Faith said. "Ice fishing?" she said. He nodded.

"What about the sheriff?" James shrugged and said, "Don't worry about it." She gave him a funny little smile but said, "All right."

They made cocoa together, Faith watching the milk heat on the stove while James fetched the chocolate syrup from the refrigerator and the thermos from the cupboard. He handed her a wooden spoon, and she stirred the syrup in. "More," he said, taking the can from her and inverting it over the pot till the milk was dark with chocolate. Faith looked at him with that funny smile again. "You like chocolate," she said.

"Hmm," he said.

"Me too," she said.

He made her dress in layers this time, piling on some of his things and some of Tante's, till he was sure she would be warm.

The sky was clearing. He found that heartening. The day's dry snowfall billowed behind the truck as they drove to the bait shop. It felt good to have Faith in the truck beside him, good to know they would be making love again later. He wondered a little at himself, at what right he had to feel good so soon after Tante's death. Then he tried to imagine how he would feel if she were still alive and realized he couldn't know. So he stopped thinking about it.

He expected Faith wouldn't last long. Ice fishing wasn't the kind of thing a lot of women enjoyed, at least not the women he knew. Tante was the only exception, and she had enjoyed it because she liked the notion of something for nothing: fish on the table that you caught yourself, no middleman, no one to exchange money with. For him, the thing was being alone. Out there on the ice, you could spill your mind into the fish hole the way you would a mop bucket into a sink, sink your thoughts with the bait, and contemplate life. How risky it was. How a man could just as easily have been born a fish. Or how a man, born a man and thinking himself safe and superior, could find himself at any moment trapped beneath the ice just as if he were a fish. It reminded him that he was neither more nor less important than anyone or anything else. It renewed the close fit between himself and the universe. It kept him humble.

He wondered how it would be for Faith. Whether she, like Tante, would like the fishing part of it only, bringing home good food to eat. Or whether she would feel what he felt, see what he saw. The mystery of it, the draw. He was surprised, after losing his family to it, that he still loved it. He had needed it ever since he was a kid. That moment of stepping onto first ice, not knowing whether it would support you or not. Solid water. Black ice. The plants still green below, waving there in the current. The fish swimming among them. Walking on water. He did not believe that Christ had walked on water, but he could believe He had walked on first ice, smooth and transparent as glass.

Faith stayed in the running truck while he went into the bait shop. The air inside steamed with the stink of fish. Minnows glittered in five bubbling tanks, schooling up, swimming, shifting silvery direction. "Morning, Warren," James said to the bait man. "Morning, James Jack," the bait man said back. It was all they said; there was nothing more to say. Warren knew what James wanted; James knew how much money to put in the bucket by the door. When the net went in, the minnows scattered like mercury spilled.

He remembered the last time Tante came fishing with him. It had been more than a year ago—or was it two? He'd been almost afraid to take her, he remembered that. She seemed so breakable, her bones so thin and close to the surface. And she moved so slowly: one foot at a time, a pause after each step. Yet she had wanted to go fishing. She looked funny in the big rubber pac boots, the shiny windproof pants. Her old parka. Her head swathed in a red scarf underneath the hood so that only her eyes and nose showed. Underneath, the layers were so many that they had almost restored her to her former size and shape. She'd made a good catch, he remembered that, too. And back home, she had insisted on cleaning the fish and cooking them up for him, just as she used to do, except that, too, was slower now. By the time dinner got on the table, he was famished—but the wait was worth it. She could still cook.

He put the bait in the back of the truck with the auger and tip-ups. Faith had the radio on, but turned it off when he got in. He appreciated that. They rode in silence.

It had been a good cold winter. He knew the ice was plenty thick. Still, if Faith hadn't been with him, he would have left the truck on shore and walked out to the shanty. But he wanted the truck close by in case Faith needed to warm up. He drove out slow; you didn't want speed on the ice. Faith's eyes went wide anyway, and he knew what she was thinking. "Seven, eight inches will hold a truck," he told her. "We've got a good two feet most places."

"If you say so," she said.

His father's shanty had gone to the dump years before. The new one reflected his own preference for simplicity, economy, sturdiness. He'd built it himself, out of excess lumber and roofing. This year it was painted gray-blue, because that's what he'd had left over from painting the Chalmers deck. In spots, last year's green showed through. Next year it might be purple, for all he knew. But never red. That had been the color of his uncle's shanty, and he would never have it for his own.

Inside, four by eight, a six-foot peak to the roof. A wood-plank bench on three sides. Three Plexiglas windows, for light and so you could watch the tip-ups. A stovepipe chimney for venting the woodstove, which he'd made, too, out of a metal drum.

Some hooks on the walls to hang gear on. A door. Two holes in the floor. That was all.

They got out of the truck, and he helped Faith put on her creepers, then she helped him unload the gear. Inside the shanty, he showed her the wood and gave her some newspaper, and while she worked on the fire, he drilled two fresh holes in the ice. When all that was done, he said, "Let's go out and set some tip-ups." Inside her layers, Faith shrugged, nodded, smiled a thin smile. She was still afraid—he could see it in her eyes. "What's a tip-up?" she asked. He showed her. "Like a little fishing pole," she said. "One for each hole we drill," he said. He offered her his gloved hand, and they walked out onto the ice.

For a moment, James wished he could see it through Faith's eyes. Wished he could feel what she felt—fear or awe. He felt about the lake, winter or summer, ice or water, the way most people seemed to feel about family. Sometimes he hated it, mostly he had a kind of affection for it, but either way he didn't see it for itself anymore, the beauty, the power of it. It was just a part of his life, like the wind, like the island, like Tante. Only in the dream did the lake become something else.

The dream had started when he was very small, not long after his parents' deaths. Then it had come almost nightly; now it came just once in a while, and he was never sure what brought it on. In the dream he was swimming with his parents and his uncle Homer beneath the ice. The sun came down through the ice and lit the water a beautiful green. There were no fish in the water, no weeds, only the four of them, swimming in the green. They wore, at first, their winter clothes, but gradually they stripped them off, layer by layer, until their skin was colored green, too, by the iridescent green light of the sun. It gave them scales, like fish. They were not fish, yet they could swim under the water indefinitely. Looking up through the green ice with green eyes. They all had green eyes.

The dream always left him both comforted and sad. It wasn't a nightmare. Just a dream of death.

But the lake in his dream was not the real lake. The lake in his dream was friendly, gentle, quiet, safe. The real lake was none of those things, although it could seem them at times. But he had grown so used to its crotchety nature, its change-ability, that it didn't matter to him now. He just knew the lake, and he responded to it instinctively, and always did the right thing.

But to Faith it was unfamiliar, and terrifying. Through the layers of gloves that separated his hand from hers, he could feel her trembling. "You all right?" he said.

"Fine," she said.

He got the sled ready, put the rope in Faith's hand, took the auger in his, and they started. The wind blew the snow a little and flakes settled into their eyebrows and lashes. They put out eight tip-ups, twenty yards apart, in a line straight out from the east window of the shanty, so they could see them from inside. They were drilling the seventh hole when the ice let out a deep boom. Faith was so startled, she almost fell. "Jesus," she said, catching her balance. "What was that?"

"Nothing, nothing," he said, standing and taking her elbow to steady her. "Just the ice talking," he said. Faith's breath came out in quick little clouds. "Ice talking," she said, and inhaled deeply. "Right."

He couldn't help but laugh. "Expansion," he said. Then he pointed to the hole in the ice. "You saw how long it took me to drill that? See how thick the ice is? Two inches can support a person walking. You really don't need to be afraid." She gave him a look. "That is, unless you don't trust me," he said.

"You know, funny thing about that," she said. He took off his glove, stuck a bare hand into the minnow bucket, baited the hook, and balanced the tip-up over the hole, and they started walking again, this time with Faith's hand hooked on his arm. "I do trust you."

"Oh," James said, keeping his voice light, "but I'm so dangerous." He paused to kiss her.

"Yes," she said. "I know." Her voice more serious than his. He knew she was thinking of Tante then, of what they were to do that night.

When the last hole was done, he stood and turned to Faith, who was gazing out across the lake. "It's like a white canvas," she said. "So flat."

He looked with her at the white stretch of ice and snow. Far off, the figure of another fisherman moved, small and gray against the white. For a moment James felt that small, reduced to a stroke of paint on the canvas, Faith another stroke beside him, nothing more. Then they started back, his hand on her arm steadying her, and he felt large again.

They were coming up on the first tip-up when the orange flag popped up. "Fish!" James said. He ran toward the hole and knelt by it, waited for the reel to stop spinning. When it had, he lifted the line and let it run through his bare fingers till he felt the weight of the fish on it, then let it run a few seconds more. Then, with a snap of the wrist, he set the hook and slowly pulled the fish in, hand over hand.

It was a pretty perch, no trophy but large enough to eat, yellowish with dark-green bands. He held it out, arching and flipping, for Faith to see. "Pretty," she said, smiling, and he knew that fishing at least had won her over. He took out his cleaning knife, slit the fish's belly. Twin pillows of pale orange roe came bursting out. "A mama," James said. "Oh," Faith said. He dropped the fish and the roe into the bucket. He reset the line, and they went silently back to the shanty.

It had warmed up inside. He got out two jigging lines, baited one for Faith and handed it to her. She sat on an overturned bucket and lowered the line into the green-lit water. He poured her a cup of cocoa, dug into his pocket for something he knew was there—a package of hard candies, lemon drops—and gave her one. She took it and put it into her mouth. "You remembered," she said.

Looking at Faith's hooded head bent over the fish hole, he pretended that she didn't love her husband anymore, that she loved him instead, and that they were married, and happy. She looked up at him again. "What?" she said.

"I was thinking," he said, "that Tante was right."

"About what?"

"About us," he said.

The night after he first met Faith, James had told Tante about his day as he always did, over supper, leaving nothing out but telling nothing that did not have to be told. Still, the news of Doc's death didn't seem to affect her as much as the news of Faith's arrival. "Tell me more about her," Tante said. "She has red hair? I don't recall that."

"Probably not her own color," James said, concentrating on cutting his meat.

"Probably not," Tante said. When he looked up, she was peering at him. "I see," she said.

"See what?"

"I see that you like her," she said.

"Of course I like her," he said.

She rolled her eyes.

"She's married, Tante," he said, serving himself some more potatoes.

Tante shrugged.

The next day, he stayed away from Doc's trailer. Found things around the house that needed doing. A loose shutter to fix. Wood to split. Went down to the store and bought some oil and a filter and came back and changed the oil in his truck. Kept busy. Worked hard. But could not sleep that night.

At breakfast the next morning, he said, "I think I'll take Doc's daughter some wood. I don't think she's got enough to last her out the week."

"She's staying a week, then?" Tante said, her eyes sly at him.

"I don't know," he said, realizing that he hadn't asked.

Tante nodded. "Well, then," she said. "I think you ought to take Doc's daughter some wood. And find out how long she's staying."

It took him an hour to load the truck. The dawn air was frigid, but the work made him sweat. The thought passed through his mind to clean up before he went, but he shoved it out. Foolish to clean up just to sweat again when he stacked the wood for her. He got in the truck and drove over.

Faith opened the door before he got out of the truck. "Hi," she said. She was dressed, but in clothes she might have slept in, and she looked sleepy.

"Brought you some wood," he said.

"Thanks." She said it as if she had a right to expect it; he saw that she was used to people doing things for her without her asking.

"I'll stack it on the lee side of the trailer," he said. "That'll keep the snow from drifting on it."

"If we get any," she said.

She was standing in the door in her jeans and T-shirt.

"You're gonna catch a chill," he said. "Standing there like that."

"I'll put my coat on and come out and help you." Before he could tell her there was no need, she'd gone inside.

He backed the truck around to the other side of the trailer. This was where his father had always stacked the wood; he remembered that much from his early childhood, from the time when his parents had rented this place from the farmer who owned the land before Doc did. What wood Doc had left was piled here, too, but not well; he pulled that out first. Since it was older and dryer and would burn faster, he wanted to stack it last. He'd begun to unload when Faith came around the corner.

"What do I do?" she said.

"Well," he said, and then he showed her how to stack the split logs so that they fit together tight and stable but still had some air between them, the wedge of each piece between the curves of the two below it, keeping space between the pile and the trailer for circulation. She learned fast, and between the two of them the wood was stacked in half the time it'd taken him to load it. "Well," Faith said. She brushed the wood chips off her gloves and coat front, and when she spoke was a little breathless. "That's a good job well done."

James nodded.

"Come in for cocoa?" asked Faith, and James nodded again.

Later that day they went for a walk along the road. When he asked how long she was staying, "a while" was all she would say. The next day, he found another excuse to see her, and the next. She talked easily to him, the way strangers did sometimes; all he had to do was ask a question, and she opened up. He realized he was trying to learn about her, learn everything he could—researching her the way he researched a truck when he bought it, the way he'd researched Tante's condition when she was in the hospital.

He learned a lot of things. Faith liked the taste of sweet and sour, tea with lemon and sugar better than coffee, lemon drops, that pink pineapple sauce on Chinese food. She liked the color blue and had a set of blue glass dishes at home. She got cold easily, especially the tips of her fingers. She loved animals but had never had a pet because she was mildly allergic. She had a job she didn't like at an insurance company that paid her well, and why quit? what else would she do? When she was a small girl, she'd touched her tongue to a frozen flagpole and had waited there for more than an hour before anyone had come to help her. Her mother had died not long after she was born. As a result, she had loved her father too much, and missed him now more than she missed her husband. She referred to the place where she and her husband lived as the "condo-minimum."

Her husband. That was the one subject Faith avoided. James learned a lot of little things about her, but not the biggest thing. He imagined what anyone could imagine—to him, bad marriages were all alike in some way—but couldn't know until she told him.

On the fourth day, Tante said, "Invite her to dinner," and so he did. That night, he made a fire in the front room and cooked a nice meal—venison stew, green salad, pie for dessert—Tante advising him from her kitchen chair.

He was unaccountably nervous about their meeting, maybe afraid that Tante would offend Faith in some way, or vice versa. But Faith sat right down next to Tante and struck up a conversation, and from the kitchen he could hear them laughing together like girls. He wondered then if they were talking about him, and he felt self-conscious but also proud.

The only tense moment was at the table, when Tante leaned forward and said, "Why'd you dye your hair?" He winced at her presumptuousness.

But Faith rolled with it. "I don't know," she said, gazing at the ceiling thoughtfully. "To irritate my husband?" She smiled, and Tante smiled back, two knowing women, cutting him out. But he liked that.

Faith had had a little too much wine, she said at the end of the evening. "Could you drive me home?" He avoided Tante's eyes as he helped Faith out to the truck; he knew she'd be smirking.

The truck's roar kept them silent for the few minutes it took to get to the trailer. There, he shut it off and turned to tell her good night. "Thank you," she said, and he was saying, "For what?" when she leaned toward him, pressed her cheek to his, put her hand on his neck. And it felt natural for him to put his arms around her, return the embrace. They stayed like that for a long moment, longer than they should have. He did not want to let go. Did not want to ask her the question in his mind. But he did. "What about your husband?" he said.

She pulled away then and he was sorry he had said it, because he did not want to hear her answer. "What about him?" she said.

He looked at her and waited. "I love my husband," she said, "if that's what you're wondering." He let out his breath. "But I don't think he loves me," she said. He put his hands on the steering wheel. The windshield was fogging up. "Why not?" he said.

She blew out a breath, adding to the fog. "I don't want to tell you that," she said. "I don't know you well enough to tell you that yet."

He nodded.

"I'm sorry," she said, and then, clumsily, she was letting herself out of the truck, stumbling toward the trailer. As he leaned across the seat to shut the door she'd left open, she turned to him and called, "Maybe tomorrow, all right? Maybe tomorrow." And then she was gone inside.

So she was staying another day, he thought. And drove home happy just to know that.

He returned Faith's car before dawn the next morning and

then went fishing. Sunrise made the ice red. Sitting in the shanty with his jig line and the woodstove and his view of the long white body of the lake, he listed in his mind plans for the next summer: reshingling the barn, painting the windows, planting the garden. Last year they'd tried some Indian corn—pretty but useless. This year he wanted more Silver Queen, with its fine sweet white kernels. And cherry tomatoes. There was a gold variety that was so sweet it tasted like candy.

In this way he avoided thinking about Faith. Whether he wanted her, whether she wanted him. Whether it was only the wine that had made her do what she did. He was avoiding thinking about the sensation of her hand on his neck, her face against his. The faint scent of her hair. How close they'd come to kissing. It had kept him awake most of the night.

He had two strikes in the first hour and lost both fish because he tried to set the hook before they had really taken the bait. Halfway through the second hour, he noticed a flag up on one of the tip-ups, and realized that he had no sense of how long it had been up, whether it had just popped up or had been up for minutes or longer. He thought twice about getting up and going out into the cold to check it. But he couldn't be cruel, even to a fish.

He was on his way back from releasing the fish when he saw Faith coming across the ice, slow and small in her blue coat. No creepers on her boots against sliding, but the good sense to follow his tracks.

He wanted to go help her, but he stood his ground and watched her make her way. She looked up from the ice once and saw him there, and smiled. An uncertain smile, a deliberate smile. To set him at ease. When she reached him, she stopped and stood still, and he could see the relief in her as her body relaxed its fight against falling. She took off her gloves and pulled a pack of cigarettes from her pocket. "Tante told me where you'd be," she said.

"Tante'd know," he said.

With shaking hands, she lit a cigarette. "You cold?" he said, and she nodded, and he waved her inside the shanty.

They sat facing each other, as far apart as could be in the small space. He took up his jig line again, and played it a little. She warmed her hands by the stove. "About last night," she said. He waved her words away. "No," she said. "Let me apologize. I'm sorry. I shouldn't have done that."

"No harm done," he said. "Nothing happened."

"I think I should explain," she said. "Let me—"

"There's no need." He concentrated his attention on the hole.

She didn't say anything. He looked up. Her eyes were red, but from cold or tears or sleeplessness he couldn't tell. He didn't want to know, didn't want to hear—it was none of his business—but she seemed to need to say. "All right," he said.

She gazed down into the fish hole. "The night before I came here, I set the bed on fire," she said. "Our bed—my and my husband's."

She looked up for his reaction; he tried not to look shocked.

"We haven't . . . we haven't spent much time there lately," she said. "At least he hasn't. Not for a year."

He nodded, trying to pretend—to himself, at least—that it was an innocent thing, this conversation, a kindness he could do a friend. As he asked, "Why not?" he tried to think of her that way—as a friend, not as a woman—tried to put away any feeling beyond friendship, beyond kindness. But another part of him wanted to pull her to him.

"I don't know," she said. She laughed again, tapped some ashes into her palm. "Short story, huh?"

"There must be more to it."

"No," she said. "Not really. I mean, yes—we have our problems. I have my theories." She looked up. "But I don't know why we stopped having sex."

"What does he say?"

"He doesn't. He just says he doesn't want to." She sighed a long sigh. "I'm thirty-four, he's fifty. Maybe that has something to do with it. I want to have a baby; he doesn't. That probably has a lot to do with it." She shook her head, stared out the door of the shanty. "Anyway," she said, her tone apologetic again. "That's a short part of the long story I don't think you'd care to hear. And last night—last night I just wanted someone to touch me. Just wanted to touch someone. I'm sorry."

He shook his head. "No problem," he said. "No offense taken."

"Of course," she said, "I do like you. But I can't do anything about it. I love my husband. I still have hope."

James nodded. "I see," he said.

They were quiet for a few minutes, looking down into the fish hole. When James pulled his line up, the bait was gone. He looked at it a moment, thinking. "Let me walk you back to your car," he said.

He gave Faith some ice creepers and held her hand to steady her as they crossed the ice. On shore, she leaned against a tree while she took off the creepers. "There you go," she said, handing them back. She went to her car. "Listen," she said, turning back before she opened the door. "I'm not leaving the island till Monday. Couldn't get a plane till then." He felt a little leap as his mind calculated—today was only Friday, he had two more days. But then she said, "I'd like to see you again, but we probably shouldn't." She gave him a weak smile. "Right?"

"Right," he said, as firmly as he could. She got in, shut the door, and started the car.

He stayed away. He had to stop himself, several times, from driving along the lake road, just to see her car in the driveway. He had to stop himself, several times, from thinking about little things he wanted to do for her. Places he wanted to take her, views he wanted her to see; things he could make for her, take to her. A bird feeder, to hang in front of her window; kindling for her fires. Things would just pop into his mind, as if she were his lover, already a part of his life. He had to keep reminding himself that this was not the case, but it was as if another level of him had leapt ahead to some imaginary future. He couldn't stop the thoughts from coming.

But Saturday he kept busy. Sharpening tools. Organizing the barn. Running errands for Tante, who kept her eyes on him as if he were a pot she wished would boil. But he was silent on the matter, told her nothing. And she had enough sense not to ask.

It wasn't necessary, but he toured the houses he was care-taking that winter. Checked shutters and doors. Went inside their elegant interiors and double-checked to see that the water had been shut off, the pipes emptied. At one place he was happy to discover that some ice from the last storm had fallen off the roof and damaged a porch railing; it took him all afternoon and part of the evening to repair that. Or anyway he let it take that long. It felt good to be working, good to be far away from her. For a while he was able to forget her.

Sunday was harder. He woke up angry with himself for mooning over a woman he had known only a few days. He lay there, counting their encounters, going over them in his mind. There was nothing there. And yet he had this feeling for her. And now not seeing her only seemed to make it worse. Did he love her? How could he? He tried to figure out what it was, exactly, he felt. A longing. But for what? For sex? That would be the obvious thing. But that was nothing new; he was old friends with that kind of longing. Something about her got to him some other way, and he couldn't shake it off. She had set the bed on fire.

Tante was irritable, too, Sunday morning. She crabbed about some newspapers he'd left in the summer kitchen, where he'd been painting the railing for the Clark place. When he crumpled them up and rammed them into the stove to burn, she complained about that. "If you can't do something right, don't bother," she said. She called him "James Jack" all morning, which was what she had called him as a boy when he was in trouble. After lunch, she went into her room and shut the door, as if being with him had just become too much of a trial to bear.

Sunday at Tante's had always been a day when nothing could be done. It wasn't that Tante was religious. It wasn't even that she allowed no work. It was, instead, as if the day itself refused to cooperate. As if the fact of it being Sunday broke momentum, brought things to a halt, slipped a hood of inertia over the house. No matter what they planned, nothing came of it.

As a boy he hadn't minded the slow, quiet day. As an adult he had come to enjoy it—a day of rest without guilt. But today he felt the way he had as a teenager: restless, anxious, uneasy. He wanted it to be over, and Monday to come.

He had it in mind that he would go to the trailer Monday morning. He hoped she would already be gone, but if not, suspected that when he saw her, the bloom would be off the rose. He would see her for what she was, whatever that was, and this feeling would die of its own accord. He thought he should tell her good-bye, if nothing else.

And then Tuesday would come, and everything would go back to normal.

But here was Sunday to get through, Sunday that seemed to last forever. He lay down on the settee in the front room and pulled Tante's old silk quilt over him. A quilt of blue diamonds sewn in broad herringbone, like waves flowing back and forth across its surface. The shiny ocean he'd slept on as a baby, shivered under as a sick child, made a tent of as a boy. Stained and worn from many washings, still the quilt had the smell of memory. Surrounded by that smell, he slept what felt like a long time. But the clock on the mantel told him otherwise. The afternoon still stretched before him.

He took a walk up to the lower quarry. He'd dropped some trees there back in the fall and left the wood to cut up and the brush to burn in spring, so he thought he'd go remind himself how much. The day was midwinter solemn and gray, the wind playful along the path. But the quarry ice, protected, was smooth and flat under a thin layer of perfect snow. In the summer, this was his swimming pool, the dark ledges of marble rising up around him in the cold, deep water. Now he walked out onto the ice, paused, looked over his shoulder, and walked backwards, fitting his boots into the footprints he'd left. The Man Who Disappeared in a Quarry. Risen to heaven? Taken by aliens? An alien himself? Someone seeing the prints would not know what to think. He both liked the idea and felt silly for having it. He hardly glanced at the downed trees as he headed home, refreshed by the exercise.

It was near dark by the time he got back. Tante's door was shut. He knocked on it. "What?" she said, her voice sharp. He heard the bedsprings. "What is it?"

"Checking on you," he said.

In a moment the door opened and she appeared. She seemed wide awake. "You just want your supper," she said, and came out as if to make it, even though for a long time it had been he who cooked the supper. But he let her help him, trying to stay out of her way and keep her out of his.

For as long as he could remember, he and Tante had played cards after supper on Sunday nights. While he was clearing up, Tante got the cards out and put them on the table in the front room. Remembering the night Faith had been there, he made a fire. The chill went off the room. Tante seemed to approve. "I'll make some tea," she said, and he took that as a sign that he was forgiven for whatever it was that had angered her that morning.

They played gin. Tante won the first few hands. "You're not concentrating," she said, and he won the next three, as if to prove her wrong. The anniversary clock swung its pair of twins this way and that, sweeping the minutes away, sending its gleam over the walls. He found himself thinking about Marion. And then about Faith. If he could hold Faith, just once. If he could put his hands on her bare shoulders. If he could put his arms around her and give her what she needed, what she wanted—whatever that was. Even a baby. He tried to shut the thoughts out. "This room needs painting," he told Tante, who only glared at her cards and said, "Do it when I'm dead and gone."

He put down his cards. "All right," he said. "What's the matter?"

She moved a card from one place to another in her hand. "Nothing," she said, pretending concentration. She reached out to take a card from the pile, discarded, said, "Gin," laying the cards down.

He looked at her cards. "Tante, that's not gin," he said. "You're thinking this three is an eight." He pointed.

"Don't you tell me what I'm thinking," she said. She pushed her chair back and stood so quickly it made her unsteady. "If you knew what I was thinking, you'd know what's the matter." She gripped the edge of the table.

He felt his own anger surging, kept it back. "All right," he said. "Tell me what's bothering you. I can't read your mind."

"That's right," she said. "You can't." She sat down again and pulled the cards toward her. He gave her his and watched as she tried to stack and shuffle them. "I'll tell you what the matter is," she said. "The matter is you're a thirty-year-old man with nothing to show for your life." She laid the deck on the table; he cut it.

"Thirty-five," he said. "And that's an unkind thing to say." It was the same old argument. Tante would say she was holding him back, that he ought to leave her, go do what he wanted, get on with his life; he would tell her he already was doing what he wanted, and she should mind her own business; she would say he was her business, and he would say that she was his. "What if I told you," he said, "that you were a ninety-four-year-old woman with nothing to show for her life?"

She began to deal, the cards spinning down on the table. "I had a life," she said. "I had a whole life before you." She set the deck in the middle of the table, turned over the top card. "You, on the other hand—you've never had any life but me."

"What brings this on?" he said. She didn't answer, pretending to look at her cards. The answer came to him. "Ah," he said. "This is about Faith, isn't it? Tante, she's married."

She peered at him over her hand. "That wouldn't stop you if I wasn't around."

"Yes, it would," he said.

She shook her head. "You're in love with her," she said. He shook his head. "Don't tell me no," she said. "I know what I see."

"I hardly know her," he said.

"Doesn't matter."

"She's married," he said.

"Matters less."

"She doesn't love me," he said.

She just looked at him. "Maybe not," she said. "But she might." She took a card, discarded it. "I think you should go see her," she said.

"I am going to go. Tomorrow," he said. "To say good-bye. She's leaving Tuesday." He felt the lie roll off his tongue like a ball that could just as easily have choked him.

She put down her cards. "Go now," she said.

"Come on," he said. "It's late, we're playing cards."

"Go now," she said. "Go to her or go someplace else, but go."

"Tante, come on."

"I want you out of this house," she said.

"Goddamn it, Tante." His turn to stand up angry. "Goddamn it. Mind your own business."

She turned a cold eye up at him. "Don't you talk to me that way," she said.

He'd been angry enough to do it, angry enough to put on his coat and slam doors behind him. Leaving her at the table with the cards. He went not to Faith, but to the cabin. Made the fire and fell into bed and after a fashion slept a dreamless sleep.

That was it. That was all. A little argument, one of hundreds of little arguments they had had in the thirty-five years they'd been together. A little argument, that's all.

But Tante had come after him. To forgive him, or to carry on with what she had to say? Or had she gotten lost? Or had she been walking in a dream?

No. She hadn't come after him at all. And she knew where she was going. She knew what she was doing. When he'd found her dressed in nothing but snow and roses and her own blue skin, she'd been on the quarry road. She'd been on her way to death.

He admitted that to himself now, accepted it.

And tomorrow Faith would go. He admitted that too. But for now, her face flushed with cold, her eyes intent on the fish line, she was here with him. For that, if nothing else, he could be thankful.

It was nearly dark when they stopped fishing. At the house James stoked the fire again while Faith stripped off her layers; when he looked up, she was nude, and despite himself he smiled. So odd to see a beautiful woman naked in this house. "Let's take a bath," she said.

Marion was the only other woman he'd been in a tub with, but he didn't tell Faith that. So he could pretend—to himself, to Faith—that she was the first. He let her get in first, then climbed into the big footed tub so that he faced her, his back to the faucet. She had her knees pulled up as he came in; as soon as he sat, she straightened them, and he felt her slippery feet between his legs, touching him. There was nothing he could do about his reaction, except watch the smile grow on Faith's face. "Men are so easy," she said.

"Great idea," he said. "A bath."

She laughed and splashed him, and he laughed and splashed her back.

They washed one another, shampooed each other's hair. The water felt hot and good after being outside so long. Faith's head felt good under his hands. Her shoulders felt good too. Her breasts, all the rest of it. He thought about how happy it would make her if their lovemaking produced a child. He'd like that. He'd like to have a child of his own. He knew that was dangerous thinking, but he liked thinking it anyway. So when she pulled him toward her in the tub and climbed onto his lap, he didn't resist. They were like two fish copulating, wet and slippery and awkward. But that too felt good, and made him happy.

Dressed, they went back down to the kitchen, fixed some tea.

Outside, as the night cooled off, the wind rose, rattling windows and making the house moan. "Winter trying to come inside," Tante always said. "Trying to get warmed up, like a ghost that's had enough."

After the bath, Faith had put on one of his flannel shirts. Not a shirt taken fresh and clean from the closet, but one she had found in the laundry basket in the closet. "I want to smell like you," she'd said. The tails of it came down to her knees. Underneath it she wore her own pants, and she had put her big wool socks on. She sat now with one sock foot up on the chair, the other dangling, looking like a little girl. Looking at her, he knew how much he would miss her when she was gone.

"What's the matter?" she said.

"Nothing," he said. "What do you want for dinner?"

"It's too early to think about that. I'd rather have a cigarette."

She got up and went to her jacket and found a half-pack of cigarettes in her pocket, brought it back to the table, took the matches from under the cellophane, and lit a cigarette. She was careful to blow the smoke away from him, but she smoked nonetheless, as if she'd forgotten his request earlier. "I was thinking, out there on the ice, what it must be like to drown. It seems a relatively peaceful way to die."

"I suppose so," he said. "If you choose to die that way. Most people who drown don't."

She nodded. "Yes, I suppose I was thinking of suicide," she said. He must have frowned, because then she said, "You don't approve of suicide?"

"No."

"Never considered it?"

"No."

"Well," she said, "you've always had a good reason to live. Someone to take care of. Maybe now that you don't, you'll feel differently."

He could hear the anger in her voice, knew it wasn't meant for him, but felt his own anger rise anyway. He decided not to let it. He put his hand out and took the cigarette from her and stubbed it out in the saucer. "Right now, I have you to take care of," he said.

In the momentary stillness that followed this statement he could hear nothing but the small, regular sound made by the anniversary clock in the next room. It was not a tick, exactly, but the sound of taut wire unwinding, one second at a time. It was the sound of waiting.

The waiting ended when she picked up the half-smoked cigarette and relit it, inhaling deeply. "Taking care of me is not so easy as all that," she said.

James shrugged. "It's never easy to take care of someone who doesn't want to be taken care of."

She stubbed the cigarette out again and came to him. "I could take care of you," she said, her lips close to his ear, her voice low enough that he could not be certain whether he heard her or only felt the motion of her lips against him. Then she said, more loudly, "For instance, you could use a haircut." She tangled her fingers in his hair. "Scissors in the desk drawer," he said.

He moved his chair to the center of the kitchen; in a moment she was circling him. "Tante always cuts my hair," he said. "I'll be careful," she said. The hair dropped away, sifting down to the floor. "Like heavy silk," she murmured. She pressed her warm fingers into his neck; the scissors hissed through his hair like silver wings. "Voilà la beauté," she said at last, whispering. He got up and looked at himself in the bathroom mirror. "Not bad," he said, and saw her smile behind him.

They cooked. Fresh fried fish, potatoes, bread, wine. They ate in the front room, at the big wooden table. The fire crackled and spit in the fireplace. The frost inside the windows was melting from the top down, from the heat. He should have felt groggy—

from the wine, the heat, the long day—but instead he felt wide awake, aware of everything. Not nervous, but attentive. The way he felt the first morning of hunting season. Wide awake before the alarm went off.

After supper, James brought Tante's will out to the table. They opened it, read it together. Night had long since fallen. The sky was clear, the stars were out; it was time to do what they needed to do. But they didn't move from the table. He wanted just to sit there with her, time suspended. Forget for a moment the past and the future too. Just talk. "Did you like ice fishing?" he asked.

She took a sip of wine. "I've been trying to figure out what I was so afraid of," she said. "Not the water. Not the ice. Falling, maybe. I've always been afraid of falling. I don't like losing control. You know?" He nodded. "But the fishing. Yes, I liked it. I can see why you like it, too."

He waited for her to tell him.

"You like the quiet," she said. "You feel free. You've got space."

He had to smile. "Shanty's a pretty small space," he said.

She laughed. "It's not necessarily walls that hem you in," she said.

"How about you?" he asked. "Why did you like it?"

She raised her eyes toward the ceiling for a moment. When she brought them down, she looked right at him. "Because I was with you," she said.

The phone jangled like a distant alarm clock. James went into the kitchen to answer it. It seemed to get louder, more insistent with each ring; he thought it would be the sheriff calling. He almost didn't answer it, but something told him he should.

When the caller asked for Faith, he hesitated. Then the voice said, "She's there, isn't she?"

"Yes," James said.

"Well, this is her husband."

"Yes?"

"I'd like to speak to her."

"I'll see if she can come."

"Wait," the man said. "Are you the one?"

James knew what he meant, wondered how the man knew—
or if he was guessing, assuming something he didn't know.

"Yes," James said.

"Do you know why she's doing this?" the man said.

"Yes," James said.

"I doubt it," the man said. "And you should know. She's doing
it for revenge. She thinks I'm having an affair."

"Are you?"

"No," the man said.

"I'll get her," James said, and turned to call Faith.

She had already come into the kitchen. James saw her now,
face washed of color. She took the phone from him.

"Yes?" she said.

James left the room. "How did you find me? Where did you
get this number?" he heard her ask, and then he tried not to hear
the rest. The conversation went on forever, a long low murmur
of words, Faith's voice rising and falling, angry then soft. He
thought she was crying, then he thought she was not. He stared
into the fire, into the coals blinking at him, black and red. He
tried to think ahead to what they had to do that night, how they
should do it; he tried to focus on something more immediate,
more important to him. He put his hand on Tante's quilt where
it lay folded on the couch.

Then Faith was back.

"You all right?" he asked.

"Yes," she said.

"How did he get the number?" he asked.

"The sheriff gave it to him, apparently."

James nodded.

"He wants me to come home," she said. "Tomorrow. I should go," she said. "I should go. His mother's ill. She and I are close."

James nodded. "You'd better go. Lucky you already have the flight."

She placed her hands one on either side of his neck; he felt the heat of his skin under her palms. "I don't have to," she said. "I could stay. Or I could come back."

"Go," James said. "They need you."

"You need me, too," she said.

He lifted her hands away from him and she moved back. "Look," he said. "I can't tell you what to do." He took a deep breath. "I can only tell you that I'm not your husband, and this" —he waved his hand, at the room, the house, the island— "is not your life."

Faith began to cry.

"But what if I want it to be?" she said.

Then don't go, he wanted to say, but don't ask me to tell you not to. He felt as if he were being whittled away, bit by bit; he felt that when she was gone, there'd be nothing left but the empty house. He felt they were each other's last chance. He felt he could make it right for her, and she for him. He felt so many things that he wanted to tell her.

Instead, he put his arms around her, intending to hold her until they had to go.

There is a saying, "to sow your wild oats." The wild oats I know are not oats at all, but lilies that bloom in May, drooping yellow at the edge of the woods. . . . Perhaps in the saying "wild" refers not to the oats at all, but to the sowing, the wild spreading of oats to places where they are not meant to grow but sometimes take root anyway. And why oats? Not wheat, not corn, but oats. Because oats grow so easily.

Six

I read somewhere once that innocence is not virtue. Perhaps that explains me, or rather describes the girl I was. For although I was innocent, I was never virtuous. My mother taught me that.

When I was small, at night I often lay in bed listing the ways in which I would improve my behavior the very next day. *I will mind, I will not sass, I will not eat more than my share, I will work hard, I will be prettier, stronger, smarter, cleaner, quieter, quicker.* I did not pray, mind you; it never occurred to me to pray. More evidence, I suppose, of my lack of virtue. Instead of turning to God for help, instead of submitting myself to a higher power as I had been taught, I fought with myself to find ways to please a lower power: her.

I remember my confirmation and first communion. I was six, and proud of having learned the catechism. It was a sunny day in June. I sat tall and careful in the wagon, my parents on either side of me and a thick blanket over me to keep the dust off my white dress for the hour and more we rode. When we came over the rise, the lake gleamed before us, a mirror to the sky. My father helped me down from the wagon and led me to a spot beneath a tree, where my mother straightened the bow at my waist and smoothed my hair with a spitty palm and lent me her arm for support while I removed my dirty boots and put on the thin white slippers she had made for me, along with the dress—a week's labor. "Marguerite," my father said, taking my face in his sandpapery hands. "The priest will give you two new names today, instead of one. Bernadette and Marie, after my twin sisters. They died infants." I thought about the dead baby whose funeral we had attended earlier that spring, gray-faced in the tiny pine coffin, and how the priest had said babies went straight to heaven. Maybe my namesakes' deadness would make me more holy, would make me good, even saintly.

My father had built the church himself, using the fine rare marble from our quarries. Though not large, the church was elegant, its black walls shining, its tall windows framing views of woods and lake more beautiful than any stained glass, its altar made of smooth-planed and whitewashed maple wood, a fine Italian Jesus hanging above it, complete with bloody feet and hands.

Despite all this, we were fortunate that my father had been able to convince a priest to serve so small a population—barely six dozen of us. It didn't matter that the priest we attracted was one of somewhat dubious distinction, his sermons sometimes incoherent and his robes never entirely clean. What mattered was that he said the Latin mass, took confessions, and cleansed us of our sins, bringing us closer to God and heaven. And that he pleased my parents, and especially my father, who sponsored him and without whose monetary support there would be no church at all.

As I entered the church that day, I felt myself rising toward heaven, my white dress floating around me, the cool air inside the church lifting my hair. But under my slippers were not clouds but cold stone steps whose roughness—carved by my father's chisel—testified to their earthliness, as did the eyes of the priest and the congregation, on me as if in one judgmental gaze. It seemed I would never be allowed to forget even for a moment how full of sin I was.

The ritual passed in a dream. I made no errors. In fact, all went well until the moment when the priest—hands shaking from some early intemperance—spilled three drops of wine on the front of my white dress. I had been taught to believe that consecrated wine became Christ's blood. I saw the droplets as blood. Three drops: Father, Son, and Holy Ghost. My head swam. Gazing up at the crucifix, I thought I saw Christ move, sending more blood splattering down toward me. Breath escaped me in a gasp. I swooned. I let go of the railing and fell unconscious to the stone floor.

When I opened my eyes, my father's kind, rough face was smiling above me. "It's a blessing from God," he said, and gathered me into his arms.

In the wagon, my mother barely spoke. It was only when we reached home that she looked at me. "Ruined!" she said. I knew she meant the dress she had worked so hard to make. But the word stung as if she had applied it to me.

I was born in 1903. By then my mother was nearly forty and had been married twenty years to my father. How a devout Catholic couple avoided the glut of children of so many devout Catholic families, I can't say. In any case, my mother told me many times about those early years of struggle, when my father's business was still new. I was lucky, she said—at the same time telling me that she would not let me become spoiled by that good fortune. Hard work had made her the person she was, and if I wanted to be strong and virtuous and make some man a good wife, I would have to work as hard as she had.

Our lives did revolve around work. That was how it was here early in the century, when we lived off the land. There was no respite. We rose before dawn and worked till dark every single day, spring, summer, fall, winter, except Sundays, of course, which differed only in that our work was interrupted by church.

Before my birth, my mother had labored alone, the house and garden and barn under her domination, my father vanquished to the quarries, a division of labor that suited them both. Nothing changed when I was born. My father spoke proudly of how she had risen from the birthing bed after only a day and a half, intent on doing the morning milking; how she carried me on her back like a papoose. The farm was her life—even a baby would not change that. She would have borne me in the field, I think— except that ladies, real ladies, never would have done such a thing.

As soon as I could walk, I began to work too. I worked hard, but I was a child, and always insufficient to the task, not quite able to understand why tomatoes were to be set into the basket, not dropped; kindling laid parallel in the box, not willy-nilly; weeds pulled but not carrots. I was a child, but she measured me against the yardstick she used for herself, and punished me with it on more than one occasion.

Once—I was seven or eight—she asked me to walk to the next house, about two miles off, and collect some sewing notions the neighbor had been so kind as to bring back from the mainland. It was early spring, the road muddy, the thaw gurgling all around me—everything moist and suggestive and inviting. I thought—I knew, I know—that I walked as quickly as I could, did not stop on the way, received the sewing notions without pausing for conversation, and returned promptly. I knew that I had followed my mother's strict instructions to the letter, despite my yearning to play in the mud, to trace the trilling stream to its origins.

Yet when I returned home, it was to her fury. She paddled my bottom as soon as I was through the door. "What did I tell you about dallying?" she began, pointing at my muddy boots. Tears sprang to my eyes. Yet even then I could not be sure if her accusation was unjust; maybe I *had* unconsciously done as she said I did: maybe I had dawdled, maybe I had sought out puddles. To add insult to injury, somehow the neighbor had given me the wrong color thread, black instead of brown. I had not looked in the bag; I did not know what color was wanted. But this was my fault, too. That night, she prepared my favorite meal, ham steaks and potato pancakes—then sent me to my room without supper. But it did not matter because I could not have eaten anyway. Injustice had spoiled my stomach.

Injustice might have killed me, or at least my soul, had it not been for my father. He loved me with a love I could take for granted. Often he told the story of the first moment he held me—my head fitting round in his palm, my fingers wrapping themselves around his big thumb. "Your hair was as fine as if a spider spun it," he said. He was my protector, testing the water in my bath, rescuing me when I climbed too high a tree, chastising my mother when she left me alone too long. In fact, when I was only three, he saved my life.

I remember it clearly; it is my first complete memory of childhood. It was spring. I stood in the dooryard, letting the warm air waft around my face. The ground was muddy and I had been told to stay on the grass, which was not yet green but was, at least, dry. Of course I found the mud more attractive; I remember setting my little boot into it and watching as the mud splushed up around it, like bread dough when you press your hand into it. Mother was inside; Papa was in the barn, occupied with some chore or another. I pushed my foot further down into the mud, then pulled it out, laughing at the sucking sound. I stepped in again, both feet now, and looked down at my boots disappearing into the muck.

When I looked up, I saw a dog—not ours, we didn't keep pets. This one was muddy and wet but seemed to be smiling, its foamy tongue hanging out between its big teeth. When it came trotting toward me, I tried to lift my feet to meet it, but my boots were firmly stuck. So I just put out my hands to touch it. We yearned toward one another, that dog and I, as rabid dogs and children do everywhere.

My father seemed to come out of nowhere. Before the dog could so much as growl at me, he'd swung a shovel down on its spine. The dog gave a terrible yelp and ran off; my father chased it down to the road, hollering, waving the shovel. Now I was frightened and wanted to run, but I could not move. I burst into tears. Papa dropped the shovel and came back to me, scooped me up, held me close. "Don't cry, angel," he said, over and over, stroking my hair. I remember looking at my empty boots, still stuck in the mud, and my dirty stocking feet, and crying all the harder, believing Mother would punish me for my disobedience when she saw them. But Papa got the boots out for me, cleaned them, put the boots back on, and she was never the wiser.

A few years later I overheard my mother recounting the dog story to a family who'd just bought a nearby farm; rumor was they had several dogs that also roamed freely. My mother had always hated dogs—why, I don't know, though she gave plenty of excuses—and the purpose of our visit was less to welcome the new neighbors than to warn their dogs away.

In Mother's version of the story, my father came off part hero, part villain. "He's given to fits of temper," she said, then dropped her voice. "I don't mind it, but when it comes to Marguerite . . ." She gazed at me, her face sorrowful; I wondered what she meant, since he had never raised his voice to me. "Poor man can't control himself; he has native blood, you know," she went on.

Till then the neighbor woman had looked on with sympathy; now she stiffened. "My husband does too," she said in an icy tone, "but he would never beat anyone, not even a dog." Mother looked a bit stunned; after that, it wasn't long before we left. As we walked up the road, my mother snorted. "I'll have your father shoot the first mongrel that comes on our land," she said. "They'll learn that way."

Somehow my mother's view of my father never altered mine. How could I help but admire him, when everyone else but she did? He was well regarded in the county, not only for squeezing money out of stone but also for his physical prowess. His French ancestry had kept him short, but his native blood and years of heavy work had made him powerfully strong, with knotty muscles in his arms and legs and across his shoulders. Every year we traveled hours to the state fair, where he pitted himself against the best in the countryside, performing a variety of skills with a variety of tools: ax, sickle, sledgehammer. Chopping down trees, hand-mowing hay, splitting logs. And then—this is my fondest memory of him—he would enter the pie-eating contest. It was comical to see his face smeared with blackberry, cherry, rhubarb pie, but many times he out-ate a youngster half his age. The prize: a half-dozen pies to take home. People loved it; their applause made him grin. And I loved him all the more.

When I was twelve years old, a school came to the island, or rather a schoolteacher did, a widow whose husband had left her a small sum with which she purchased a homestead where she set out her shingle. I pleaded with my mother to let me go, but she would not hear of it. "I need you too much," she said. "Who will do your work?"

By that time my father's fortune was well made. We could easily have afforded to hire help for my mother, as well as pay the small sum the teacher would charge to have me in her class. But my mother clung to her territory and to her native frugality, giving in only when my father insisted that what I learned at school would make me even more useful to her. So he hired a farmhand to help her, and I began my formal education.

Each morning he himself drove me to the teacher's road, down which I walked the several miles to her house. I did not mind the walk, not even in inclement weather. In solitude with nature on the small, rutted lane, I discovered joy in the small changes that showed the seasons passing: in the fall, the green leaves shifting to yellow and red, then sailing down; the road growing harder underfoot as winter came on; the snow, fresh and white and soft at first, then gleaming with a sheen of ice when its surface melted and refroze; the buds reddening and bursting as spring warmed the air and melted the road to mud; the tiny wildflowers that bloomed unseen among the greenery. As much as I learned in school, it is to these walks that I owe my curiosity about nature. Of course, I might have observed such things at home, too, but only my walk to school gave me the time and necessary freedom of mind.

The teacher was a kind woman, young to be widowed. When she discovered that at twelve I still could not read, she set to teaching me. I learned quickly. Within weeks, I had consumed the early texts as if they were tins of Whitman's candy, and in half a year I was ready to join my peers.

I loved the shape of letters and the sound of words, but better still was the joy I took in doing something my mother could not do. She had never been to school. Now my father and I had something in common that she could not share, and in the evening as I sat with him before the fire and read from the Bible or from his books on geology and agriculture, her jealousy fed my passion to learn.

Mathematics also appealed to me. As soon as I had learned enough, my father took me once a month to his "office," a shed at the edge of the quarry, where he set me to work at the ledgers. So I learned the art of careful accounting, by which I would later make a living. My father said I had a special talent for it, but I knew I loved it because it pleased him and displeased my mother.

Over time, school changed me. It was as if I divided into two selves: the little child who was eager to please, cheerful, hardworking, and suitably female, and a new, private self full of rebellion, self-righteousness, and determination, in control of its own destiny. Goodness, saintliness, virtue were no longer things to strive for, but requirements to rail against. I walked down the road kicking stones out of my way, sometimes talking aloud to myself like a lunatic, full of ideas about life. The other children—most of them younger than I—passed me quickly and at a distance, looking over their shoulders with trepidation.

In short, I was a normal adolescent. By today's standards, if not by those of the time.

Changes came to my body as well. Mysterious changes, and frightening. When the bleeding came, I went to my mother, somehow knowing that she and not my father would be able to explain it. I found her in the kitchen. "Mother?" I said, and she turned from the stove where she was boiling maple sap, her face red with the steam and her hair frizzing.

"What?" she said, sharp.

I showed the bloodied undergarment to her.

"Dirty girl," she said, smacking my hand with the wooden spoon she'd been using. I had shocked her, I realize that now; her response was instinctive. But at that moment I felt only rejection and hurt and a terrible rage, feelings all the more powerful because I could do nothing with them. I dropped the panties to the floor; she looked down at them. "Oh, you stupid thing," she said, her voice softening as if she had just realized what I was there for. And she explained what was happening to me.

But I never forgave her that moment.

As I became, physically at least, a woman, the private half of me became more than half, the public part shrinking till it was no more than a thin veneer, a skin. It was a tough skin, like an elephant's, but one whose puncture I did not want to risk, and so I became even more careful, even more of an actress. And soon enough I truly had something to hide: genuine proof that virtue was forever beyond my grasp.

Like many evil things, that proof came to me in my sleep. Unbidden. Unsought. But this time, not unwelcome.

The farmhand my father hired had been sent over one day by a neighbor who knew we were looking for help. He brought with him a small satchel and one letter of recommendation that said he was quiet, efficient, reliable, and capable. Although my father did not know the former employer himself, he knew the family name and that was adequate recommendation.

I had been at school that day and so learned of the hiring indirectly, through my parents' conversation that night. "Tomorrow he'll repair the harrow," my mother said, passing the potatoes and informing my father at the same time. "Have him fix that barn door hinge, too," Papa said. "What's his name?" I asked, since no one had said it. "You've no need to know that," Mother said. "He's only help." We ate in silence for a moment. Then Mother went on. "I hear they have a way with animals," she said. "They?" I asked. "She means Indians," my father said. "The full-blooded ones, anyway," Mother said, and I saw then why she was so careful to distinguish the farmhand from us—not only because he was help but because he didn't have the European blood that made us better than those who had not sprung from such roots.

After that, the farmhand all but disappeared from my consciousness until one winter day, when I caught sight of him mucking out the barn, steaming manure flying off his shovel into the fresh snow. He couldn't have been more than fifteen, but I was only twelve, and he seemed fully grown to me. He had dark hair and a heavy brow; when he turned to look at me, it was with a quiet, clear gaze that embarrassed me into looking away.

At first I wasn't even curious about him. The gap between our ages was large enough that I thought of him as an adult, not a boy, and in any case I was not interested in boys, or "the creatures," as I called them to myself. I was too self-absorbed, too caught up in my own world, to notice much more about him than that his hair tended to be greasy. When I did begin to notice more—to become interested, in a vague but more directed way, in the nature of these "creatures"—it was with a kind of disgust, especially in summer when he would sometimes work in his undershirt. Why were his muscles so smooth, so unlike my father's? Why did he have such protrusions at his wrists and collarbone, shoulders and neck? Why did he sweat so? Did he have a single intelligent thought behind that brow, or was he as dumb as the cows he milked and fed?

He never spoke to me. Even when my mother imposed me on him, made us work together in the haying fields, for instance. When he wanted me to do something, he would gesture or demonstrate, then wait for me to deduce what was wanted. At first I found this irritating; gradually I grew accustomed to it, and came to enjoy the kind of silent partnership, the mindlessness, the wordless communication that allowed us to work together like two dray horses combining their obedience, their strength.

Three years went by like this, and then I was fifteen.

That summer the topic at the dinner table was always the war in Europe, but to me nothing seemed further away or less important. Kept home from school to help with the spring plowing, I chewed on nothing but the injustice in my own life, my own imprisonment by circumstances not my making. I found solace only when I was alone and outdoors—weeding in the garden, pumping water from the well, carrying my father's lunch up the hill through the apple trees and to the quarry, or—very rarely—permitted to wander off to the lake, where I would sit on the boulders and read, the words boiling on the page in the sun. But most of the time I had to work with my mother in the kitchen, or with my father in the office, or with the farmhand, haying the fields, caring for the animals, or doing any one of the dozens of tasks that seemed to materialize in warm weather.

People say that on the island there is no spring. Just a sudden leap from winter into summer, like the flick of a switch. My fifteenth year, last snow fell on May Day, and our first heat wave rolled in on the fifth. (If it seems strange that I remember so particularly, consider that weather was the stuff of conversation, year after year: such details were the center of our lives.) One day the hickory buds were tight, glossy fists; the next day they were open palms. The maple leaves overnight lost their red and their wrinkles and tripled, quadrupled in size. Dicotyledons spread like a green moss over the damp forest floor. Native violets and trillium bloomed. All in the blink of an eye. Yes, of course a slow, subtle greening had preceded this, but still there was a magical, overnight transformation, as if all that had been carefully growing—trees, plants, insects, animals—suddenly threw itself into life with abandon. It may be a short growing season we have, but it is a vigorous one.

We had an unusually late lambing season that year. As it had been the previous spring, my job was to help the farmhand when needed. He was staying in the barn, sleeping in a roll of blankets in the hayloft above the sheep, so he could hear when one of them began to bleat; I slept in the summer kitchen, where he could wake me without waking my parents. A lamb could come any hour of the day, but usually they came at night, and often several ewes went into labor in a row, as if inspired by one another. It was exhausting, bloody work, and I pretended to hate it, but I had long since grown used to blood, and was of an age where I did not mind, but rather liked, the idea of being rousted in the middle of a warm night. When the hand needed me, he tapped on the window; I was a light sleeper, and usually woke immediately.

In retrospect, of course, I am amazed by this arrangement. How could my parents—my father, especially—have trusted me with this man, a mere farmhand, so blithely? But I know the thought never occurred to them to trust or mistrust: they were almost willfully oblivious to the changes in me, to the fact that I had become a young woman—my father because, likely, he did not want to lose his little girl, my mother because, I realize now, she could not bear the competition of another woman in the house. And the farmhand? To them, he was another species altogether, and no more threat to my innocence than a ram was a threat to the virginity of a goose. An Indian, after all, would never dare touch someone like me. Besides, farm work trumped everything those days; I was needed, so I would serve.

One night there must have been a hatching, for beetles began battering the window, bludgeoning themselves against the glass, hovering, whirring, frantically attracted by the light. I had made myself a little corner in the summer kitchen: a cot, a table, a lamp, a book to read. Restless, warm, distracted by the racket of those pathetic beetles, I read longer than usual and fell asleep with the lamp still burning beside me.

I dreamed. About what, I don't recall, could not recall even a moment after I woke. But I know it was in a dream that I first heard a voice both familiar and strange, a voice saying my name, calling to me gently.

I opened my eyes. Close to my face was another face, a face I knew and did not know. A face with dark, loving eyes. Despite how quickly the face drew back, I saw that. And then I saw that it was the farmhand waking me, calling me out to the barn. He'd been unable to rouse me amid the sound of the beetles, had come inside, had looked on me sleeping, had spoken my name to me. And then was out the door and gone into the night.

I got up, and everything seemed as it always had been. But in those few moments—those moments when I heard his voice, saw his face so close to mine—something had changed. It was as if what I had assumed to be reality had revealed itself in fact to be merely a curtain, a scrim that hid something else, another reality—a more real, more important, more interesting reality. A reality in which I had heard that voice, seen those eyes: the reality that the farmhand was a human being, and that he cared for me.

We delivered eight lambs that night. Then it was dawn. I could barely walk, so thorough was my exhaustion, yet I stayed in the barn, watching him as he began the morning chores. "Do you want me to help?" I said to him. He looked me in the eyes again for the first time since that moment in the summer kitchen. I was leaning against a post; I felt certain that if I let go of its support, I would collapse. "No," he said to me. "You sleep."

I had spoken to him; he had spoken in return. Our voices had mingled in the air between us. He had looked at me; our eyes had met. As I dragged myself back to the house and my bed, I hugged this to me.

Outside the summer-kitchen window, several beetles lay on the ground, their legs pedaling the air. I crushed them under my boot. They were known to eat my mother's hollyhocks.

When I was small, my mother told me that moths were butterflies that had been banished to the night, where they lived tortured lives dreaming of the day. In this way she explained why they sacrificed themselves to flame: it was both an end to their suffering and a reunion with the light they longed for.

The parable, of course, was meant to warn me against wanting what I should not have. Now, as the end of lambing season put an end to my chaste but nightly trysts, I felt like a moth banished from the night as well as the light. I returned to my bedroom, he returned to the cabin in the woods where he stayed during the rest of the growing season. To all outward appearances, nothing had changed. But although we did not speak any more than we had before that night, now when our eyes met, they lingered. Whenever I was near him, a strange ache filled my chest. I imagined that it was the same for him. It surprised me that my parents could not see the connection between us, which to me was like a massive and rapidly spreading web. Each evening when he went up the hill, I felt the strands tugging at me; each morning when he returned, I felt them growing stronger. But I was careful, and my parents remained oblivious.

I did not entertain fantasies. I had nothing to feed them, not even stories from books; I was not, of course, allowed to read novels. I had no conception of a love affair, no notions about or knowledge of sex except what I had observed in animals, and the idea of marriage was alien and distant from me. This was something different. I did not think about it, did not create an "us"; I only lived within my heart, feeling what I felt without naming it.

Worst was late at night. Lying in my bed one wall away from my parents, with nothing to occupy my mind but my feeling, the distance between him and me seemed unendurable. I sent messages from my mind to his, hoping he would sense them. I lay perfectly still and tried to feel the messages I was sure he was sending me. In this fevered state I fell asleep each night. And so I began to dream.

What I could not imagine, my dreams began to supply. At first I could not remember them; I only knew I woke bathed in sweat—not afraid but strangely agitated. Each night it got worse, until I could not bear anything touching my skin. I flung the sheets from me, tore off my nightgown, but even the air seemed too much pressure; there was nothing I could do but lie there awake and angry. The hot air, the wind in the trees, the chorus of peeper frogs in the pond down in the pasture: all of it irritated me beyond proportion. I found that the only way I could sleep was to lie naked on the itchy horsehair rug that covered my floor. One irritation canceled out the other.

Then came the dream of water. In this dream, I was lying not on my rug but on the shore somewhere, with the water lapping up and over me. Soothing my skin, stroking me. The sun warm on me but the water cool and friendly. In the dream, I opened my eyes. The water became a fluid hand stroking me, my breasts, my belly, my legs. I felt a pleasant tingling that intensified, expanding into a kind of pleasure I had never felt before: the sky above me, infinite, and myself rising up into it.

I woke feeling ashamed, without knowing exactly why.

That morning at breakfast, my mother bustled about, her usual brisk self. "I want you to help the hand today," she said to me. It was not an unusual thing for her to say. But at the word "hand," blood rushed to my face, then left again in the same rush. I recalled my dream of the watery hand touching me.

Dizzy, I dropped the spoon with which I had been about to eat my oatmeal. "Marguerite?" my mother said. "Are you ill?" She touched my forehead, and lowered her voice as if my father might hear, all the way from the quarry. "Is it your time?" I shook my head, knowing she was referring to the monthly bleeding. "You'd best spend the day abed if it is," she said. I shook my head violently. "No, no, I'm fine," I said. I could not imagine a worse torture than going back to bed. "It's just the heat." "Well, it will only get worse," she said; as usual, her way of alleviating current distress was to predict worse to come. "Yes," I said.

I knew even then that dreams could predict the future—or, at the very least, tell what the dreamer wanted the future to bring. So I went to the barn not knowing what would happen, but knowing that something would. He was hanging up a bridle in the tack room; he had his back to me and did not hear me. I liked him this way best, in the morning when his shirt was clean and his hair still wet and combed from his morning bath in the quarry pond. Without thinking, I came up behind him, put my hands on the flat muscles of his back. He stood motionless. The tack room was almost dark, and sounds inside it were muted by the old soft boards of the walls. I let my hands follow the curve of his body forward until I was embracing him. I held my breath. He took my hands in his and put them to his chest and pulled me close against him. I began to breathe again. The smell of him filled me. My ear to his back, I listened to his beating heart and felt a deep and unfamiliar joy.

That day he told me his name: Daniel.

Life takes on a strange quality when you begin to live for certain moments—between them, nothing seems real. As the summer fulfilled my mother's prediction and grew even warmer, I moved through the air and heard my parents' words and ate and worked as though nothing had changed. But all this served only to preserve the sanctity of those moments when Daniel and I came to each other. I was asleep, I was dream-walking—except when I was with him; only he seemed solid to me, real; only then did I feel awake. I felt the muscles and bones under his skin and understood their purpose; smelled the smell of him, the smell of straw and manure and sweat and the sweet pomade he put in his hair—the smell that was all of those things and none of those things—and I loved it. For his part, he seemed both unable to contain himself and determined to contain me, for if it had been my decision we would have lain down on the dirt floor of the barn that first day.

But he put me off. He restricted our embraces carefully to those times when mere coincidence put us alone and safely out of view, in the barn or in the fields or in the woods. He always made me come to him, and even then at first he resisted me, stiffening his body against me. I learned quickly how to overcome him, how to press my breasts against his chest, how to slide my hand under his shirt, where to put my lips, and it was only a moment, usually, before he would pull me to him, grip my shoulder blades in his strong hands, open his mouth and press my lips apart, and slide his hands under my blouse.

But he wouldn't let it go on. At some point always too soon, he would push me away. "Work to do," he'd say, and we'd resume whatever we had been doing; there was no more arguing with him than there was with a tree, or with my father or mother.

It seemed to go on forever, this in-between state. And if I had imagined that it would stop my nighttime torture, I was wrong; if anything, that became worse. I all but stopped eating; my mother, expressing rare concern, tried to put me to bed during the heat of the day. "May be sunstroke," she said, pressing a palm to my brow. I brushed her away. "I'm fine, Mother," I said, revealing more irritation than I had intended. She squared her jaw. " 'Fine' is not what I would call it," she said. " 'Sassy' is more the word I would use." But she let me go.

I suppose she had suspicions even then. But a part of her still thought of me as a child, and what those suspicions were, I'll never know. At supper one night she tried to tell my father that I ought not to be working on the farm anymore, that I ought to be cultivating the behavior of a young lady. All he did was look at me and smile. "I don't want her to get soft," I overheard him tell my mother later. "Life is hard on soft people."

A letter came for Daniel.

Those days, the island had only one center of business, and then it was called Keller's General Store. A crowded little storefront at the ferry landing, there you could pay your taxes, use a telephone or send a telegraph, and buy flour and sugar, dry goods, nails and tools, paint, boots, pickles, penny candy, toiletries, medicines, ferry tickets, and dozens of other items. But Mr. Keller was most proud of the fact that he was official postmaster for the island, although this generally meant very little except that he sold stamps and exchanged outgoing for incoming mail with the ferry pilot. There was no mail delivery in those days; if a letter came in, it might sit there behind the post office counter for weeks, sorted into a box labeled "A–E," "F–Q," or "R–Z," no one even bothering to notify you. For that reason we made a weekly trip to Keller's.

When I was a small child, I made the trip with my father, who, despite my mother's protestations that it would spoil my teeth and me as well, would inevitably buy me a candy or two. I loved those trips, not just for the candy but for the pleasure of watching my father and Mr. Keller converse. To me, they were the kings of our island, discussing as they did the past and what it meant, the present and how it should change, the future and what it might bring. They predicted the coming of electricity long before it happened; they discussed the levying of taxes and the building of bridges and roads and schools; they prognosticated on wars and debated government, both national and local. (Papa was a selectman and had been so as long as I knew, Mr. Keller was both town clerk and treasurer, and on town meeting day their words carried great sway with the population.) Sitting on the counter with my legs dangling and a sweet dissolving in my cheek, I watched their faces and heard their words, thought to myself that my father was a great man, and loved him all the more.

As I got older and my father busier, I usually made the trip alone, but looked forward to it no less. I loved to look at the bolts of fabric, the ladies' shoes, the mail-order catalog that opened the world of purchases to me. Then I would spend the few pennies my father had given me on a bonbon or a piece of licorice, feeling childish for doing so, gather the mail into my satchel, and walk home.

When I came in that day, Mr. Keller was distracted by two ladies sending a telegraph. While he was busy, I wandered about, contentedly perusing new stock and old. Finally he called to me, an unfamiliar tone of curiosity in his voice. "Got an interesting letter here," he said, shuffling through the "A–E" box. "For your farmhand," he said, and gave me the envelope. The handwriting was large and childlike, but the letter was clearly for Daniel. In the corner was a return address on the mainland.

It occurred to me suddenly that I knew nothing about Daniel's family, and little enough about him. I hurried home, the letter tucked into my blouse so that my mother wouldn't see it. Then, as soon as I could, I went to find Daniel.

He was loading hay into the loft. To do this, he used an inge-
nious device of his own invention, involving several rope pulleys
that he operated from below while the hay was moved up on a
platform that tilted and dumped through the open window. Normally I would have been at the top, grabbing the bales and stack-
ing them, but because I'd been gone all morning, he'd been
doing it himself. It was a hot day; sweat had soaked through his
undershirt; his face and arms were ruddy, his face with exertion
and his arms from the hay poking and scratching them. But
when he saw me, he smiled and jumped down from the loft. I
got him a ladle of water from the rain barrel, and he drank.

"Daniel," I said, reaching into my blouse, "you have a letter."

The smile faded from his lips. He took the envelope and
shoved it into his back pocket.

"Aren't you going to read it?"

"Later," he said, his tone telling me not to push.

I sat down on a bale of hay and gazed at him. "Tell me about
your family," I said.

"Marguerite."

"No, really—I want to know."

He sighed. "Marguerite, there's nothing to tell."

"Do you have brothers and sisters?"

He nodded.

"How many?"

"Two of each," he said.

"How old?"

"Older than me," he said.

"Where do they live?"

"On a farm."

I stood up, disgusted. "You know everything about me," I said.
"Would it be so hard to tell me about you?"

I couldn't tell if the half-smile, half-smirk on his face repre-
sented amusement or capitulation. That became clear, though,

when he spoke. "They're dirt poor," he said, "and too dumb to do anything about it. Let's leave it at that."

I changed tactics. "Who's the letter from?" I said.

"My oldest brother," he said. "Only one besides me who can read and write."

"Why don't you open it?" I said.

Exasperation finally pushed him over the edge. "Because," he said, "I already know what it says. I told him to write me when our pappaw died. That's the only reason he'd send me a letter."

He stood up. I was gazing at him, waiting for him to say more, or at least for his face to show his emotions. But he only took another ladle of water from the barrel, wiped his mouth, and gazed out at the hay wagon. "You'd best go back to the house for your lunch," he said. I nodded and went.

After lunch I changed into work clothes and went back to the barn to help with the hay. But Daniel was nowhere to be found. I called to him, and when he didn't answer, I climbed the hill to the cabin where he stayed. The door was open; I went inside. He was there, sitting on his cot, face buried in hands. "Daniel," I said. He looked up, and there were tears in his eyes.

I picked the letter up from the floor where it had fallen. In the childish script, it talked of a "grip" that had taken the lives of both parents. "We berried them Sunday," it said. "Sorry you cldn't be with us."

"Oh, Daniel," I said, and sat beside him.

He came into my arms then, and I stroked his hair while he sobbed like any orphaned child.

Summer was waning. The hot days of August were followed by cooler nights. Sometimes now, walking, Daniel and I held hands like any courting couple. We still stole silent moments, kissing, embracing, but now we also spoke as we worked. Talked about our dreams and interests, even about my parents. "I admire your father," Daniel said one sunny afternoon. I was surprised by the envy in his voice. "Any man who could make this land pay"—he kicked a rock out of his path—"is a man to be respected." My father had recently signed a lucrative contract to provide the marble for a great new building in Manhattan, and he had been boasting of this to everyone, even to Daniel.

"But does it seem to you that it makes him really happy?" I said.

As he did sometimes, Daniel smiled at me as if I were only a child—a child to whom he could explain the ways of the world, if only I would listen. "Of course not," he said. "But look what else it gives him. Land, a wife, a family. That is what makes him happy."

At dinner one evening my father, still beaming with his success, announced to my mother and me that he himself would be taking the first load of marble to the city, riding with it on the barge down the lake and into the river, a trip of many days. My father rarely left the island, so this was a momentous announcement. I could not imagine him in a city; could not imagine the city. But quickly I lost interest in trying. Somehow, the thought of my father being away thrilled me, as if it had been he, all along, who kept me away from Daniel.

The morning my father left for New York, we gathered to see him off—my mother, Daniel and I, the quarry crew. My father looked down at us from his seat behind the team of eight huge dray horses and said, "Mother, you take care," and then he looked past me at Daniel and said, "You watch over them as if they were your own, mind you. Keep a gun by your side," and Daniel nodded, and it was then I realized that Papa had instructed him to stay in the barn again, as he did during lambing season.

Papa was gone. He took with him two of his crew, and left

behind his second foreman and another crew to oversee the quarrying of the next load to go. As these men thundered back up the quarry road in their wagon, my mother turned to me and Daniel. "Well," she said, "God willing, he'll be back in time for apple harvest." Then she looked at the two of us in a way that made me wonder what she saw. But I kept as still as I could, and the look faded. "You two had better finish haying," she said, and went to the house to do her chores.

We could not stay in the barn.

It would not do. I did not want to give myself to him in that dark and musty place where animals ate, defecated, breathed. So that night when I went to him, I called him down to me, and heard his feet on the rungs of the ladder, then felt his touch before I saw his face. "Come on," I said. He said nothing, but took my hand, and I knew I had been right. With my father away, Daniel was mine.

I led him through the woods. This is crucial: I led him. I cannot say he was innocent, but neither was he guilty. If anything, I should take responsibility; I should take blame.

We both knew the place, it's true. The quarry pond. A quarry that had been shut down and left to fill with rain, and in the night now was filled with stars, mirrored by the sky. A thin moon— "God's fingernail," my father would have called it—gave us just enough light to see. We stood there at the water's edge, and I put my hands to the buttons of his shirt. It fell away from his shoulders, and I undid the buttons of my own dress, underneath which I wore nothing at all. He pressed his palms toward me till they barely touched my nipples. I laughed. Not a nervous giggle, mind you; a full-throated laugh. I was happier than I had ever been.

We swam first. There'd been little rain since early July, so the water was warm as a bath. We found each other in the black and came together and kissed more deeply and more freely than we ever had. I felt him against me, all his fleshy parts. I wanted to touch him, but as I tried he pulled away and swam some more. I loved the sound of him slipping through the water. It made me want him. I swam, and swam, looking for him, but he was eluding me now. I called to him: *Daniel, Daniel*—but he stayed silent, playing with me. I treaded water, as quiet as I could be, listening for his breathing, and heard nothing. I called to him again, afraid.

And then he was behind me, his arms around me and on my breasts, bursting up through the water, laughing, kissing me, turning me around.

We went up onto the mossy rock where our clothes lay. Spread them out under us, and lay down. I held his face in my hands a moment. In the moonlight, it was a dark face with eyes as black and shining as the water. I want to believe I said, "I love you," but I can't remember now. He bent to me, and we began to make love.

It was not what I imagined it would be. Afterward we lay a long time, only our fingers touching. The cool air wafted around us; I shivered, and he came back to me and covered me with his body. I liked the weight of him on me, the warmth of him. Then I felt him pressing against me again. I wasn't certain I could, I wasn't certain I wanted to. Then he began to do things that made me want to. I pressed myself against his hand, against the wave of sensations, nearly unbearable sensations. When he stopped, a moan escaped my lips; I did not want to stop. And then he was on top of me again and I was moving under him, pressing up when he pressed down, until at last the wave crashed over us, drowning us, drenching us, draining us.

We fell asleep there. Woke just before dawn. In the gray light, I saw the blood on my thighs, my dress. Ignorant as I was, I thought it was my time of the month, and felt embarrassed. But he only took my dress to the water's edge—how beautiful his body was, all bone and sinew, paler where the sun hadn't reached it, darker where it had—and rinsed it there, till almost all the blood was gone. And called me to the water's edge, where he began to wash me clean as well.

Which is what Mother must have seen when she came upon us. An Adam and Eve, naked in that Eden. The tenderness of Daniel as he cleaned me, turning me this way and that. I know I had just put my hand on his nape to draw him to me for a kiss when I heard her. The guttural rasp that came from her throat. The sound of betrayal discovered. When I turned to look at her, when I saw her face aghast, when I saw the ash of anger and dismay there, I did not feel what I had imagined I would feel. I felt no shame, no desire to cover myself. I felt, instead, proud.

By the time my father returned, the apples were ripe and it was time to pick. My father grumbled a bit when he heard that my mother had fired Daniel—"caught him stealing" was all she said—but relented and let her hire the daughter of his foreman to help us with the harvest.

The girl was as unlike me as any girl I knew. Tall, thin, with a beaky nose and small chin, she was surprisingly strong and could carry a full bushel alone. But it was her mouth that surprised me. Around my parents she was soft-spoken, obsequious, but as soon as they were away and we were alone with the trees, words came out of her that I had never heard before, even from my father. "Fuggin' bugs," she'd say, swatting at the horseflies that harassed us. "Bleedin' roots," she'd say, every time she stubbed a toe on the knobby roots that stuck out of the thin soil. She was called Gwenny, short for Gwendolyn.

Mother packed us a lunch each day so that we wouldn't waste time coming back down to the house to eat. Sitting together in the shade, Gwenny and I conversed in an odd, lopsided way. She asked questions of me, one after another; before I could get the complete answer out, she asked another, the whole time looking behind and around me as if expecting any moment to be interrupted. I never knew if she was really that curious about me or was trying to make friends by expressing interest, but it was flattering to be subjected to such interrogation. No one had ever wanted to know so much about me.

Most of her questions were about the way we lived. I gathered that her parents viewed mine as royalty, wealthy beyond belief and therefore godlike, despite the fact that we worked every bit as hard as they did. Gwenny wanted to know about everything from the sheets on our beds to what we ate, from my mother's wardrobe to my father's education. It was as if she were planning to model her life after ours by mimicking the details.

One day the topic turned to me. Had I traveled? Where? When? How? What books had I read? Then, out of the blue: "Did you ever get kissed?"

I must have blushed, for she grinned and said, "Ah!" Then: "Did you ever do more'n that?"

Another grin.

"You done it all, then," she said, in a satisfied voice. Then she lowered her tone to a more conspiratorial one. "Me too," she said. "I did it just last night."

It had been more than a month since the night Daniel and I "did it." Later that morning, consigned to my room for the day, I had watched him leave, his things in a sack over his shoulder. He had paused in front of the house for just a minute, looking back, looking up—but he didn't see me, didn't know where to look. And then I heard my mother come rushing out of the house, hollering for him to "get away, get away!" Waving her hands at him as if shooing a wild dog. And he was gone.

After that, every time I thought of him I began to cry, and so I had sworn to myself not to think of him, and had succeeded— more or less—until the moment Gwenny raised the subject. Now the dam broke and the tears flowed again.

"Ooh," Gwenny said, and put a dirty but sympathetic hand on my knee. "Is you knocked up, then?"

Through the tears I looked at her. "Knocked up?" I said.

She nodded. "You know—stuffed." I was still perplexed. Were these terms for being brokenhearted? She lowered her voice even further, put her face closer to mine. There was a sweet, understanding kindness in her eyes. *"Has you got a baby in you?"* she whispered. I simply stared at her, the tears drying up of their own accord. She sat back, satisfied again. "I thought so," she said. "You have the look."

Since then I have heard stories about women who can look at a person and tell, immediately, that she is pregnant. Maybe Gwenny was one of those, or pretending to be. In any case, as soon as she said the words, I found myself wondering if she were right.

I knew the basic mechanics of it from animals, of course. Sheep, horses, cows, pigs: I had seen them all go into estrus—the rut, my father called it; my mother called it heat; I had learned the scientific term from one of my father's texts. I had seen the animals mating, had seen the offspring they produced. But what had happened between Daniel and me, as earthbound and bloody as it had been, had somehow seemed different from that—an expression of feeling, not an act of reproduction. I had never, till that moment, made the connection between love and biology, never considered that the desire I had felt might be no different, say, from the desire our cows felt for the single bull that inseminated them all.

And now I found myself counting: counting days, months.

How long had it been since I had bled? I couldn't be sure. I turned to Gwenny. "How do you know?" I asked her.

"Oh, I can just tell. Always been able to."

"No," I said. "How do *I* know? How can I tell for sure?"

She shrugged her shoulders. "You'll know," she said. "First you'll start to feeling kind of dizzy and queasy all the time. Maybe you'll even heave up. Lots of girls do. Won't be able to keep a thing down. Then your tits'll start to swell, and your belly." We both looked down at me. Gwenny nodded assuredly. "You'll know," she said again.

Lunch over, we went back to work. Was the light-headedness I felt caused by standing up too quickly, or something else? Was the knot in my stomach the beginning of nausea, or just fear? Suddenly unsteady on my feet and in my thinking, I climbed the ladder and reached for apples with a new awareness of my body as a vessel, a vase, a bottle into which could be poured fluid far more precious than water or wine. If I fell, and the vessel broke, the fluid would spill. At the top of that ladder, I hovered briefly between air and ground, considering one and the other and deciding between them. If it was true, how did I feel about it? I took one foot off the top rung and felt how easy it would be to swing out and let go, crashing the ten or twelve feet downward. Would it be enough? Probably not. Would I want it to be?

No.

I wanted the baby. I wanted Daniel's baby. I wanted *my* baby.

Once I felt sure, I tried to find him, to let him know.

I had never been allowed to ride horses, for fear I'd "damage" myself—a point that seemed moot now, but still, I had never learned the art of horseback riding. This left me two options: the wagon or my feet. My feet would take too long, as Daniel's family lived on the mainland and I would have to return by nightfall. So I stole a wagon.

A girl my age didn't have freedom to come and go at will. So I chose a day when my mother was at a quilting bee and my father was caught up in his work at the quarry. I knew he might wonder where I was, when it came lunchtime and he descended to eat and found me gone, but I didn't care. Once I had told Daniel, I wouldn't care about anything; once I had told Daniel, he would marry me and we would be together, and all would be well again.

It was nearly November by then, and days were shorter, but they felt long to me. The nausea had indeed begun not long after that day Gwenny taught me about life, and it continued unabated, day and night. Luckily I did not "heave up" as Gwenny predicted; instead, I was simply unable to eat.

It was late morning when I hitched the horses up and pulled the wagon out of the barn and onto the rough road. Each bounce and jerk made me wonder if I would be able to keep down the eggs my mother had insisted on feeding me, saying I looked "pale." She eyed me with suspicion often those days, and for good reason, of course. I had thus far been able to hide my condition from her, but soon I would not be able to; already my breasts were tender and swollen. I was thankful she had never raised the question to me; maybe she hoped that if she remained silent her worst fears would prove unfounded.

The ferry took longer than I'd thought it would, and from there I wasn't completely certain of the way. I'd found Daniel's letter left behind in the barn, but the return address was not as specific as I would have liked, so it was well after noon by the time I found the farm. It did not look a prosperous place—the barn unpainted, the house too, and some of the fencing in need of repair—but it was relatively neat and orderly, and I took solace in that, thinking that I could live with poverty if other values did not have to be sacrificed.

I stopped the horses and tied them up and climbed the worn steps to the porch.

I should have known from the silence that they were gone. But I knocked and knocked, my knuckles raw on the cold wood, hoping against hope. No answer. I looked around me at the desolate place and understood why they had gone. But where was Daniel? How could I find him now?

I climbed back into the wagon, unsure what more I could do. All I had with me was the letter—no pencil, nothing to write with. But I climbed down again and slipped the letter under the door. If Daniel came back and found it, he would know who left it. And he would come to me then. I wanted to believe he would come and save me from what was sure to be a tempest when my parents discovered the truth. But this had not been the happy reunion I had planned, and now nothing else seemed assured either.

As I rode toward the ferry, I watched for him, hoping irrationally that fate might throw us together. It didn't. The day grew dimmer, unusually dim for the time of day, but I was so distracted I did not notice the storm approaching. As I disembarked the ferry, a cold rain fell, drenching my coat and clothes to the skin and making the horses shiver with nervousness and chill. I had to close my eyes against the rain and let the horses find the way. The going slowed as the roads grew muddier, and by the time I got home, it was well past dark and the supper hour.

My mother was standing on the porch with a lantern, waiting for me, my father having gone off on horseback to search. When she saw my blue-lipped face, she whisked me upstairs to my room, where she stripped my clothes and dried me off and wrapped me with a blanket and brought me some thin soup to drink. When the quaking stopped, I looked up to see her sitting on the chair across the room, watching me with quickened eyes. "What?" I said.

"You went to see him, didn't you?" she said.

There was no point denying it.

"Why?"

I just looked at her, daring her to speak what I sensed she already knew. How could she not see, when even Gwenny had?

"Oh," she said then. "Oh Mary, Mother of Jesus," she said, the closest I had ever heard her come to swearing.

She got up and came over to me and took the blanket from my shoulders and let it fall so that she could look at my naked body. Once again I shocked myself by feeling no shame. But the anger I expected to materialize on her features never did. Instead there appeared a kind of smirking knowingness. "Do you have any idea what your father will do?" she said. I nodded, although I did not in fact know. In making love with Daniel, I had shamed my father in so many ways: I had had concourse with the hired help; I had had concourse with a native; I had had concourse out of wedlock; I had given away my virginity (a gift not mine to give, as I had been taught in church); I had an illegitimate child in my belly; and, no doubt worst of all, I had kept secrets, I had deceived him, I had grown up and begun a life of my own without his knowledge. It was hard to imagine the extent of his response, but I knew it would be terrible—despite, or perhaps because of, how much he loved me.

"Help me," I said to my mother then.

She stepped back. "Help you?" she said, looking down at me. "*Help* you?"

"Yes," I said. "You are my mother. I have no one else."

She averted her eyes then, turned them to the window, outside of which the first winter storm lashed the trees about. What she saw there, aside from our reflection, I don't know, but when she turned back, she said, "All right, Marguerite, I will."

She left me alone in my room then. I extinguished the lamp and sat there in the darkness, waiting for my father's return. I knew he was beside himself with worry; he was not a young man even then, and I felt ashamed of having sent him out into the storm in search of me. My mind roiled with the difficulties that lay before me; I prayed to God for guidance. Then, exhausted by my journey and my situation, I fell asleep.

I woke to hear my father shouting "Marguerite! Where are you?" and his boots fast and heavy on the stairs. By the time he reached my room, I was shaking with fear. The door opened. He held a lantern, and in its swinging light I could see his face, ruddy with cold and wet with rain, and his drenched coat dripping on the floor. I had never seen him so angry.

"I'm sorry, Papa!" I cried. "Forgive me!"

He stood in the doorway a long moment, silent. Then he came toward me, holding the lantern out. Still naked under the blanket, I shivered, but not from cold. I was afraid. He raised his free hand. I lowered my head, cowering before the blow I felt sure was to come. But when his hand descended, it only rested on my crown, holding my head in its palm again, as if he were measuring how much I had grown over the years—as if he were noticing, for the first time, that I was a woman, too large to keep and hold.

I felt the weight of his touch lift, saw the lamplight drifting toward the door again, and looked up. He stood there another long moment. I could not see his eyes, but I felt them looking at me. And then he was gone, the door slammed shut behind him, and I sat in darkness again.

Later that night I heard their voices through the wall, his angry and blaming her, hers conciliatory and mollifying. She admitted to him that I had taken the wagon and horses without permission, but for a laudable purpose: to go to the church and pray for a sick friend. Not being used to traveling alone, she said, I had gotten lost in the storm. I was to be pitied more than censured; he should blame her, rather than me. Slowly his anger dissipated and her voice became but a murmur. And then I heard them making love. It was not what I needed to hear at that moment. Into the chamber pot went the soup Mother had given me. Back in bed, I used a pillow to muffle the noises and fell into restless dreams.

The next morning, my father came to see me again. I feigned sleep. I could not bear to face him. When he was safely gone, I went downstairs in my nightclothes. My mother gave me unbuttered toast and some weak tea, the first breakfast that had appealed to me in weeks. As I ate, she told me that we were going to see a doctor that day, "to make sure," she said, so I should wear something "respectable," dark and modest. I only nodded. I felt myself in safe, experienced hands. It was a great relief to shift the weight from my own shoulders to hers, to know she loved me after all and would help me.

We took the ferry to the mainland and rode to town under a cold gray sky. Over the years I had made a few trips to town, but I was always still taken with the swarms of people, the buildings that stood cheek by jowl, the busy-ness and business. It seemed so full, so lively compared to the island. "Don't stare," my mother said. We passed a woman pushing a perambulator carrying two toddlers, bundled up and motionless; a third was on the way in a belly so large that the buttons of her coat did not close. "Don't stare," my mother said again, and this time she pinched my arm so hard that my gaze was torn away.

The doctor's office was itself in an impressive building of reddish stone. We passed through the double oak doors and went up two flights of stairs and into a room furnished comfortably if not extravagantly, with blinds drawn and lamps lit, though it was daytime. I wondered how my mother knew of this doctor; I had never known her to be sick, and her visits to town were as rare as my own. But the nurse who greeted us seemed to know her. "This is my daughter," Mother said, and the nurse nodded, and replied, "The doctor will be right with you. Come this way."

Mother accompanied me. I felt a little flutter in my belly, different from the nausea, and thought it was nervousness. But then the excited thought came to me: was this the first sign of life, the little fish swimming inside me? Gwenny had told me of this too, when I plumbed her for more information. I took my mother's hand and put it on my belly. "Can you feel that?" I started to say. But she pulled her hand away and said, "Not now, Marguerite."

The nurse helped me to remove my skirts, which Mother took and folded onto a chair. I had never been to a doctor before. I did not realize that I would have to undress. But I did as I was told and put on the thin robe. They sat me down in a chair and went into the hallway for a moment, as if to discuss something outside of my hearing. But I strained and heard no voices, and within moments Mother had returned, followed in more moments by the doctor.

He was the handsomest man I had ever seen, tall, thin, with blond hair going gray and an elegant mustache, white teeth, a strong chin, clear blue intelligent eyes. I trusted him.

"All right," the doctor said. "We're just going to check you here, make sure everything is all right." He gave the nurse a look, my mother another. I was helped onto the examination table, and then everything happened very fast. Mother drew up one of my knees, the nurse the other, and they pried them apart. I could not imagine what was going to happen next, and was shocked when I felt the doctor's hands, and then something inside me. "Let's just see," he said. I felt something push, then some pain.

"Mother!" I said, turning to her; she kept one hand on my knee and used the other to brush the hair from my forehead. It was the most soothing thing I remember her ever doing. "Shh," she said. "It'll soon be over."

The pain grew worse. "Mother!" I said again.

The nurse handed the doctor something, he grunted, and then I felt moisture below. "What's happening?" I cried.

"Oh, no," the doctor said. "Oh, dear."

I wasn't sure how much time passed before I spoke again. "What's the matter?" I said, my voice slurred now by the pain.

It was the nurse who spoke next. "The baby's dead, dear. There was nothing the doctor could do."

Dead. The word resounded in my ears. What had I done wrong? What had I done to kill the baby?

The doctor kept on, doing something more. "Don't worry," said the nurse. "The doctor just has to clean you out, so that you won't get infected." I felt them pressing my knees apart, so far apart I thought I would break; I heard my mother murmuring, saying, "Better this way, far better"; the pain grew worse again, worse still; I heard sounds coming from my mouth; and then all was black.

When I woke, it was the doctor's face above me, much as Daniel's had been a few months before. "Marguerite," he said. "Marguerite." I smelled something sharp, inhaled, gasped. "There," he said, disappearing from view, speaking now to my mother. "She's fine now."

Then he appeared in my line of vision again, that sweet smile on his face. He put his mouth to my ear. "Marguerite, dear," he said in a whisper, "this will never happen again. Do you understand? Never again."

I thought it was just a warning, or a word of advice. I thought perhaps he was extracting a promise from me.

Decades later, back on the island, I read in the paper how some doctors had taken it upon themselves to eliminate, as the article put it, "the degenerate bloodlines," by sterilizing poor women, retarded women, alcoholic women, and especially native women—in many cases, without their knowledge or consent. In 1931, the state even made such sterilization legal. My mother's doctor, it seems, was ahead of his time. I didn't know, then, that he had killed my baby and, with my mother's help, stolen all the other babies I might have borne.

Mother took me for a special treat: ice cream. It was a blustery day, almost winter, but we sat in the sweet shop and ate ice cream with chocolate sauce ladled over it. I shivered—from loss of blood as much as from the cold, I think. "I'm so sorry," Mother said to me, not particularly sounding it. "But it's for the best. You'll see. It'll be all right."

I bled for days. Mother kept the cloths changed; I lay in bed, wan and emptied. She brought me soup and toast. The nausea of pregnancy faded, but hunger didn't return. I did not want to eat.

Daniel may have come during that time, I don't know. I was so sunk in my own despair that I doubt I would have heard him, as much as I had once longed to.

One morning I awoke with the smell of blood in my nostrils. My own bleeding had stopped; it was animal blood I smelled. "Your father shot a deer," my mother told me. I'd been hunting with him many times; I knew this meant he'd be in a fine mood. "Come down and eat with us," she said, and I agreed, and rose shakily from my bed.

It was the first time I had seen my father since my mother had taken me to the mainland; she'd kept him at bay by telling him I was suffering from "women's problems." Now, at the table, he was so solicitous of me that I thought I might cry. Taking for embarrassment the shame that kept my gaze on the plate before me, he soon rose and left me alone with my mother. Her remonstrance was sharp and quick. "Only pigs wallow," she said, taking away my cold eggs. I lifted my eyes and chin and gave her a false smile. "Better," she said. "Now, get yourself dressed and take some air. It's time to get your strength back."

I did as she instructed. In the dooryard the smell of blood was even stronger. The deer hung from its legs in the barn door, its belly split down the middle and its rib cage exposed. From deeper inside the barn I heard the sound of my father sharpening his knives, as he always did after the first kill of the season. Normally I would have offered my help, but that day I left him to his work.

It was a bright November day. A few clouds hung motionless over the shorn fields, like beasts grazing in the chicory-blue sky. Crystals of ice crunched underfoot. The air was sharp and clean and cold in my nostrils; my breath came out in little white puffs. I began to feel alive again, as if, as Mother insisted, everything really would be all right.

I heard the horse before I saw it, and then there was Daniel, right in front of me. Seeing his face again after all that time was like seeing a stranger, by which I mean that I saw with new objectivity both his flaws and his virtues, his strong chin and weak brow, his integrity and his naïveté. I felt suddenly older than he; felt I had grown old in the days since I had seen him last, old and sad and cautious.

As soon as he saw me, his forehead knotted with concern. He jumped down from the horse and led it the rest of the way, until we were standing facing one another.

"Marguerite," he said.

You can tell someone loves you by how he says your name. Daniel said my name as if it were a prayer.

When I told him what had happened in the doctor's office—

that our baby had died—his face fell, and all my own sorrow was renewed. But then he smiled and put his arms around me again, and I pressed my face into the rough wool of his jacket, into his smell. "It's all right," he said. "We'll make another."

I stepped back from him and looked up into his eyes, so black. "You'll still have me, then?" I said.

When he told me yes, I felt an incomparable joy.

Together we went back to the house to tell my parents. I knew Mother would be angry, but at least to her it would not be news. It was my father's reaction that scared me most. Still, with Daniel beside me, I imagined we would be all right.

They were both at the house. My father had come in from the barn with a worker who'd been injured at the quarry; my mother was bandaging the wound. When Daniel and I walked into the house, hand in hand, Papa lifted his head to look at us and, as soon as Mother was done, sent the injured man off. "Family business," he told him.

The four of us went into the front room. Papa would not sit, so none of us did. Daniel told him our intentions. Papa listened silently, but his lips were set and his face reddened as Daniel spoke. After Daniel was finished, there was not even half a moment of silence before Papa spoke. "No" was all he said. He strode from the house, doors slamming behind him.

"Let me try," my mother said, and followed him out.

Daniel and I held each other until she returned "I'm sorry," she said. "He won't hear of it. I told him about the baby. But it didn't soften him a whit."

My heart sank as I realized that my father now knew what Daniel and I had done, knew it all. Daniel squeezed my arm and said, "Your father is a reasonable man. I'll convince him," and went out. Mother and I looked at each other and followed.

My father had gone back to butchering the deer, working on a makeshift table of sawhorses and planks. Daniel stood before him, straight and square. With Daniel between us, I could not see my father's face. Nor could I hear Daniel's words—only the tone of his voice, respectful and confident. He made me confident; I ventured closer. "Marguerite!" my mother hissed, half whispering, but I pulled away and all but ran to Daniel's side, where with pride I took his arm.

The deer still hung in the doorway but was skinless now, all its muscle and sinew exposed. Papa had one leg on the table and was cutting the haunch into chunks for venison stew. We had no freezer then—no electricity—so Mother would cook and can the stew meat and store it in the house cellar in sterile jars, as she did lamb and mutton and beef and chicken. The other deer meat— the steaks and roasts and chops—would be saved for holidays and company dinners, salted and stored on ice packed in hay in the root cellar.

Papa's face had returned to its usual color and he seemed calmer, but he kept his eyes on the meat as if it required all his concentration. "I know I don't have much to offer," Daniel was saying. "But I am a good man and a hard worker. And I love her." I watched Papa's hands, big and rough and precise as they did the cutting. "I wouldn't take her from you," Daniel said. "If you'd have us, we'd live here. I could keep on as help. I'd earn your trust, I promise. If only you'll forgive the way we started—"

Papa lifted his head so sharply that I jumped back. I saw now that his eyes were still dark with anger; they grew darker when he saw me there. "Forgive?" His voice broke as if it had been a long time since he had spoken. "You ask too much," he said. He stepped around the table now, came closer to us. Daniel stood his ground, and me with him. "Only one Father could forgive what you've done," he said, "and that's our Father in Heaven." He was looking at me as he said this.

"Papa," I said. "I pray for God's forgiveness every day. But it's yours I want more."

For a moment I thought I saw his eyes soften; for a moment I thought I had wedged open a crack through which his love could shine again. But as quickly as I had glimpsed it, it closed.

"Don't blame her," Daniel said, pulling my hand over his heart and holding it in both of his. "If you must lay blame, blame me."

"I do," Papa said, and then he moved.

The knife went through our clasped hands first. I screamed with pain. When my knees buckled under me, Daniel tried to hold me, tried to keep me from falling, but our hands slid apart, slippery with blood. So he turned and fell over me, sheltering me from the blows that followed. I felt his weight on me, his body shuddering each time the knife came. It came again and again and again. My consciousness drained away with my blood. I heard my parents shouting, but as if from far, far away. Then, close to my ear, I felt the sudden exhale of Daniel's breath. His body went limp and heavy.

The last thing I heard was the sound of someone crying. I don't think it was me.

I did not want to rise from the blackness, but rise I did.

And the first thing I saw, in the light of a dim lamp, was my father.

He was kneeling beside my bed, his eyes closed and his hands clasped before him. He was murmuring: "Hail, Mary, full of grace . . ." Over and over again. I let him go on for quite some time before I spoke.

"Papa," I said.

He opened his eyes. I could see fear in them. Daniel appeared before me, his face, the way he'd looked at me before he fell. I closed my eyes, but the vision remained.

"Marguerite," a voice said.

I opened my eyes again. My father was still there, and now I understood what he was afraid of. Me. I didn't speak.

He took my hand between his hands. "Marguerite, forgive me," he said.

I pulled away. Beneath bandages, my hand throbbed. I unwrapped the bandages then, curious but strangely distant from my own sensations. When I saw what had happened, I felt like laughing. Perhaps I did laugh. My father looked away. He had not intended to harm me, he said; he hadn't known what he was doing. He spoke without meeting my eyes, his voice a drone of shame.

"When your mother told me what he did, I . . . How could I do otherwise? My child. I left you alone with him. I am to blame. I should have protected you. And now look what I've done . . ."

I heard what he said but did not hear it, because at that moment, for the first time in my life, I saw tears in my father's eyes.

For the next few days, I slept. A healing sleep. Or a sleep of cowardice, avoidance. I had no dreams. It was as if I too had died.

I woke early one morning feeling quite calm. I was alone in my shadowy room. I sat up with some difficulty, weakened, I suppose, from days of not eating. I looked down at my bandaged hand and remembered all that had happened. An aching exploded in my heart. I thought of Daniel, not just of his death but of how his last thought had been to protect me. And the horror he must have felt. And my complicity in it.

And then I remembered my father's words: *when your mother told me what he did*. And then, as if my mind had been working out the problem while I slept, I knew what had happened.

I found my mother in the kitchen, stoking the fire. When she heard me, she turned quickly, the stick of wood in her hands thrust out like a weapon. "It's only me, Mother," I said. The fear I'd seen in her eyes faded and was replaced by a look of concern. "Marguerite," she said, coming toward me. "You worried us so—"

"You told him Daniel raped me," I said.

"Yes." The concern fell from her face; there was no regret in her voice. She turned and chucked the stick of wood into the stove, straightened and wiped her hands on her apron. I stared at her, disbelieving. "What?" she said. "Surely you don't blame me? You know your father's temper." I did not; I knew only that she alone could have driven him so far. She moved to the table, where dough was rising in a bowl, removed the towel, and began to knead. Without meeting my eye, she spoke again. "Of course," she said, "I never expected him to kill the boy. It's not my fault if he did."

Waves of rage and grief, then shame and guilt swept over me; I sank into a chair, my face in my hands. After a long pause, she spoke again. "What now?" she said.

I looked up. Her question surprised me, implying as it did that the choice lay in my hands. Quickly I realized that, since I was the only other witness to the crime, it did. But soon I saw how terrible it was to have such power.

If I reported my father, she told me, there would be a trial. My father might go to prison. But even if he was found guilty, he might not. "Remember," she said, "that boy was an Indian." They would all believe her, she said, when she told what Daniel did to me. And they'd believe my father, she said. He might have native blood himself, but he was a good French Catholic and a pillar of the community. They'd forgive my father for what he did, even if I could not. But the shame would still be on him, on me, on all of us. The shame of my sins, the shame of murder.

"You brought this on us, Marguerite," my mother said. "*You* did this to our family."

I wanted to claim otherwise—wanted to blame her. But hadn't my own sin preceded hers? If I had only been good . . .

She was sitting at the table with folded hands. Now she spoke in a whisper, as if someone might hear. "No one knows yet. No one will, unless you speak. You are young; you can start again. We cannot. But if you go away—"

With me and Daniel both gone, they could say we had run away together, eloped. If anyone asked. And my father would be saved. And our family reputation would be saved. I would be saved.

I found myself wishing I had never awakened. I found myself placing the words "Daniel" and "reputation" next to one another, and "unless you speak" and "saved." I tried to turn them into an equation, but the numbers would not yield. My father's praying voice echoed in my head. I felt dizzy, as I had at the altar the day I received my first communion. But now the blood was on my hands.

I wish I could say I stayed; I wish I could say I had the strength of character to fight, to set the record straight, to tell the truth at least to my father. But I was too afraid, then, of hurting him too. I was afraid of everything then. And I didn't think, then, that he would have believed me.

I didn't know who to hold accountable, who to punish or how. So, late at night when witnesses were unlikely, I went away. My father rowed me across to the mainland himself, in our little skiff. The lake had not yet frozen, but the wind that cut across it was sharp and bitterly cold, already a winter wind. I carried a lantern to light our way, but its flame flickered so that I could barely see Papa's face, much less what lay ahead of us.

Yet we found our way. At the silent ferry dock, Papa looked at the bandages still wrapped around my hand, gave me a small sack, and went. I knew he wanted to embrace me but did not dare; I made no move to embrace him, the distance between us too great for me to cross. I stood alone there a long moment, listening to his oars splashing in the black water.

When I could hear him no more, I looked down at the sack he had given me. I knew what it contained: money, and quite possibly a good sum of it, enough to see me to a new life. I could not keep it; I wouldn't keep it. It only compounded my guilt. I was leaving for his sake, but saving him did not erase Daniel's death, nor my silent part in the crime of it.

I looked around. The ferry was shut down for the night. All was silent; I thought I was alone. But then I saw someone huddling next to the dark shed. Moving closer, I saw it was a woman, wrapped in rags, sleeping. I tucked the money bag beside her; then, after a moment's thought, left my small satchel of clothes as well. She didn't wake.

I knew I might regret this act later; I did regret it, a little, during those cold nights in the railway cars. But as I walked away with nothing but the clothes I was wearing, I was ready to begin my penance, to pay for my sins with the rest of my life. Even though I believed that God—if He did exist—would never forgive me.

I sowed one wild oat, reaped it, then tried to put it all behind me. But the crime would not be put behind, no matter how far I traveled.

It was an early spring day, sun shining on columbine and leopard's bane blooming purple and yellow in the border. I was digging your strawberry bed when my shovel hit bone.

Clavicle.

Then: tibia, ulna, pelvis.

So many bones, so cold to my lips, the warm flesh gone, gone, nothing to hold them together, nothing to show whose bones they were or how they came to be there. Daniel. I dug up that profane grave—and as I dug, watered the soil with my tears.

I couldn't bury him right; I didn't know how or where, didn't know the ways of his people or mine. Instead I took the bones to the quarry that night. Carried them out in my arms, remembering the night he loved me there, the night we loved each other. The water deep and cold rising around me as I went. I could have joined him. I wanted to join him. It was what I deserved. But who would have taken care of you? So I set the wooden box on fire and let it go.

His spirit lit the water for a while, then rose to the starry sky and was gone.

It's my turn now, little bird. Let my spirit rise.

Seven

He was a deputy again, come to get the boy, who was sitting with Marguerite Deo on the sunny stoop, the two of them all dressed in their warm clothes and playing with a piece of string. He moved toward them without effort, floating above the snow, stood there looking down into the cat's cradle that the boy had woven in his child's hands. It was as intricate as a spider-web, and with each move they made—Marguerite's fingers moving quickly, surely, the boy's hands equally adept—it became more so. The boy seemed unaware of the deputy, and Marguerite spoke to him without meeting his eyes, her own eyes on the web they were spinning. "Fire or water," she said. He didn't understand. "Fire or water," she said again, more loudly. It was a question. "I don't know," he said. "Fire," she said. "So the soul can rise." He nodded then. The boy looked up. His eyes were sky-blue. "Your turn," the boy said, and put his hands out for the deputy to take the web. But the deputy fumbled; his fingers would not fit, and the web fell to the porch boards, a shapeless pile of string.

Just before midnight, the sheriff woke. At first he thought he was in his own bedroom; but no, he was in Linda's apartment downstairs, in bed with her beside him, sleeping, one arm flung over her eyes against the light that came through the window, the other curled over her belly as if to protect the baby, her hair spilling across the pillow like a dark waterfall. He thought what a beautiful bride she would make when they got married in the spring; he thought what a beautiful mother she would make. He thought what an odd father he would make, gray-haired and grizzled. "You're young for your age," Linda always told him. Young for his age—not young. He hoped to live to see the child grown, to see him—or her—graduate from college. That was all he asked.

He thought about the image that had wakened him. When he drove up to fetch James Jack that day, they *had* been sitting in the sun, dressed in their warm clothes. Walking toward them, he'd rehearsed the words in his head, hating that he'd be the one to break the news. But Marguerite said they'd seen what had happened, and they'd been expecting him. "Here's the deputy, James Jack," Marguerite said. "Come here, let me spiff you." She'd taken the boy in her arms, hugged him briefly, then straightened his hair and the collar of his jacket. "You go sit in the deputy's car now," she said. "I need to speak to him for a moment."

James Jack had gone down to the car, the deputy waiting, respectfully, to hear what Miss Deo had to say. She stood and came down the steps to face him.

"I take it they're all dead," she said.

He nodded.

"Did they die in the fire or drown?" she said.

It was a curious question. "We don't know," he said. "I suppose when they find the bodies, there'll be an autopsy."

She nodded, impassive. "The boy," she said.

"We'll take care of him," he said.

Now he sat up on Linda's bed, groped on the floor for his clothes. Linda woke and turned on the bedside lamp. "What's the matter? " she said, sleepy-voiced. He leaned across the bed and kissed her. "I'll be back," he said. "I just remembered something I need to do." "Sheriff stuff?" she said, smiling, and he nodded.

She watched him put his uniform back on. "I never understood that thing about men in uniform," she said, "till now." She got out of bed and helped him with his tie. Ran her hands down the front of his shirt. "A sheriff," she said, touching the badge. "Imagine that."

As silly as it was, he felt himself swelling with pride. He felt large and in control as he left the apartment. The smell of her on his hands, in his hair. The taste of her in his mouth. He didn't care anymore what people would think—the sheriff marrying again, marrying his tenant, marrying a much younger woman. All he cared about was how good she made him feel.

The windshield was thick with frost. He started the engine and got the scraper from the floor of the backseat, and as he leaned over the windshield he saw Linda in the window of her apartment. She waved and pointed, and then in a second she was at her door. He left the car running and went back to her, stood below her on the steps. "I heard that men whose wives kiss them good-bye have fewer accidents," she said, her face flushing just a little, and leaned forward to kiss him. He tugged the lapels of her robe together. "Don't catch cold," he said. He felt pleased that she had come out to kiss him good-bye. Glad that she would be there when he came back, keeping the bed warm. "I'll leave the door unlocked," she said.

"No need," he said, and smiled. "I'm the landlord. I have a key."

The snow had long since stopped, the sky had cleared, and the winter darkness crackled with stars. The wind was calm for a change. The plowed road had that dry, frozen feel. Every sound was small and contained. Like organ notes with the damper pedal pressed. The cedars along the lake road seemed to be hold-ing themselves back, pulling into their own shadows, hiding from his headlights. He got on the radio to let Gina know where he was headed.

It had been a busy day; he'd never had time to go back to the Deo place. But the memory had wakened in him his premoni-tion of the morning, as well as a thought about where he'd find James Jack, if in fact Marguerite had died. Being sheriff, he had to follow up every lead. Even if it meant going out in the middle of the frigid night.

He drove past Doc Milton's trailer. No lights, the woman's rental car gone. He drove on. To his left the lake was a vast white field, perfectly level, with the matte finish of new snow inter-rupted only by a few fish shanties. In the new moon the snow seemed to generate its own blue light. He peered into the dis-tance. He had almost given up when he saw what he was look-ing for.

He parked the patrol car at the boat landing and took a few moments to pull on some extra clothes before heading out onto the ice. From the trunk he got a flashlight and the long-handled, three-pronged cultivator he used for gardening in summer, and then he went down to the water's edge and stepped out. He'd never liked the ice, not since that day Homer Wright's shanty had caught fire and gone through it, taking James Jack's parents down. So he took the cultivator with him to test the ice and to pull him back onto it if he fell through. A simple precaution, that's how he thought of it.

The snow squeaked under his boots. The flashlight spilled a yellow pool onto the undamaged snow but could not touch the blackness beyond. He kept the light low so as not to spook who-ever was out there. Kept his eyes on the yellow flicker in the dis-tance, at first no bigger than a candle flame. Every so often, he swung the claw of the cultivator ahead of him, just in case.

The ice was utterly silent. He began to forget that it was ice at all; it felt like solid ground. But that was a dangerous illusion. He listened to his footfalls, felt himself growing farther from the shore.

The smell of wood smoke came to him first, and then the faint tinkling of music. He could see the flames now, spitting out of a darkness that slowly took shape as a barrel, next to which he now saw a man, sitting, bent over a fish hole. A transistor radio by his side spewed trebly lyrics. Oldies station. *You're just too good to be true, can't take my eyes off of you . . .*

The man was dressed in a black snowmobile suit with a hood, his face hidden by a ski mask. His hands and feet were oversized in gloves and boots; it was hard to tell, looking at him, who he might be or how big. The sheriff cleared his throat. "Evening," he said, and the man looked up. With one mittened hand he pushed the ski mask up onto his forehead, and the sheriff saw that it wasn't James Jack, but Warren, the bait man. "Hello, War-ren," he said. "Evening, Sheriff," Warren said, peering at him. "Cold night for gardenin'," he said, and broke into a grin.

The sheriff looked down at the cultivator. "Suppose so," he said. "Cold night for fishin', too."

Warren pursed his lips and shook his head. "Never too cold. Not if you dress right," he said. "And bring some heat." He nod-ded toward the fire burning in the barrel, flames visible through rust holes in its sides.

"That burn barrel looks less than legal," the sheriff said.

"Arrest me, then," Warren said, jiggling his rod confidently.

"I will," the sheriff said, "unless you've got something hot you can give me to drink."

"Ah," Warren said, "so you're the kind that takes bribes."

He got the sheriff some cocoa, gave him a bucket to sit on. They sat looking out at the lake stretching before them, bounded on two sides by the black shoreline and at the top by the black sky. The last time the sheriff had been out on the lake at night, it had been summer, and he had been in the little motorboat he and Alma had when they were first married, and she had been with him, and it had been the Fourth of July, and a dozen other boats had floated around them, voices oohing at the fireworks that bloomed above them. Nothing could be more different from this black, silent stillness.

"You're not out here for fish," Warren said, jiggling his line again. "Far as I know, you're not a fisherman."

The sheriff shook his head. "I'm looking for James Jack," he said.

With comical exaggeration, Warren looked around at the emptiness.

"What's he done?"

"Nothing I know of," the sheriff said.

"I see," said Warren. "Well, last time I saw him was this afternoon. Came by for some minnows." He put his rod between his knees while he poured more cocoa for himself and the sheriff. "It was right around here it happened, wasn't it?"

"Yes," the sheriff said.

"Long time ago."

"Yes," the sheriff said.

"I was a boy then," Warren said. He wiggled his fish line. "Ten years old. The ice was green that day."

"Was it?" the sheriff said. "I don't remember."

"It was melting from beneath," Warren said. "Still safe, though," he said. "Except for them."

"You saw it happen," the sheriff said, "and here you are."

"You can't let things get up on you," Warren said. "Things

happen, or they don't. If they happen, they happen, and that's that. If they don't happen, then you're lucky, and that's that too."

"Story never bothered your wife?" the sheriff said.

"Mainlander," Warren said. "Story she heard, but she didn't see it. She makes me wear these, though." He put the rod between his knees again and shook his hands: twin screwdrivers fell from his sleeves and hung there. "Handy if you fall through," he said, tucking them away again.

"Doesn't mind you night fishin'?"

"Doesn't complain. That I know of, that is," Warren said. "I think sometimes she just likes to get me out of the house."

The sheriff nodded. "Wives do," he said.

"Besides," Warren said thoughtfully, "she's got three kids and seven grandbabies that give her plenty of love and mush." He jiggled his rod. "All women care about," he paused to jiggle it again, "is love and mush."

"Suppose so," the sheriff said.

His own wife had changed after Marguerite took the boy away from her. After the tears stopped, after he'd suggested and she'd rejected adopting a baby or taking in a foster child, Alma had changed. She didn't act unhappy, not the way most people would; that wasn't her way. Instead she tried too hard to be happy. Smiling and cheerful. Keeping an immaculate home. Volunteering until she was the mainstay of the church. Cooking and sewing for others. Organizing a fund drive when someone's kid was stricken ill or a house burned down or a farmer lost his arm in an accident. Thirty turkeys roasted for a Thanksgiving dinner for the homeless; food baskets delivered on Christmas morning. She won awards for her good works. And was always smiling and cheerful and sweet and kind and neat as a pin. That's what everybody saw.

They didn't know what it was like at home. That she rose every day at four to begin work. That even as she slept her hands were working. They didn't know what it was like to live with someone who felt that God had forsaken her but would not forsake Him back. They didn't know what it was like to live with someone who lived by the Bible even as she hated it. They didn't know what it was like to have a wife who hated you because you'd done what you thought was right.

Once a month, as if he were a charity, she came to bed without her gown and gave herself up to him. But no matter how he touched her, she did not respond. Ashamed, embarrassed, he went to a mainland drugstore for the "female lubricant" he needed to make it possible to achieve his own satisfaction. She never complained, but he always felt ashamed, and finally he stopped.

To leave her would hurt her; to hurt her would hurt him more, and so he stayed.

The day before she died, she'd been making doughnuts. She was legendary for her doughnuts, which were feather-light and greaseless because she always got the deep-fat fryer to just the right temperature, so the dough hit the oil with a sizzle and cooked fast. They were never for him, although she saved him some—usually a dozen of his favorite, maple-glazed yeast, to take to the office. This time the church ladies had requested them for a Saturday bake sale.

But when he came home that Friday, the kitchen was dark. The bowl full of dough sat on the counter; the oil was cold in the fryer. He found Alma in the bedroom, sitting in a chair, her hands full of knitting. She looked up when he came in. He tried to put his arms around her. "I'm fine," she said. She wouldn't stop what she was doing, just sat in the chair and repeated herself. "I'm *fine.*" The needles clacking.

He went back out to get some dinner, coaxed her as far as the living room to eat it. They watched television. He thought fleetingly about calling a doctor to check her over. But he didn't. He'd wanted her to be as all right as she said she was.

He woke at dawn, briefly, and was surprised to find her still asleep. He touched the broad plain of her flannel back. She'd been alive then, he was sure of it.

But an hour later, when his alarm went off, she wasn't.

It was as if some nut with a gun had come in and shot one of them at random. It was that sudden, that *over*. He felt death had missed its target, but only by a few inches. He felt that he alone had survived the disaster that had struck his bed.

The regular doctor was away. Doc Milton—that woman Faith's father—signed the death certificate. Heart attack, he said. The sheriff nodded. But thought to himself: No. Whatever the autopsy says, she died from grief, and shame, and the lack of love. Took a long time, but it killed her finally.

And suddenly he was free. He'd sold the farm, bought the apartment building, met Linda, and started a new life. Just like that.

"You know," Warren said, "I think I'd sooner have a divorce than have to give up fishin'."

The sheriff stood, stiff with the cold, and handed back his empty cup. "If fishing is all it takes to make you happy," he said, "I guess you're a lucky man."

"Guess so," Warren said, jiggling his line. "But then again," he said as the sheriff walked away, "I sure would miss my grandkids."

The rental car was still in the drive at Marguerite's place, where it had been that morning. All was quiet. A few lights were on—one upstairs that he could see, one in the kitchen, the outdoor light by the summer-kitchen door. Two sets of footprints led from the house and toward the barn. He knew he'd have to follow them. But first he knocked on the door, just to see. No answer, of course. He let himself into the kitchen. Two mugs of cold tea sat on the table, a saucer with cigarette ashes and one butt in it. He checked the stove; the fire was low but not out. They hadn't been gone long. He threw on a couple of logs. After the ice, heat felt good. He took off his jacket and sat a moment, warming up.

James Jack had left a bad taste in his mouth that morning. He'd seen that shell-shocked look before, in the mirror last year after Alma died. Marguerite Deo was dead, he knew it. How she had died, he wasn't so sure, but she was so old he wasn't sure it mattered either. He did know one other thing, though: James Jack had taken care of her all his life, and he was taking care of her now. The sheriff just hoped he wasn't doing something foolish.

He didn't bother going upstairs. He went back out to the car and called in and told Gina what he was going to do but not why. "You need backup?" she said. He smiled at her use of the term; Gina loved to dramatize. He told her no, he didn't think so. He just wanted her to know where he was and why he'd be out of radio contact for a while. "If anything comes up, you call Dicky," he said. Dicky was his best deputy.

He got the flashlight from the trunk again, snugged his hat down and wrapped his scarf around his nose. By the thermometer outside the summer-kitchen door, it was close to twenty below. Who knew how long this would take. But as long as he kept moving, he'd be all right.

Behind the barn he found the truck. No surprise to him; he'd noticed the tracks that afternoon. Had figured that James Jack was there hiding, that the woman Faith was covering for him. Two mugs on the table. And she had known he knew. She was sharp, like her father. But she had chosen to play the game out, and he couldn't help but find that endearing. Like two children, covering for one another. He hadn't wanted to give her husband Marguerite's number, but felt duty-bound to do so. Still, he hoped things would work out for James Jack. It was time he started a family of his own. That's what the sheriff would have told James, if he'd asked.

The footprints went around the barn and followed the old road up the hill and into the woods. At one time, he knew, part of these woods had been Anna Deo's orchard. As a boy, he'd come here to pick apples, sometimes for pay, sometimes for fun. The trees then had been low and well pruned, their arching branches hanging to the ground, the apples so large and so red he understood how Eve had been tempted, how the devil had used them against her, why God had forbidden them to be eaten in the first place. When you were picking it was hard not to eat them, and more than once he gave himself a bellyache. But oh the pleasure of sinking your teeth through the skin and into the crisp white flesh.

The forest had gone wild since then, and the apple trees allowed to grow up. Now they blended into the wild woods, visible only in early spring when they bloomed white and pink. The wormy apples fell and rotted on the forest floor. Marguerite Deo had let her mother's orchard disappear, the same way she had neglected her father's quarries. He supposed that since she didn't need the money, she didn't care about preserving what her parents had built. But maybe it wasn't right to expect a child to be your extension into eternity. Maybe that wasn't what having a child was about. He thought about Linda again, and smiled.

The flashlight caught something in its beam. Something that was not the white or gray or black of everything else. He hurried toward it, feeling the strain of the hill in his legs and his lungs. When he got there, he squatted, panting. It was a slipper, a pink slipper. The kind Alma had worn, what she had called a "mule." Pink terry cloth, no back, no heel. Marguerite's, maybe? He pushed it with the flashlight, rolled it over carefully, shone the light around the area to see if there was anything else. Nothing. If the slipper belonged to Marguerite, what was it doing out here?

He felt a sudden rush of pity for Marguerite Deo. No one had ever extended kindness to her, except—in a strange way—James Jack's parents, who had been taking advantage of her at the same time. And Caroline Wright, when she let the woman keep the boy. But that had been an act of self-preservation as well as kindness.

In small ways even the sheriff had made her life difficult. He could not call what he had done harassment—for it had all been within the law—but he had taken more pleasure in it than he should have. Ticketing her whenever her truck was in the slightest violation—a broken headlight, a nicked windshield, tires not quite bald but still not quite legal. Visiting her house with a "friendly" reminder the one time her taxes were a day late. Using his position as an excuse to check on her, to make sure that James Jack was registered for school, had his shots, was cared for properly. He had been her conscience, or so he thought of himself, making her toe the line, watching out for James Jack's best interests, if only from a distance. He told himself he did it for Alma's sake, so he could report to her that the boy was all right. Even though Alma never responded to the news as if she cared. "Don't be unkind," she'd say to him if he criticized Marguerite, and he hated Alma for that. And then felt guilty for hating her.

Once, when James Jack was a teenager, the sheriff and Marguerite had almost come to blows. A bunch of kids had trespassed on Doc Milton's land to have "a boonie," a keg party in the boondocks. There was a rash of such parties that summer; the kids'd found someone to buy kegs of beer for them, nobody knew who, and they moved the party from site to site, weekend to weekend, so it was hard to track them down until the morning after, when some farmer would call in complaining about the mess. It'd been sheer luck, stumbling onto this one, finding the cars parked behind Doc Milton's trailer, following the sound of faint music back into the woods. He'd been elected sheriff by then, had taken a deputy with him, but still they hadn't been able to catch any of the kids, who scattered into the dark woods and went silent and invisible.

When the flurry of movement was over and the only sound was the tinny music from a portable radio, James Jack alone remained, standing next to the fire, roasting a marshmallow on a stick. He suspended the stick well above the flame and turned it slowly, so that the marshmallow browned gradually and evenly. Then he waved the stick toward the sheriff. "Like one?" he said. The sheriff shook his head, and started in with his usual speech about the dangers of drinking and driving, and the illegality of trespass and underage drinking. "My folks used to live here," James Jack said.

"I know," the sheriff said. Surprised, in a way, that James Jack remembered.

"I guess it's still trespass, though," James Jack said.

The sheriff nodded.

James Jack drew the marshmallow off the stick and put it into his mouth. For a moment he stood there as if in profound contemplation, gazing off into the trees. Then he wiped his mouth with the back of his hand. "Well," he said, extending his wrists, "I guess you better take me in."

The sheriff hadn't arrested him, of course, but had taken him back to the house, where Marguerite came to the door in her nightgown. She was in her seventies by then, her hair wild and gray over her shoulders. He was reminded of stories about how she played the witch on Halloween, and for a moment he felt intimidated.

"James Jack, go on in," she said, and James Jack went.

The sheriff launched in. "Illegal drinking," he said. "Trespassing."

"Kids will be kids," Marguerite said.

He had a notion then. "Marguerite, have you been buying those kids beer?"

She arched her brow at him. "Maybe I have, maybe I haven't," she said.

He knew she was taunting him, daring him to arrest her finally. He decided to sidestep the issue for the moment. "The boy needs a father," he said.

Marguerite raised her finger like a gun and pointed it at his chest. "What would a father do that I don't do?" she said, coming at him. "What would *you* do, Sheriff? You think if you had a boy, you'd be able to control him? You think you'd *want* to control him? Every creature has its nature, Sheriff. Let a child be a child till it's time to grow up, won't you?"

He stood for a moment looking down at Marguerite's finger. If this old woman so much as touches me, he found himself realizing, I'll hit her. But she did not.

"Sheriff," she said, dropping her finger, "I am sorry that you and Alma could not have children. Truly I am. But this child is mine, and I will raise him as I see fit. And over my dead body will you take him away from me."

The door had shut behind her like an ax falling.

At the time he found the exchange funny. James Jack Wright was no boy. He was seventeen years old, and with the looks and physique to pass for older. Old enough to leave home whenever he was ready. And the sheriff was long past hoping to take him away from Marguerite. Yet she had stood there defending him as if he were still a helpless child.

Later on the sheriff figured out that it was James Jack himself who was driving to the mainland with a fake ID and buying the kegs of beer for the parties, with money he earned on his first construction job that summer. So Marguerite *had* been protecting him. Would Alma have been that good a mother? Would Alma have known how to rise up against powerful forces and keep her child safe? He thought she might have, even though she and Marguerite were different as day and night—Alma like a bitter almond covered in milk chocolate, Marguerite like lemon candy, sweet and sour all the way through.

It wasn't that story about her running off with the farmhand that had turned people against Marguerite. Islanders were forgiving of youthful mistakes. It wasn't even that she'd come back citified, with airs—it hadn't taken long for her to lose them. No, what it was was what she'd done to her parents: abandoning them, breaking their hearts, never so much as visiting, letting her father die alone. Dear people, good Catholics, they hardly seemed worthy of such treatment. Anna Deo had taught Sunday school; Marcel Deo had been a selectman many years running. It was they who brought the Catholic church to town, and the first real school, Ville D'eau Public School, called after their ancestral name. (These days, the kids called it Billy Doo, or "the watering hole" if they knew French.) They ladled soup at church suppers, gave Christmas parties for the small children; when they were very old, walked hand in hand down their road at sunset, tiny and hunched and surely harmless. Mr. Deo had a temper— everyone knew that from town meeting days past, like that once when he all but punched the moderator for not recognizing him to speak—funny, sad sight, the little old man strutting up to the table, fists flailing. But Mrs. Deo was sweetness itself, hardly spoke a word in public, and he couldn't imagine what they could have done to make Marguerite abandon them.

Couldn't imagine it, that is, until she told him the rest of the story.

He was standing next to Alma's casket half listening to the priest when he caught sight of Marguerite at the edge of the crowd, her face craggy under a black hat. He looked around for James Jack, didn't see him, and wondered how she had gotten herself there, how she was managing alone, old as she was. But then it was time to lower the coffin, and in the moment he forgot about her.

It seemed everyone wanted to talk to him afterward, wanted to take his hand and offer condolences. He understood that, and he stood it as long as he could, but then he had to get away and slipped off into the trees at the edge of the cemetery. Leaning against a trunk, he closed his eyes, and was surprised to hear someone say his name. It was Marguerite. "I'm sorry about Alma," she said.

"I appreciate your coming," he said to her, as he had to so many others.

"We go way back," she said, nodding. "Do you remember the day you brought me home from the ferry?"

He hadn't forgotten.

"You were just a boy. And the day James Jack's folks died—you were there then, too."

He nodded, peering into her face. The sharp eyes he remembered were rheumy now, faded—he thought her sight must have deteriorated—but they were looking at him with the same sense of purpose and determination they'd always had. "Are you just reminiscing, Marguerite?" he said. "Or is there something you want to say?"

She sat down on a stump. "Yes," she said, reaching up and taking off the black hat. "Yes, there is."

And she told him the story then. About the baby she'd lost. About the farmhand—Daniel was his name. About what her mother had said, and what her father had done because of it. The murder. Why she had gone away. She told it to him as if he were a priest, as if she were confessing—as if it were her fault, as if she were to blame. Told him about the day she'd found

Daniel's buried bones, told him what she had done with them. She'd kept it secret, he gathered, just because that was her way—because it wasn't anybody's business, what happened so many years ago. And because she hadn't wanted the scandal, which might have cost her James Jack.

The story didn't take long to tell. He could not tell if it was tears or cataracts that made her eyes shine as she spoke. "Does James know?" the sheriff asked.

"Some of it," she said. "That I loved a boy and that he died. Not how."

He nodded.

"I wanted you to know," she said, rising from the stump stiffly, "because I want you to understand." She put her hat back on and gave him another long look; he felt sure now that the water in her eyes was tears. "So that maybe you can forgive me," she said, "for what I did, to you and to Alma."

At first he thought he would not be able to say the words, but when he opened his mouth they came easily. "There's nothing to forgive," he said.

She nodded and made as if to go. "Marguerite," he said. He had a question to ask her, wasn't sure how. Finally he said, "Is everything all right?"

Her gaze wandered toward the treetops. "I'm well enough," she said, "if that's what you mean. Of course, that's the problem." He waited for her to continue; he knew better than to press. "It's long past time he had a life of his own," she said. "But he won't go. Says he wants to take care of me till the end." She paused a second, smiled a crooked smile. "Which doesn't seem to be coming anytime soon."

"James is a good man," the sheriff said.

"Yes," she said. "Too good for his own good."

"You raised him well, Marguerite."

She suppressed a smile—he could tell she was proud to hear

him say that—and gazed past him. "You hear stories now about desecration," she said, lifting her chin toward the cemetery. "People disturbing Indian graves. Digging them up so fancy houses can be built." She shook her head. "I wouldn't want that," she said.

He followed her gaze to Alma's grave, where people still clustered about. "I don't think there's much danger of it here."

"Still," she said, "better to go up in smoke." Now the smile came, small and ironic, and she went off, moving slowly and with care.

Better to go up in smoke. If that's what she wanted, if that's what James Jack was up to, the sheriff thought, looking at the pink slipper in his hand, at least two laws would be broken. One: cause of death needed determination. It would look suspicious if it weren't; might even lead to a murder trial; after all, James stood to inherit a pretty bit. Of course, the sheriff didn't suspect that. But only an autopsy could tell.

Two: by law a body had to go through a mortuary for disposal. Stupid law, penalties not as great, but still, it was the law, and his to enforce.

Would considerations like that stop James? Stop Marguerite's boy? No. James Jack resembled her that way, if no other. Just this side of wrong but always in the right.

He put the pink slipper in his pocket and started up the slope again.

The quarry road ended, narrowed into a path, and the tracks continued, but mussed up now—hard to tell coming from going, and they were filled in, as if something had been dragged over them. The hill was steeper now, but he kept going up, feeling his heart pound in his chest. He slowed down, paced himself. The new snow was not as deep here where the trees were thicker, but it was still rough going.

Finally the flashlight beam caught something else, up ahead. A building of some sort. An old cabin.

The door was ajar. He went in. There were a woodstove, a cot, some rudimentary shelves. The place did not look unused, but neither did it looked lived in. This was James Jack's retreat, he thought, a place for him to get away. He followed the flashlight beam around the room, getting a closer look at things. Touched the stove as he passed it. Cold. The mattress was bare, sagging. He swung the flashlight across the foot of it, down toward the floor and back to the doorway. Then back to the floor at the foot of the bed. Something there. Pink.

He fingered the second pink slipper, put it in his pocket with its mate.

James Jack had brought Marguerite here, then had taken her away.

He left the cabin, walked around it. The only tracks led back the way he had come. He stood for a moment, thinking, then started down the slope. He knew now where they were; he realized now what Marguerite would have wanted.

T he new snow helps them get the body down.

They've wrapped the quilt around her, tied it in place with rope. He's rigged a harness by which they can lower her before them, letting her slide down the hill.

She makes an awkward package, arms and legs akimbo, but there is nothing they can do about that.

The wind has died. The night is still, clear, cold. They walk side by side. They go slowly down the path, the beam of the flashlight flitting across trees, rocks, flashing blue as it crosses the dark bundle.

They don't speak, except those small words of caution and encouragement that people use when undertaking a difficult task together.

They stop where path widens to road. He takes off a glove, and puts the palm of his hand to Faith's face. Unties her scarf and reties it. Then they begin the last leg of their journey, pulling the bundle behind them now.

When they reach the quarry, its walls are as black as velvet curtains, receding into space around a stage lit by starlight. The snow is undisturbed until they step onto it, pulling her behind them.

Marguerite lies there on the ice, waiting, while they make a small fire to give them light. Then they begin the real work.

The sheriff stays in the shadows, watching. In the flickering light he sees them moving back and forth, building the pyre from downed wood. They pull the branches over the ice, strewing leaves and twigs on the white surface. It takes them a long time. Motionless, the sheriff feels the cold seeping into him, into his lungs and extremities, and envies them the work that keeps them warm. But he won't join them; he won't intrude. That is not his place.

Smoke is the soul of the tree, and fire sets it free. Tante told James that. *The soul feels,* she said, but not what the body feels. Something is gone now, something is gone. What's left is no more feeling than a piece of wood. Does wood feel the fire? *No, it can't. And I won't either.* She told him that, too. Yet something leaves the wood when it burns, and something leaves the body when it dies. What's left? Not sight or sound or taste or smell or touch. Not life. What color will her soul be, rising into the night? *Let me be with him,* she said. *Let me join him in the sweet hereafter.*

A voice singing him to sleep: *A trip to the moon, on gossamer wings* . . . The moist continuity of breathing. The softness of a baby's neck.

The warmth of a fire. Love. A love so hot as to incinerate all doubt.

. . .

It's a struggle to get the body on the pyre. He can't tell exactly how they accomplish it. But then all is still and they are lost in the shadows. And he hears the fire before he sees it. Crackling and popping, splitting the silence into fragments. And then he sees them, silhouetted against it, holding each other. He doesn't see their faces; he doesn't want to. He won't testify. But he can witness, and does.

As if nine-tenths of her weight is soul, Marguerite bursts into flame and rises from the fire. Yellow, orange, purple, red: in the colors of her flowers, Marguerite burns, and her soul rises white to the stars.

She stepped out into the frozen night, placing her feet where James had placed his, then stepping finally out of the house's glow and into the moonless dark, the snow slippery under her flat soles. She ought to have brought a walking stick, ought to have worn boots; the slippers slowed her, made it harder than it had to be. And it was hard.

But she kept on. And soon the night was not frozen at all, but warm as spring, and she was a girl, going to help with the lambing. It was warm as a New Orleans evening, and she was a woman, entering a moonlit courtyard. It was warm as summer, and she was Tante, breathing air filled with the scent of sweet alyssum, walking through a flower garden blooming more profusely than any she had ever grown. It was easy now to follow the path. Nothing hindered her, nothing held her back. She was leaving, she knew that; she was leaving something behind. But this time it did not hold her back.

When she was tired, she lay down on a bed of leaves. It was only then that she started to feel the cold, wished she had someone with her. So when the little bird came, she welcomed its company. So smart, the little bird, its sharp tongue digging. She lived the truth then, her body cooling with it until she felt nothing, heard nothing but the distant tapping of the little bird. Saw nothing but the bowl of colorful petals, and the small boy raising them to his mouth. Oh, he said. Oh. They are a little sweet, he said. And some bitter, like pepper. But I like them. And the boy ate.

Appreciation to Robin Desser, Keith Monley, Michael Carlisle, Emma Parry, Joe Bellamy, Nancy Anisfield, Barbara Floersch, Susan Ouellette, Heather Kresser, Nikki Matheson, Philip Baruth, and Saint Michael's College for their help and support.